MURDER MOST ANNOYING

A CAROLYN NEVILLE MYSTERY BOOK 1

JOHN DUCKWORTH

Murder Most Annoying
John Duckworth

Print Edition
© Copyright 2020 John Duckworth

Published in the United States by Wolfpack Publishing, Las Vegas

CKN Christian Publishing
An Imprint of Wolfpack Publishing
5130 S. Fort Apache Road 215-380
Las Vegas, NV 89148

cknchristianpublishing.com

eBook ISBN 978-1-64734-882-3
Paperback ISBN 978-1-63977-092-2

MURDER MOST ANNOYING

MURDER MOST ANNOYING

To Mom, who showed the way.

PROLOGUE

I STOPPED, LISTENING. NOTHING BUT CHIRPING BUGS THAT sounded like they were the size of house pets.

Stephen moved stealthily toward the door, as if expecting the hooded white camera to lock its gaze on him, perhaps even to land a ruby laser dot on his forehead.

"I think our blogger has a thing about security," he whispered. He pointed at the door which had not one but two deadbolts.

I rang the doorbell which was loud and grating in the quiet. The noise faded, but there seemed to be no stirring inside. I rapped gently on the door. Nothing.

Stephen leaned in and knocked more forcefully. This time the door moved slightly. Looking down at the brass knob, I saw that despite the deadbolts, the door was not only unlocked but unlatched.

"Mr. Tripp's security arrangements aren't very secure," Stephen said.

With two fingers I pushed the door open a few inches, just enough to let him know we were there. "Mr. Tripp?"

Still quiet.

"I'm Carolyn Neville. From Pendleton House Publishers. We hear you've got a problem with one of our books. We're trying to find out what's going on. Can we talk with you?"

Still nothing.

"We know you might be cautious about dealing with us. But we're not lawyers or anything. Just editors."

Stephen snorted. "Yeah. There's nothing more harmless than editors, man."

I hoped hearing a young guy's voice might help, especially a cynical sounding one saying *man*. But no.

I nudged the door a little farther, enough to see the small living room and part of the kitchen beyond. A worn, blue sofa was piled with magazines. A lid-open wicker chest posed as a coffee table in front of it. Papers were scattered on the fake hardwood floor. Through a doorway I could see dirty dishes heaped in a sink.

"Looks like the place has been ransacked," I said.

Stephen looked over my shoulder. "Can't tell. He's a twenty-six-year-old guy. We're not exactly known for our housekeeping skills."

I opened the door wider. "I don't think that's it," I said. "Dishes, maybe. But all the—"

That's when I saw it.

And hoped I'd never see anything like it again.

CHAPTER 1

When the news hit that I was about to be crucified, it caught my attention.

Like most fortyish Christians with contact lenses and a weakness for doughnuts, I'd never had that experience before. They say there's a first time for everything. But when it comes to crucifixion, I guess there's never a second time.

I stood at the front of Training Suite 4B, the second-largest meeting place at Pendleton House Publishing. That put me squarely in Manhattan, the part of New York most of my coworkers thought was the center of the intellectual universe. And the cosmos, if they were honest about it.

They were sauntering or shuffling in—sauntering if they were from Marketing and shuffling if they did real work. They parked themselves at computers, making the place look like a missile-tracking station. Except that the conversations were about Thai food and shoes.

It was already one of those days you hope to look back on and laugh about but never do because you're too busy having more days like that. All morning I'd been looking in my purse to see whether I'd really eaten my last Skinny Cow Dark Chocolate Dreamy Cluster. Sadly, I had.

Now I faced down a young man who was dressed completely in black, his hair stylishly messy, his right earlobe pierced with what looked like a bloodshot porcelain eyeball. He kept tapping his laptop and glancing over his shoulder at the IMAX-sized screen behind him, apparently trying to squash the bugs out of a PowerPoint presentation three minutes before starting time.

I would have given a major limb, preferably one of his, to be somewhere else.

"I think there's been a misunderstanding," I said.

Straightening up, he managed to produce an almost-interested expression. "Oh?"

"I was invited to this meeting by mistake."

He looked at me as if waiting for the second Birkenstock to drop.

"The event notification said 'SEO Orientation,'" I said. "But we don't use SEO in Editorial."

He peered down his nose at the employee badge clipped to the lapel of my tweedy brown editor's blazer. My faded I.D. still pictured me as I'd looked my first day at Pendleton 16 years past, about four fewer pounds ago. Maybe seven.

"Carolyn Neville," he read. "Editorial." He folded his arms, smirking. "In that case you must be pretty worried about the Willow Hayly thing."

I frowned. Sure, Willow was one of our biggest authors, the brightest star in our little constellation of motivational speakers. But if there was a *thing*, I hadn't heard about it.

"What thing?"

He raised his eyebrows. "Seriously? It's been all over social media for a couple days."

"Ah," I said. *I* wasn't all over social media, at least not this week. I was fasting in that department, having seen too many pictures of people's poodles and birthday cakes.

"Some blogger in Atlanta says Willow's life story is a fake," he said matter-of-factly. "Haven't read the book. Sorry."

I squinted at the ceiling. In a sketchy sort of way, I remembered the memoir. In those days I'd just joined the company, a career move I sometimes regretted.

"Definitely a scandal," he continued. "Like Harvey Weinstein. Or Bill Cosby."

That was when it hit me. Not like a ton of bricks, but more like 25 pounds or so, just to get me used to being a victim of blunt trauma.

He looked at me with the smugness of a taxi driver who'd just beaten all the red lights on Seventh Avenue. "So, if you'll sit—"

I couldn't. The world had just changed and not for the better. Turning, I strode for the door.

"Hey!" he cried. "You can't just—"

He probably kept talking. But I'd stopped listening.

If he was right, the editor who'd handled the Willow memoir was going to be making an appearance on a cross.

I knew her well, that editor. Her face was on my I.D. badge.

There was only one thing to do.

Unfortunately, I had no idea what it was.

RETURNING to my office on the third floor, I took the elevator instead of the stairs due to a sudden lack of energy. At my desk, a dinged-up hunk of oak that looked as if it had been varnished with maple syrup around 1960, I recalled the legend that it had been used by Bennett Cerf before he co-founded Random House just 12 blocks away.

What would Cerf do? I had no idea of that, either.

I sent up a quick prayer, the kind I'd prayed a few hundred times since taking this job. The one for wisdom. I'm never entirely sure whether it gets answered, but how would I know? While I prayed, I kept my eyes open—not out of embarrassment, but because if you shut your eyes in a Manhattan office building they think you're sleeping or dead and haul you away on a cart.

I glanced around my office. What I needed was a copy of Willow's memoir. What was the title? *Worthy? Worth It?*

Rousing myself from my chair, I started searching the shelves. They'd maintained a certain order for the first decade I'd been here, but since then had fallen into chaos. After spotting three Willow books, none of them the right one, I called our administrative assistant, Alicia Romano, asking her to check the archive.

I sank back into my chair, which the Facilities Department had assured me was a managerial chair because it had arms, even though the left one kept falling off. It was time to call in an expert on bloggers.

My senior editor fit that description perfectly.

Stephen Ames was a millennial, which often came in handy. He knew everything when it came to Internet gossip… and pop culture. I liked media as much as the next person, but no book, film, TV show, tweet, or YouTube video seemed to escape his notice. When it came to entertainment, he was close to omniscient. He was also like a son to me, the one I'd never wished I'd had.

I called his extension. "Could you bring your smartphone to my office?"

His grunt sounded positive. Half a minute later he appeared in my doorway, earbuds dangling from the pocket of his gray T-shirt. His baby face was flushed, his cinnamon-brown hair begging to be brushed. He looked like the early Luke Skywalker, but without the Force.

"Need your help," I said.

"Everybody does. Usually right away."

"But this is urgent."

Sighing, he pulled the door shut behind him, then flopped into the visitor's chair. "Okay, go."

I should note that Stephen has two modes, Overdrive and Crash. At the moment he seemed set to the latter after about 72 hours of the former. In both modes he was one of the best editors I'd ever met—which I'd never tell him, since he'd want more money or his own imprint. Like most things worth having, they were beyond my power as Executive Editor to grant.

"You've edited a couple of Willow Hayly's books, right?" I asked.

He nodded.

"Heard anything about her lately? Like on the Internet?"

"Have you?"

"No, but I was just in a meeting with a guy who did. Some blogger in Atlanta is making accusations about the memoir we did with her years ago. Says her life story's a hoax."

He shook his head. "No way. My mom loves Willow. When I told her I was working on her books, she about had a coronary."

Out came his smartphone and the tapping began. "Going to the website for Willow's fan club."

I waited as he scrolled and squinted. "Willow's Upcoming Tour . . . Willow's Empowerment Pledge . . . How Willow Changed My Life . . ." He tapped again. "Not seeing anything. Too soon, maybe."

"I don't know the blogger's name, but—"

"No problem. How many Atlanta bloggers can there be

who've just accused Willow Hayly of making up her life story?" His fingers danced on the phone's screen.

Another pause. "Okay, now we're getting someplace. Blogger's name is Zane Tripp."

I slumped. "So, my informant was right."

"Looks like it. Going to his site." He read in silence, then grimaced. "*Man*," he said, as if watching a troupe of little old ladies fall on the ice in the middle of rush-hour traffic.

"Want me to read you the highlights?" he asked.

"Well, I—"

The phone on my desk rang. It was Janice Pulaski. Which might have been fine, except that she reported to the person who'd approve the purchase of the mallet, nails, and timbers for my impending execution.

"Carolyn," she said, sighing like a grade school secretary who'd had to summon a troublemaker to the principal's office one too many times. "Hunter wants to see you."

"When?"

"I *could* say ASAP. But frankly, it's now."

I shot a glance at Stephen, who seemed to be making increasingly painful discoveries on his phone.

"On my way," I said, trying to sound perky. It seemed more dignified than throwing up on my desk and sobbing.

"Problem?" Stephen asked when I'd hung up.

I grabbed a pen and a pad of paper with the Pendleton quill logo on it. "Hunter wants me. Got to be about the Willow thing."

He put down his phone. "Judging from what I just saw, I hope not."

I set out down the hall. Fifty yards lay between me and the lions' den.

I'd never seen *Dead Man Walking*. But now I knew how Sean Penn felt.

~

HUNTER THICKE SEEMED FRIENDLY. He usually did at first.

"Care for some coffee? Janice makes a mean French Vanilla with those K-Cup dealies."

He looked up from the issue of *Forbes* he was pretending to read. Mid-thirties frat-boy handsome, he was blessed with shiny black hair racing back from his forehead and the build of an ex-jock who still did push-ups. But the smile, much like one I'd seen in a picture of old-time serial killer Ted Bundy, was his most charming feature.

"Thanks," I said. "I'm trying to cut back." Not entirely true. But in this office truth would have clashed with the decor.

Sitting in his executive chair, identifiable from its genuine leather and the fact that its arms never seemed to fall off, the vice-president of content development looked out the window. No famous Manhattan landmarks were in sight, though the Benash Delicatessen was a couple of blocks away. I could almost smell the sauerkraut on the Reubens.

"We've been through a lot together, haven't we, Carolyn?" he asked.

I paused. His end-of-the-road tone had me worried.

"Guess so," I mumbled. I'd been through a lot *because* of him, but I doubted that was what he meant.

"I know you've been here a lot longer than I have. And I know we've had our differences. But I'd like to think we can be open with each other."

I stifled my gag reflex.

"So," he said, "what do you hear from Willow Hayly?"

My mouth didn't go dry, mainly because it had done that already.

"Can't say I've spoken with her in about two years. But I

did get a thank-you note a few months ago. We sent her a plaque when *You Can Be the One* hit a million copies."

He smiled, about a half-Bundy. "Keeping authors happy is important, isn't it? I'm sure that editor you're always talking about would agree."

"Maxwell Perkins?"

"That's the guy." He paused to fiddle with a small bronze figure on his desk, some kind of football trophy. "Of course, there's someone else we need to keep happy, too."

He waited, apparently wanting me to read his mind. I tried, but there seemed to be nothing in it.

"Yes," I said, hoping that covered the waterfront.

"I'm talking about the board of directors. I had a very awkward phone conversation with Ian Davies this morning. Have you met him?"

"I don't think so."

"Newest board member. Sharp guy, cool British accent. Unlike most of them, keeps up with online stuff. Lucky he called me directly instead of bringing it up at the next board meeting."

I swallowed. "You're talking about the Willow thing, aren't you?"

"So, you already know."

"A little."

He locked eyes with me, looking more like the post-smile Bundy. "Seems to me you should know quite a bit. That book was before my time, but Janice says it was your project."

I tried to look casual or jaunty or something, even though an invisible Boy Scout was using my stomach to tie a square knot. "It depends on what *your* means."

He shook his head. "Hedging? I'm surprised, Carolyn. You're a religious gal, right? Doesn't the Good Book say something about that?"

I smiled weakly. It wasn't the first time he'd referred to a woman as *gal*. Or the last time he'd poke my theology nerve with a sharp stick.

I folded my hands in my lap. "At the time I thought somebody had to be listed on the copyright page as editor. But I didn't have much to do with the project. Willow had her ghostwriter handle most of it, a guy named Philip Minor. By the time I got here, the book was already in first galleys."

Hunter frowned at his trophy, as if the little bronze man had displeased him. "Remember the guy who wrote that book Oprah loved, but it turned out to be made up?"

At first, I thought he was talking to the little bronze man, but then realized he wasn't. "James Frey?"

"Don't know the guy's name. But the book—"

"*A Million Little Pieces*."

"Whatever. The publisher took a bath on that. What's the guy doing now?"

"I don't know," I said.

"That's my point."

I doodled a meaningless curlicue on my paper as if his point were well taken.

He stared out the window again. "A leader takes responsibility for whatever happens on his watch. Or hers." I could almost see the John Paul Jones tricorn hat on his head, the rain slashing his face, the ship's wheel in his grasp. Almost.

"Are you a leader, Carolyn?"

His question hung in the air like a majestic cloud of flatulence.

"Me? Maybe not."

He nodded. "Your value to the company is mostly in your experience and your contacts. But maybe you *could* be a leader. This is your chance to find out. You could admit your mistake and work to make things right again."

"Mistake?"

"It's only human, Carolyn. You *are* human, aren't you?"

"My DNA test isn't back yet."

Forcing a chuckle, he leaned back in his chair and put his hands behind his head. "Everybody knows a publisher has to fact-check everything. In this case, maybe you gave your fellow wordsmith a pass. Professional courtesy."

I almost laughed out loud. Fact-checking was as common as five-leaf clovers. All the publishers I knew were more or less on the honor system. It was cheaper.

"Carolyn, do you know about the new cable channel?" he asked suddenly.

"Only a little."

"All Willow, all the time. Working title is WorthTV. We're close to signing a deal with her."

"We?"

"Well, our parent company, Chronicle Merkel. A PR screwup like this could torpedo the whole thing. It's not just about books. It's about leveraging the synergy going forward."

"Right." I adored buzzwords, as I did Spam, chipped nails, and melanoma.

"Ironic," I said, shaking my head. "The books themselves aren't very good, you know."

Oops. Wrong thing to say. I'd found it was best to say the opposite of what I was thinking.

Hunter drew himself up in his chair, his frown edging toward the full Bundy. "Hard as it may be to believe, your opinion doesn't mean squat to the board or the shareholders. Neither does mine. They're under the impression that this is a publishing company, not a writing contest."

"It is, but—"

"We all have to adjust to reality, Carolyn. If we can't, we're in the wrong business."

I started to draw another curlicue on my pad but put the

pen down. When Hunter reached this stage of Bundyness, all you could do was pretend to listen as hard as you could.

"You can see what's at stake here." He paused to let the words thud on the floor between us like a Gucci bag full of cement.

I nodded. The company's stock price would be on the line, along with my reputation and career. And my pathetic hope to retire someday, which in my imagination consisted of reading Anne Lamott and Tina Fey on a beach in Florida.

"Good. Then you'll also understand why you'd better show up at Willow's headquarters in Atlanta in the next forty-eight hours. I expect you to work things out."

"But—"

"It's your mess, Carolyn. You clean it up. Which reminds me of a story . . ."

He launched, as he so often did, into an anecdote he'd probably read in a treasury of awful tales for middle managers. Something about George Washington and Valley Forge and frostbitten soldiers with nothing to warm their feet except rags and gangrene.

I guess it was very inspirational.

But it was hard to hear with the pounding of nails and raising of crossbars in the background.

CHAPTER 2

I WANTED TO GO TO ATLANTA ABOUT AS MUCH AS I WANTED TO stick my head in one of the engines of the Boeing 737 it would take to get there.

Stephen felt differently. When I went to his cubicle and announced Hunter's threat, he proposed going with me.

"Why?" I asked.

"I hear Southern food is pretty good. Catfish, Moon Pies. And those Southern girls, with the way they talk, they knock me out when I'm down there."

"That's from a Beach Boys song. I thought you were too young to know any."

"Also, I've worked on Willow's books, right? And my mom's talked my ear off about her. Plus, you're nowhere near ready to show up at her headquarters. You need a crash course."

"And you're going to give me one?"

"Why not?"

I threw up my hands. "Whatever. You're not in her demographic, but then neither am I."

He smiled. "'Admitting you need help is helping yourself.' That's what Willow always says."

"You're kidding. You've memorized her sayings?"

"Hazard of being an editor."

"But do you have to brainwash me *today*?"

"'Put off procrastinating until tomorrow.' Willow says that, too."

I sighed and sat in his visitor's chair. "Go ahead."

"First thing you have to know: Willow's all about positive energy. Empowerment. Especially for women."

I nodded, wondering if my estrogen level was too low to appreciate it.

"Basically, she teaches that if she's done it, you can, too, like investing and her diet and exercise plan. She's a role model for women who want to be strong."

Well, I didn't want to be weak. I wanted to be Susan Sarandon or Condoleezza Rice. But I thought I could get there without a celebrity guru.

"Now, here's what you need to know about her origin story. The myth. In the Joseph Campbell sense, not the made-up sense."

"Yeah, I've seen PBS, too."

"Her parents lived near Atlanta. Around 1968, when Willow was three, they died in an accident. In the books and her bio it's always referred to as 'a fiery car crash.'"

"That I remember."

"Then she was raised by an aunt—kind of a weird woman with a son of her own. Willow felt alone in the world. She had zero self-esteem, zero confidence. Started eating, couldn't stop. No friends. Tried suicide at least once."

"When was that?"

He closed one eye, thinking. "In her mid-twenties. Late 1980s."

I nodded. "Okay, it's coming back now. That's when she got involved in the 'past lives' junk."

He laughed. "Boy, don't let my mom hear you say that. She'd look at you like you'd just spray-painted a Hitler mustache on Willow's publicity photo. And it wasn't past lives. It was repressed memories."

"Oh. Well, then, we're talking about *real* science. Like the Loch Ness Monster."

"Anyway, Willow knew something was keeping her in this pit she couldn't climb out of. She heard about this specialist. He retrieved memories of how her aunt had abused her. She'd blocked them out. By now, the aunt was dead."

"How fortunate for the aunt."

He aimed two fingers at the Imperial Stormtrooper bobblehead on his desk and flicked it. "Willow decided the aunt had stolen her self-worth. Knowing the truth set her free to take it back."

"And the rest is history."

"Yeah. She started believing in herself, taking charge of her life. Came out of her shell, lost weight. Discovered she had a knack for investing, especially real estate."

"And self-promotion. In a few years she was a photogenic millionaire pumping up underdogs and victims everywhere."

He flicked the bobblehead again. "Sounds like you know more than you thought."

"That's where I came in. Pendleton published the memoir and it turned into a bestseller."

"Which brings us to now. This blogger, Tripp, says the story is full of holes. There *was* no abuse. The obesity and suicidal feelings were exaggerated. And Willow's looks are thanks to plastic surgery and diet pills."

I sighed. "Bizarre. That's why I recalled so little of the book. I repressed the memory of having to read it."

"Don't let my mom hear that, either. She and the rest of Willow's fans want to be like her."

"All they need is a million dollars and a total body replacement." Closing my eyes, I smoothed my hair back with both hands. "So, when we get to Atlanta—"

"Oh, and it's not actually Atlanta. It's a little town near there, a place called Swan's Corners. Something else you have to know."

"Good. When we get to Swan's Corners, I'm going to need all the help you can give me."

"Why?"

I dropped my hands into my lap. "Because the blogger's right. Willow's story is full of holes. If we can't plug them, everything falls apart."

Just then our administrative assistant, the wide-eyed Alicia Romano, poked her head through the doorway.

"Here's the book you wanted," she said in that breathy, little-girl voice.

It was *Worth It*, with a recent photo of Willow on the cover, spotlighted onstage, her arms outstretched as if parting the Red Sea.

I flipped it over, glancing at the back cover. LIFE-CHANGING! the title said. They all said that.

I sighed.

It was certainly about to change mine.

~

BEFORE I COULD LEAVE TOWN, I had to talk with Mikki Flaherty. I hadn't seen her for at least three weeks and I needed to hear I was going to make it through this somehow.

I should explain that Mikki's my best friend but it's a little hard to explain her at all. She's the only person I know whose hobbies are interpretive dance, changing her hairstyle, and taking selfies while standing in front of other people who are taking selfies. Believe it or not, we met at church.

She's also the only one who'd drop everything and meet me for breakfast at Roundelay's, the doughnut place near my condo. Maybe that's because it doesn't take much to get either of us to eat, but I'd like to think there's a little more to our relationship.

So, the next morning we ordered two warm-from-the-deep-fryer delicacies apiece, mine a Glazed Blueberry and a New York Cheesecake plus a decaf and found a table. As usual, I found myself wishing I had her metabolism. The calories we were about to consume would be burnt to a crisp by hers; mine would be flameproof.

This time Mikki's hair was cut short, almost too short, and black. I'd seen her with everything from a red ponytail to a blonde Swiss Miss braid. I guess the import company she worked for in Queens didn't mind that the only consistent elements of her look were her dancer's slenderness and the way she turned gesturing into aerobic exercise.

She leaned forward, her eyes narrow. "This isn't about the worship dance number last Sunday, is it? I have no idea how those silk scarves with the Cinzano logos got in with the rest."

I laughed. "No. Although it did get people's attention."

"Pastor Ben loved it. But next time he wants us to advertise a nice wine instead of vermouth. I suggested Pinot Grigio."

She took an inaugural bite of her raspberry-filled doughnut. "Anyway, what's up?"

I told her. It took so long that by the time I was done, so was our food.

She leaned back in her chair and hugged herself. "Your boss is a piece of work. Is it sinful to wish he'd fall in a manhole?"

"I think so, yeah."

"Do *you* think you're responsible for the mistakes in the book?"

I frowned. "We don't know there *are* any yet. And like I told Hunter, I was hardly involved with—"

"Just playing devil's advocate. Deep down, can you honestly say you couldn't have done a better job?"

"Hey, whose side are you on?"

"Yours. We're supposed to hold each other accountable, right?"

"That was two diets ago. Right now we're supposed to be supportive."

Looking down, she chased a crumb on her napkin with a bright red fingernail. "Carolyn, are you sure Pendleton House is the best place for you? I mean, not that they make you do immoral stuff. But they don't show you a lot of respect."

"Does Icarus Imports show *you* a lot of respect?"

She shrugged. "Not especially. But you deserve it."

"So do you. But you know how it is when you're on your own. There's no backup. Besides, it's not like there are a lot of jobs in this field. I picked this occupation for a reason."

"Which is what?"

"I don't remember. Something about making America read again."

She picked up her cup and drained the last of her cappuccino, then looked me in the eye. "I think this is all going to work out."

"Now you're talking. You're full of baloney, but I like the sound of it."

"That's what friends are for."

"That and recommending over-the-counter treatments for yeast infections."

She shook her head. "Tell you what. I'll pray for you at

least twice a day while you're in Atlanta. So I hope you won't be there very long. I can't keep that up."

"I should be back in three or four days, tops."

"Good." She grabbed her purse, a tiny tan leather day clutch that matched her pint-size physique. "I've gotta get to work."

She stood, then bent down and touched her forehead to mine. Her hair smelled lemony today. "See you when you get back."

I watched her go, nimbly picking her way through the crowd. Always dancing.

My watch said it was time for me to go, too.

I wondered how long it would be until I sat here again.

And whether Mikki's prayers would make a difference.

I BOOKED THE FLIGHTS, the rental car, and the motel online. It was a task beyond Alicia Romano's limited abilities, which didn't matter because her uncle was a Pendleton senior vice-president. She was a permanent fixture.

Nineteen hours after we'd gotten marching orders, Stephen and I boarded Delta Flight 781, nonstop service to Atlanta, departing from LaGuardia. The flight was packed, but thankfully not with passengers who could remember when air travel was tolerable and wanted to reminisce about it.

Stephen sat next to me, poking his phone. I pulled mine from the pocket of my blazer. Time to renew an old acquaintance I'd never really made—with the ghostwriter of Willow's memoir.

My destination was Amazon, which immediately offered me markdowns on hydraulic shop presses and beef bouillon cubes, having apparently gotten me mixed up with someone else. Searching the Books category, I typed in PHILIP MINOR.

A stack of thumbnail covers appeared over my actual thumbnails, which seemed ironic. All but one were Pendleton books—Willow bestsellers, no doubt listed because Minor was the co-writer. He got no cover credit, though. Hardly a surprise; diluting a celebrity author's brand with a nobody's name was a bigger taboo in my circle than cannibalism.

I tapped the only cover that wasn't a Willow book. Its design screamed 1990, all frenetic white calligraphy leaping from a background of ruby and green. Something called *Stressed for Success*.

Minor's name was almost as big as the title. Small publisher probably defunct now, self-help, out of print, no reviews. He must have written it before he worked for Willow.

On *Amazon's Philip Minor Page* were photo and bio. Nice-enough-looking man, lots of dark hair, though the nose was slightly too big and the chin slightly too nonexistent. He seemed about my age, which according to my top-of-the-head calculation was mathematically impossible. Clearly an old picture.

This being my first glimpse of the man, I couldn't claim he looked familiar. I barely remembered speaking to him on the phone once, introducing myself in one of those conversations where you fake interest and sincerity while making a chain of paper clips.

After a few minutes of research, all I could say for sure was that he'd been Willow's go-to ghost for the last 16 years. If nothing else, he was loyal.

Or he didn't own a calendar and didn't realize how much of his life he'd wasted. But with 192 months under my belt at Pendleton, who was I to talk?

I put my phone away. We'd be face to face in a matter of hours.

Something told me Philip Minor wasn't going to take the blame for his boss's predicament.

He'd slip away like Barabbas, leaving me to face that cross alone.

CHAPTER 3

"So, this is Swan's Corners."

It seemed the most appropriate and unnecessary thing to say as I took Exit 38 from I-285 and turned right onto U.S. Highway 29 North. Atlanta's Hartsfield-Jackson International Airport was about 20 miles behind us and any structure more than two stories high was just a memory. So was underarm dryness.

The sun had taken over the sky. It was July, about 350 degrees, more humid than the Russian and Turkish Baths in the East Village. Only the cranked-up air conditioning of the silver Nissan Altima we'd rented was keeping us alive.

Ahead was a billboard that said WELCOME TO SWAN'S CORNERS, POPULATION 5,480. Anchored in a clearing of Georgia red clay, it was surrounded by sinister-looking, dark green vines. The sign painter seemed to have used house paint on plywood, portraying legendary lumberjack Paul Bunyan with some kind of heartbreaking skin condition, standing and grinning with his ax next to an evergreen tree. Or maybe a really moldy wedge of cheese.

"Willow's a Southern girl," Stephen said, sounding sweaty.

"You'd never know it from hearing her, though. No trace of an accent."

"A marketing decision," I said. "Would have limited her audience."

We passed a drive-in called Dairy-Freez, its faded blue marquee featuring a maniacally grinning soft ice cream cone. Just past a SPEED LIMIT 25 sign sat a used car lot, a jumble of aging Fords and Buicks simmering in the heat. Next to the road stood a reader board whose crooked and missing letters garbled John 3:16. I resisted the urge to stop and fix them.

Next came a sign that said WILLOW DRIVE.

"So, the lady has her own street," I said.

On the right, in the midst of towering trees, rose a two-story office building the size of a small cruise ship. The polished gray granite structure seemed more suited to a city, along with opera houses and carjackers.

A slab of the same granite sat by the road; its face carved with a dignified font that said WILLOWORTH INTERNATIONAL.

"Must be the place," I said, as if that were a good thing.

"Hey, check out the parking," Stephen said.

I looked where he was pointing, next to the building. Visitor spaces didn't say VISITOR. They said EMPOWERED GUEST.

Shaking my head, I guided the car into the nearest space and shut off the engine. Already I missed the air conditioning.

Stephen folded his arms. "I haven't felt this empowered since—"

BRRRRAAAAAPPPPP!

The deafening noise exploded from somewhere behind us. It was followed by a quieter *POCKETAPOCKETAPOC-KETA*, a more subdued *PUMPUMPUM*, a pop, and then silence.

"*Yow,*" he said under his breath.

Two rows behind our vehicle stood a black-leather-clad male, straddling a burnt-orange motorcycle. Reaching under the chin of the black-visored helmet that hid his face, he fiddled with a strap and lifted the whole thing from his head.

When we climbed out of the car, the heat hit us like a soggy quilt.

"Carolyn! Is that you?"

The smooth baritone came from the cyclist, who was fast approaching with an outstretched arm. It was Philip Minor, older and definitely thicker in the midsection than his Amazon photo promised. He seemed to be trying to channel the memory of Steve Jobs, the graying hair on his cranium and face equally half-shaved for that touch of innovation and rebel genius. A pair of round glasses and a black turtleneck that just cleared the collar of his leather jacket completed the outfit. It looked hot, but only temperature-wise.

"I *knew* it," he said, shaking my hand with the energy and enthusiasm of a behind-in-the polls city council candidate. "The knowledgeable Ms. Neville." No doubt he'd found my photo on LinkedIn, which looked much like the relic on my employee badge.

"And who's your colleague?" he asked.

Stephen told him, apparently thinking me incapable of making a proper introduction. They shook hands.

"The accomplished Mr. Ames," Minor said. "Senior Editor. So, Carolyn, what does that make you?"

"Editorial Director," I replied, not explaining that meant I was The Queen of Nothing.

"So, you've come up in the world," he said. "I suspect we all have since you and I worked on Willow's memoir. I have fond memories of that project."

"Yes," I said, unable to think of any.

"Have you read the book?" Minor asked Stephen.

"Sure. Edited some of the others, too."

"Excellent. We have a story to defend, so we'd better know it backward and forward." He paused. "No need to fry in the parking lot. I'll give you the grand tour."

We followed him toward the entrance. "Official tours are twice a day. We get quite a few guests, considering Swan's Corners isn't exactly a magnet for sightseers."

"Hard to believe," I said.

"Most visitors hope to catch a glimpse of Willow, but she's often on the road. She'll be doing seventeen cities in October." He lowered his voice. "Which is one reason we need to resolve the current misunderstanding as soon as possible."

We pushed our way through the revolving door, then emerged in the lobby as if reborn. The refrigerated octagon was the size of a tennis court, the floor a golden marble, the eight walls alternating between cherrywood paneling and plate-glass mirrors. Before each wall stood a life-size bronze sculpture of one or two figures striving or climbing or reaching. It was all very aspirational, as my old English Literature professor might say.

"The Eight Keys to Empowerment," Stephen said.

"You *do* know your subject," Minor replied with a smile, walking us toward the front desk. "On the left is the gift shop —books, DVDs, page-a-day calendars, other licensed merchandise. Cafeteria's on the right."

He stepped up to the receptionist. "The lovely LaShawna," he said, waving in the direction of a well-nourished young woman. Picking up a pen, he started doing something official to a sheet of paper on a clipboard.

"Welcome to Willoworth," the young lady said, handing the two of us pre-printed stickers. Where VISITOR might have been, they said EMPOWERED GUEST.

I pressed the sticker over my heart. Stephen did the same,

making a face.

"So, how many people work here?" I asked the receptionist.

"About three hundred and fifty."

"Wow," I said. "You must be the biggest employer in town."

"We are. We wouldn't if the sawmill were still in business. Government jobs are probably second. After that, maybe the Piggly Wiggly."

I did my best to maintain a somber expression. It was, after all, none of my business what some people chose to call their supermarket chains.

Minor finished whatever he'd been doing with the clipboard. "Some people think Willow should have her headquarters in Atlanta, but her roots here go pretty deep. As she says, 'If you want to change where you're going, don't change where you've been.'"

I nodded earnestly, but mostly because my neck hurt from the plane flight and the driving.

"Speaking of roots," Minor continued, escorting us down a hallway hung with giant blowups of photos and pie charts and maps bristling with light-up pushpins, "this is where the official tour usually starts." He strode past pictures of Willow as a blurry little girl in black-and-white, Willow looking empowered on the floor of the New York Stock Exchange, Willow shaking hands and matching grins with ex-president Jimmy Carter.

"Since you're up to speed on Willow and her story," Minor called over his shoulder, "we'll go directly to the lady herself."

He smiled, but there seemed to be a nervous twitch in the corner of it.

～

MINOR STOPPED at the end of the hall, where a stainless-steel elevator awaited his touch on a keypad. Seconds later we rose to the second floor.

"She's in Studio B," he said, pointing left.

A red light glowed above the oversized door with the push bar. To the right of the door stood a square-jawed man, late thirties, upright as the Washington Monument and just as animated. Dark blue sports jacket, khakis, no tie. A Secret Service agent on Casual Friday, maybe, except that it was Wednesday.

"The steadfast Mr. Yates," Minor said.

The man nodded. "Yes, sir."

Minor turned to us. "They must be shooting. When the light goes off, we can go in."

The light stayed on. We waited. I nodded at Mr. Yates, who stoically nodded back.

Minor unzipped his leather jacket and stowed his motorcycle helmet under his arm. He aimed a mechanical smile at the glowing red bulb. "As Willow says, good things come to those who wait—and better things come to those who don't."

Mercifully, the light went dark.

We followed him through the door. A white glare stabbed our eyeballs and my hand flew up to shield mine. I wondered whether heaven looked like this to newcomers.

Stephen squinted. "Must be all that empowerment."

Blinking rapidly, I saw it was only video lights with silver umbrella reflectors. They were trained on a set decorated with giant plastic arrows floating in midair, squiggling in all directions like confused tropical parasites. In the middle of it all stood a small, slender figure with her back to everyone else.

It was Willow.

She was screaming.

CHAPTER 4

THE FIGURE TURNED TO FACE THE CAMERAS.

It was Willow, all right.

The scream was a frustrated one, not a stabbed-in-the-shower shriek. To our right the sound man flinched and yanked off his headphones.

Hard to believe, I thought, that such a noise could come from such a body. She was tiny, fragile as a hummingbird with osteoporosis, looking like a casual hug might prove fatal. She still had the blunt-cut blonde hair she'd had when she'd signed her first contract with Pendleton. Still wore a charcoal business suit with pants, her gender confirmed only by the lavender scarf around her neck.

But something was different. And it wasn't just the screaming.

I couldn't tell what it was. She seemed a city block away, separated from us by several layers of technology and personnel that included the lights, three cameras with teleprompters, cameramen, a makeup artist who kept rummaging through what appeared to be her fishing tackle box, and half a dozen people with checklists and laptops and furrowed foreheads. Nearest us was another man with a white goatee and a pink face, staring at a monitor as if trying to decide whether to hang himself or take poison.

"It's been a challenging day," Minor muttered in our direction. "This whole issue with the book has been very hard on her."

The man with the goatee shook his head at the monitor, then threaded his way past the contraptions and crew and into the spotlight. Standing next to the unmoving Willow, he folded his hands behind him, bowed his head slightly, and said something.

She nodded, then apparently replied.

He reached over and patted her elbow. Stepping away, he called out, "Brian, can you slow the teleprompter down a notch? Let's take it from 'Don't let anyone tell you.'" He returned to the monitor, his grim countenance suggesting he'd chosen the noose.

"*Your New Direction*, Scene Seven, Take Nine," said someone I couldn't see. There was a clapping sound.

Willow was still for a moment, then addressed the camera in the middle. "Don't let anyone tell you you're too young or too old or too soon or too late." She sliced the air with her hand. "Let the nay-sayers bray their tomorrows away. Let the doom-and-gloom . . . let the doom-and-glue tunes—"

She stopped, then put both fists over her face.

"Oh, not the face," moaned the makeup lady.

Willow lowered her arms. "Philip!" she barked in no particular direction. "Are you here yet?"

Standing in front of me, Minor raised his hand. It seemed to tremble a little.

"Philip, your script is fabulous. But can you come up with an easier way to say that line? We've done—what, ten takes?"

I could practically hear Minor perspiring. He looked

down at the motorcycle helmet in his hand as if it were Yorick's skull and he were Hamlet.

"How about . . . 'Let the doom and gloom of the clowns and buffoons'?"

Willow chewed on her fingernail. "Better. Yes. Let's do it."

"I'm making the change," declared a woman with a laptop. Then she leaned toward a nearby man and murmured, "She's losing it."

The clapper clapped, and Willow tried again. And muffed it.

She stamped her foot. Stepping off camera, she picked up a bottle of water but didn't sip. After clearing her throat, she was back.

"Don't let anyone tell you you're too young or too old or too soon or too late." The voice was starting to get hoarse. "Let the doom-and-gloom tomb . . . let the doom and gloom of the tomb—"

She stopped. Without a word she marched over to one of the plastic arrows and kicked it in what might have been its groin.

"That's it!" she yelled. "We'll reschedule. Next week, maybe."

The man with the white goatee searched the room as if for a rope. Whether he aimed to use it on Willow or himself I couldn't tell.

She fumbled a clip-on wireless microphone from her lapel and tossed it to the floor, where it landed on an X marked with duct tape. Ten seconds later she was out the door.

Minor gave a discreet cough and checked his watch. "We're scheduled to meet with Willow in her office as soon as the shoot is over."

"I guess that would be now," I said. Reaching into my

purse, I fished out a bottle of Advil and started looking for a drinking fountain.

~

TWENTY MINUTES later the three of us were still cooling our heels in front of Willow's desk, literally and figuratively. Minor had ditched his helmet and leather jacket in his own office.

Willow's assistant was a genteel, white-haired lady introduced by Minor as "the magnificent Ms. Melodee Luther." She kept popping in, predicting that Willow would be out any minute. Her soft drawl summoned visions of Forrest Gump, grits, and banana pudding, but so far, she'd offered only coffee and tea.

I stopped after one coffee. Stephen was hard at work on his third, evidently to maintain his momentum in Overdrive.

I gazed around at the multitude of shadow boxes, photos, and other memorabilia that comprised Willow's personal museum. A golden statue on the desk caught my eye. It looked like an angel playing basketball with something stolen from a fifth grader's science fair project.

"Is that an Emmy?" I asked.

Minor nodded. "She has two more at home."

"That's three more than I have," Stephen blurted, clearly flirting with caffeine poisoning.

Finally a metallic click came from the corner behind the desk. The door of what was apparently Willow's executive washroom crept open. Out she stepped, still clad in the charcoal business suit but minus the lavender scarf.

"I don't know which is worse," she groused, making her way to the desk. "Scraping off that foundation they make you wear on camera or looking in the mirror after it's gone."

She plopped onto her chair, a tan leather throne. "I had to

put my face back together. Believe me, you wouldn't want it any other way."

She leaned back and closed her eyes. "I hate this—just *hate* it. I'm sure you folks have better things to do than fly down here and try to put out this fire."

"Actually," I said, "we ran out of Georgia peaches and peanut butter."

She smiled a little, opened her eyes, and fluttered her lashes. "Carolyn. How nice to see you," She paused. "You sent me a lovely plaque." She surveyed the walls and her desk, then frowned. "I swear it's here somewhere. I'll find it later."

Minor extended an open hand in Stephen's direction. "And this is Stephen Ames, senior editor at Pendleton House. He's very familiar with your books."

Stephen fidgeted in his chair. "Had the honor of editing three," he said quickly.

"Well, God bless you, young man," Willow said. "You've probably saved all our rear ends more than once. I don't know what I'd do without you—and Philip, of course."

I looked down at the empty Styrofoam cup in my hand. "We were at the video shoot. I'm sorry you're having to go through this."

She shook her head. "I just *could not do it*. All I've been able to think about are the lies that blogger's been telling. I could barely read the teleprompter, much less focus. People expect more from me and they have a right to."

"That trademark intensity," Minor said, as if they'd discussed the subject a thousand times.

Willow closed her eyes. "Maybe there's no point in even trying. Who's going to watch this DVD, or any of the others, if they think I'm a fake?"

"This, too, shall pass," Minor said, sounding like the unctuous voice-over in a laxative commercial. "Or as a great thinker once said, 'There is only one thing new under the sun: every single day of the rest of your life.'"

"Please don't quote me to myself," Willow mumbled.

I leaned in her direction. "You've helped millions of people. I can't imagine them suddenly turning against you. Especially not because of somebody who's trying to make a name for himself by dragging yours through the mud."

She opened her eyes. "Lady, you are a cup of cold water in the desert."

Minor gave a dismissive wave. "When we get the facts out there, Mr. Tripp will be history. The people who love you now will love you more than ever—and there'll be twice as many of them."

But then he lowered his chin and peered at Willow over his Steve Jobs glasses. "I hate to bring this up. But we might keep in mind that Carolyn isn't here solely to rescue us."

Willow raised an eyebrow. "What do you mean?"

"She has to rescue herself as well. She was, after all, the editor of the memoir. I imagine Pendleton House is demanding . . . *accountability* from her."

I could feel my blood pressure rise. The phrase *aging hack* went through my head, along with a few others never seen on the *Christianity Today* website.

Willow frowned. "I'm sure our guests have our best interests at heart."

"Of course," Minor said.

There was a pause, a kind of cleansing of the verbal palate. Finally Minor looked around as if the four of us had reached a comprehensive and permanent Middle East peace agreement. "So, it's settled, then. Our guests will gather proof of Willow's story, and we'll assist in any way we can."

I frowned. "That's not quite—"

"I owe you one, Carolyn," Willow said. "You, too, Stephen. Let me know what you come up with."

She smiled, but there was something amiss in her eyes. I hadn't noticed it before, in person or on dust jackets or on TV.

There was weariness, but also something guarded. Something tense, hiding.

A secret, maybe?

I tried to let it go, but I'd never been good at that. I didn't like puzzles, especially Rubik's Cubes, but couldn't resist erasing question marks. Especially when failing to do so would result in the end of my career.

I glanced away from Willow's face to avoid the awkwardness of being caught staring. But it was too late.

"Carolyn, are you all right?" she asked.

"Just . . . a bit tired."

She gave a slight smile. "It's been a long day. Things will look better in the morning."

"I'm sure you're right," I said, as I usually did when the opposite was true.

THINGS DIDN'T LOOK BETTER in the morning, but they didn't look worse. They mostly looked blurry without my contacts.

Having awakened at 6:13, I couldn't drift off again. Lying in the dark, I slowly remembered where I was: at the Swan's Corners Inn, a 1960s relic at the edge of town. The place had looked thoroughly unpromising during our check-in after leaving Willow's headquarters, but it was all I could find at the last minute. Two big conventions had seized control of the Atlanta area, overrunning it with two mobs of urban planners and comic book aficionados.

I pulled the cheap bedsheet up to my chin. At least the air conditioning worked, in the sense that it chilled the atmosphere while it rattled and roared. I'd brought earplugs, but they seemed to function only north of the Mason-Dixon line.

There was a noise on the nightstand. It was the wheedle of the room phone, not the *1812 Overture* ringtone of my mobile version.

"Morning!" Stephen said. He sounded perky as an animated Disney rodent, only less endearing. Apparently, he'd found the coffee already.

"Time to rise and shine," he said. "We still meeting downstairs for breakfast?"

I grunted. "I'll need about half an hour."

"Okay," he said, and hung up.

I managed to get upright. This may have been the day the Lord had made, but I'd have to work my way up to the rejoicing part. Skipping the shower for now, I did what I could with clean underwear, a hairbrush, a tube of Fuschia Flicker lip gloss, and a travel-size stick of Secret Invisible Antiperspirant Deodorant.

The tiny elevator down the hall lowered me to my first-floor destination. The latter was designed to suggest a charming Vermont inn, but with all the charm removed due to budget considerations. I entered under the sign we'd noticed the night before:

FREE COMPLIMENTARY BREAKFAST
SERVED 5:30 A.M.—9:30 A.M.

IGNORING the redundancy of following *free* with *complimentary*, I surveyed the space. It was half full of heavy-lidded travelers, most facing a TV in the corner that displayed two earnest-looking CNN news readers anchoring away.

Spying Stephen at one of the tables, I slid into the dented metal folding chair across from him. To my surprise there was no coffee in front of him. And no trace of his earlier perkiness.

But there was a copy of *USA Today*.

"I take it they had no *real* newspapers," I said.

He offered no response, except to hand me the Life section. "Read it and weep." The headline wasn't in Second Coming type, but may as well have been:

WILLOWGATE?

THE SUBHEAD WAS SMALLER:

BREAKING SCANDAL HITS POPULAR SPEAKER, AUTHOR

I DIDN'T WEEP. I just wanted to.

"Something nasty has hit the fan," he said.

I sighed. "I need some coffee before I read this. And maybe one of those gluey-looking Danishes. Do you want some?"

"Yeah, I guess."

We went to the breakfast bar. The coffee smelled a little like bug spray, but we got some anyway. My pastry had a blob of red goo in the middle. Stephen opted for petrified Raisin Bran.

After silently asking the blessing, which always made me wonder whether I was being a coward, I ate a few bites and lowered myself into the bad news.

The article was about 500 words. Mostly basics—the

blogger, the accusations, the photo of Willow playing Moses with lots of lens flares.

When I looked up, Stephen was picking a raisin chip from his teeth. "So," he said. "What do you think?"

"Probably not Pulitzer material. But remarkably free of typos."

"Calling it 'Willowgate' doesn't seem very original."

"This is *USA Today*, not Ursula LaGuin."

"Didn't say much new. But the sidebar on Tripp is kind of helpful."

"Too bad there was no picture of him. We already know what Willow looks like." I folded up the Life section and stuck it in my pocket.

"So what do we do now?"

I shrugged. "That depends. What did you take away from our meeting yesterday?"

"Not a whole lot. Willow stands by her story and Minor stands by Willow."

"The malignant Mr. Minor. I trust him about as far as I can throw his motorcycle."

"Sounds like they're expecting us to prove Willow's innocent," he said. "But practically everybody who knew her when she was little is dead now. If you don't believe in repressed memories, you won't believe in hers. And some of the stuff—like how suicidal she was—only she would know. How are we supposed to prove she's telling the truth?"

I took another bite and stared at the TV, thinking.

"We may not have to," I said after a few moments. "If we can prove the blogger isn't."

He frowned. "Come again?"

"We have to assume Mr. Tripp discovered—or was given—information that led him to believe Willow's a fraud."

"Right. Although he hasn't said what his source is."

"So, we need to find out. See what evidence he has, and poke holes in it."

"How do we find out what his evidence is?"

Another bite, another sip. "Ask him."

"Why would he tell us?"

I smiled. "Hey, he'll probably tell you anything. You guys have a lot in common. You're not much older than he is. You both have umbilical connections to the Internet."

"Ah. Right. And you and Sandra Bullock are twins."

I scoffed. "*Sandra Bullock?* I'm nowhere near as old as she is. And my hair's a totally different color. And—"

"Please don't have a stroke. I'm just saying that ageism is a bad thing."

Setting my jaw, I told myself for the thousandth time what a good editor he was, and that the pepper spray in my purse was for emergencies only.

He downed the rest of his coffee. "So, what are you suggesting?"

"That if we're going to visit Zane Tripp, we'd better do it as soon as possible."

He sighed. "No time like the present," he said, pulling out his phone. "Maybe I can find him."

I finished my breakfast and went back to drooping in my chair, staring at the two talking news heads in the corner.

I wondered whether Hunter had seen the paper yet. I wasn't sure he could read, but he'd gotten all those inspirational anecdotes somewhere.

Next time I heard from him, he wouldn't be telling me motivational stories. He'd be setting the date of my public termination.

CHAPTER 5

HAVING POSTPONED MY SHOWER, I RETURNED TO MY ROOM while Stephen tried to locate Mr. Tripp. Unfortunately, the plumbing system of the Swan's Corners Inn couldn't cope with the doomsday scenario of hosting more than one guest. The result was a torrent of water that felt as though it had been piped directly from Glacier National Park.

I warmed up by gazing wistfully into space and trying to remember the good old days before I was born. Then I called Stephen.

"Are you still downstairs?" I asked.

"Yeah. I've been trying to find Tripp's address. If I can just . . . Oh, hey, hold on."

I waited.

"Got it," he said. "Want to know how I did it?"

I didn't really but all the management seminars had taught me to pretend I did. "Tell me."

"I went to Tripp's website and looked at the bottom of his home page. Found the name of his LLC. Looked that up in last year's notices of incorporation in the Atlanta paper. They have to list an address for each one."

"Sounds complicated."

"It is. But if that's his address, we can go find him. Right now."

"Shouldn't we call to make sure he's there?"

"His number's unlisted. Either because he doesn't have a landline or he doesn't want anybody to reach out and touch him."

"He's probably at work," I said. "The sidebar said when he's not blogging, he works in a coffee shop."

"But it doesn't say *where* he baristas. And yeah, I know *barista* isn't a verb."

"Okay. Meet me at the car."

A few minutes later we were sitting in the Altima, waiting for the air conditioning to kick in. I'd traded my editor's blazer for a teal linen jacket with the sleeves rolled up.

"So," I said. "According to that sidebar, before Willow came along Mr. Tripp's biggest exposé was about a childcare center that didn't disinfect its toys every day. Not quite WikiLeaks."

"Not even Drudge," Stephen said.

"Sounds like muckraking hasn't been too profitable so far. Otherwise he wouldn't be working as a coffee shop barista."

"Well, he's hit the big time now. Maybe he'll quit his—"

Suddenly the ringtone was playing from my pocket. Retrieving the phone, I knew without looking whose number I'd see onscreen. I also knew I'd better pick up.

"Carolyn!" said the voice, sounding suspiciously chipper. "Hunter. How are things in Atlanta?"

"Not too hot," I said.

"Really? I heard it was pretty steamy down there."

"I'm not referring to the weather."

There was a pause. His cheerfulness withered like a weed. "Frankly, neither am I. Have you seen *USA Today*?"

"Just the bad parts."

"Then you know why I'm calling. What have you found out so far about the book?"

"Willow's sticking to her story," I said.

"That's good, right?"

"I guess, but it's no defense. We need to hear what the blogger knows or thinks he does. We're trying to find out."

He paused, then came back as if he'd just changed roles in a one-man show. He was The Old Storyteller again.

"Carolyn, have you heard the saying, 'The buck stops here'?"

"Many times."

"U.S. President Harry Truman said that. Do you remember him?"

"Not personally. I'm not that old."

"Of course not. You probably can't even remember Eisenhower. He was the bald-headed one."

"So I've heard."

"Well, back to Harry Truman." It was the smoothest transition since the French Revolution. "I'm sure you understand the moral of that story. At this moment in history, the buck stops at *your* desk. A lot of people are depending on you. This is your chance to be our hero."

Ow, I thought. Even *he* sounded embarrassed to say it. Maybe Philip Minor had been moonlighting, writing Hunter's motivational speeches, too.

"I'll keep the image of that U.S. president before me at all times," I said.

"See that you do. I'd hate to lose you." The line went dead.

I turned to Stephen. "Hunter," I said.

"What was that about a president?"

"Never mind. Let's go."

It was time to meet the young man who'd caused all this turmoil.

And to find out why.

~

HE WAS A CLEVER FELLOW, Zane Tripp.

Or so he seemed on his website, which Stephen revisited as we headed for the street address he'd found. It was about half an hour away, he said.

The blogger's site was called *Tripped Up*, which I had to concede was inspired. *Trip* worked on so many levels for a muckraker with his last name, especially if he was also clumsy, drug-addicted, or fond of travel.

My admiration was a problem, though. Tripp was my employer's nemesis, an assumed liar who had to be stopped. But here I was giving him points for originality.

I turned to Stephen. "Do me a favor. Tell me this guy is a four-hundred-pound man-child living in his parents' basement. Tell me he lives on pizza and jalapeño poppers."

He swiped his fingers across the phone screen. "Not that I can see from his picture. Seems to be in pretty good shape. Looks a little like Ansel Elgort, but skinnier."

I didn't ask who that was. I'd look it up later on IMDb.

He tapped the screen again. "Considers himself an 'indie journalist.' He's 'chasing stories wherever they lead, telling truths some people don't want to hear.' Bachelor of Arts from Georgia State University. Majored in journalism and communication. Interned at CNN Digital."

I steered gradually onto Interstate Highway 285. "You'll have to try harder," I said. "I don't dislike him yet."

"Just a minute." He poked and swiped. "You'll be going south on I-85. Stay on it for fourteen miles." He tapped again, then paused to read. "He calls Pendleton House 'a festering cesspool of corruption and greed. Just another corporate octopus with its tentacles squeezing the life out of the rest of us.'"

"Subtract points for mixed metaphors," I said.

"He doesn't 'trust this so-called publisher to do anything other than harass me and my sources.'"

"Probably right. Maybe he won't talk to us after all."

Stephen put the phone in his lap. "Or maybe he will. He's never had this much attention, this many followers. Willow-gate is his dream come true."

"Then why does he need us?"

"He can't afford to let the controversy fade. Gotta keep it alive. I've been looking at his posts. No new information. Just keeps rephrasing everything."

I nodded. "So, he needs new content to keep people coming back. His fifteen minutes of fame are almost up."

"Exactly. He'll meet with us so he can write that we harassed him and festered like a cesspool and tried to squeeze him with our tentacles."

"I hope you're right. If not, our job will be a lot harder."

Stephen put his earbuds in his ears. "The hard part won't be getting him to talk. It'll be getting him to shut up."

THE CLOSER WE got to Atlanta, the closer we got to the rear bumper of the SUV in front of us. Soon traffic was stop-and-go, almost as slow as the hypervigilant brake-stomping of my daily commute to Manhattan.

I sighed. "At the risk of sounding like a five-year-old in the back seat, are we there yet?"

Stephen studied his phone screen. "I think we're getting close to Home Park. That's Tripp's neighborhood."

After a dozen turns or so, we passed a rustic wooden sign

with white letters that said HOME PARK. Then a bunch of storefronts, one of which said VALHALLA DONUTS. The misspelling bothered me, but I was willing to put up with anything where doughnuts were concerned.

Stephen swiped his screen a few times. "I've got the website for this place. Man, I can't believe these pictures. Peanut Butter Cup Doughnut. Chocolate Wild Berry Fritter. S'mores . . ."

I swallowed, not from anxiety but to conceal the fact that I was drowning in my own saliva.

We passed a bazaar of businesses catering to twentysomethings, from Vaper's Paradise to Starbucks. "Wonder whether Tripp works there," Stephen said.

"He doesn't seem fond of corporate monsters that strangle the life out of the little guy." Before he could reply, we passed another one.

Soon the storefronts yielded to a tree-lined residential zone, the shadows of oaks and hickories dappling the windshield as we passed beneath.

Stephen checked his phone. "In 500 feet, turn left at Hackberry Street Northwest."

I did and the canopy of foliage was so dense it seemed like twilight.

Tripp's mailbox was the start of a long driveway, gray gravel. The forest and the darkness thickened further. I was tempted to turn on the headlights.

"He must like his privacy," I said.

"So did the Unabomber."

I pulled up to a small, olive green duplex. No garage, just a carport. A boxy subcompact, sky blue, sat there looking old.

When I turned off the engine, the rain-forest climate rushed back.

"Somebody must be home," Stephen said.

We got out, stretched, and stood there, saying nothing. The stillness seemed to make the heat even more oppressive. We took in the leafy dome overhead and the profusion of that nasty Southern vine that had commandeered the chain link fence between this property and the next.

"Is that what I think it is?" Stephen said, keeping his voice low.

"What?"

"Over the door. A surveillance camera."

"Seems to be."

"It's not moving."

"Are they *supposed* to move?"

He shrugged. "Maybe not."

I stopped, listening. Nothing but chirping bugs that sounded like they were the size of house pets.

Stephen moved stealthily toward the door, as if expecting the hooded white camera to lock its gaze on him, perhaps even to land a ruby laser dot on his forehead.

"I think our blogger has a thing about security," he whispered. He pointed at the door which had not one but two deadbolts.

I rang the doorbell which was loud and grating in the quiet. The noise faded but there seemed to be no stirring inside. I rapped gently on the door. Nothing.

Stephen leaned in and knocked more forcefully. This time the door moved slightly. Looking down at the brass knob, I saw that despite the deadbolts, the door was not only unlocked but unlatched.

"Mr. Tripp's security arrangements aren't very secure," Stephen said.

With two fingers I pushed the door open a few inches, just enough to let him know we were there. "Mr. Tripp?"

Still quiet.

"I'm Carolyn Neville. From Pendleton House Publishers. We hear you've got a problem with one of our books. We're trying to find out what's going on. Can we talk with you?"

Still nothing.

"We know you might be cautious about dealing with us. But we're not lawyers or anything. Just editors."

Stephen snorted. "Yeah. There's nothing more harmless than editors, man."

I hoped hearing a young guy's voice might help, especially a cynical sounding one saying *man*. But no.

I nudged the door a little farther, enough to see the small living room and part of the kitchen beyond. A worn, blue sofa was piled with magazines. A lid-open wicker chest posed as a coffee table in front of it. Papers were scattered on the fake hardwood floor. Through a doorway I could see dirty dishes heaped in a sink.

"Looks like the place has been ransacked," I said.

Stephen looked over my shoulder. "Can't tell. He's a twenty-six-year-old guy. We're not exactly known for our housekeeping skills."

I opened the door wider. "I don't think that's it," I said. "Dishes, maybe. But all the—"

That's when I saw it.

And hoped I'd never see anything like it again.

There was a leg on the floor, sticking out from behind the wicker chest. I could see it only from the knee down, clad in faded denim and what looked like a leather deck shoe.

Nothing moved, least of all me.

"Oh, my God," Stephen whispered.

I forced myself to step forward. The unmoving young man with the black hair was wearing a blue-and-white checked shirt. There was no mistaking the fist-sized patch of dark red that soaked his chest. Or the finality of all the dark red that pooled beneath his body.

"It's him," Stephen said.

Despite the heat, I shivered.

CHAPTER 6

"Did you know Mr. Tripp?"

The man asking the question was an Atlanta Police Department homicide detective who'd introduced himself as Sergeant Luis Valenzuela. He looked to be in his mid-thirties, cleft chin and high cheekbones, short and wiry as a jockey but less flamboyantly dressed in a white shirt and narrow maroon tie.

When he sat, as he was doing on a tree stump in the front yard, he kept leaning forward as if spurring a thoroughbred to the finish line.

I was standing, my outfit not conducive to stump sitting, feeling numb, a little dizzy. I tried not to think about the body that lay on the other side of the door.

"Ms. Neville?"

"Uh . . . no, we hadn't met Mr. Tripp yet. We came here hoping to."

He clicked the ballpoint pen he was using to take notes. "You and Stephen Ames?"

"Yes."

I glanced down the driveway at the Altima. Stephen sat in

the front passenger seat with his window down, the two of us having been separated for interviewing. "Standard procedure," Stephen had whispered to me before walking to the car. "Otherwise we might influence each other's accounts of what we saw. If our stories were different, they could catch us in a lie. Saw it on *Law and Order*."

Now he seemed to be napping in the car or at least in Crash mode. Lined up behind him were two black squad cars, the detective's unmarked black sedan, a white ambulance that said GRADY EMS over the cab, and a white van from the medical examiner's office. Still dazed, I kept thinking about how monochromatic it was.

The detective clicked his pen again, repeatedly. "Ms. Neville?"

I pulled my gaze back to his. "Yes. Sorry."

"What happened here today?"

"I don't know. I guess Mr. Tripp was shot and killed."

"I mean what happened to *you*."

"Oh." I felt stupid. "We . . . got here around 10:15. Rang the bell and knocked, no response. Called to him. Discovered the door wasn't locked or even closed." I swallowed. "When we opened it, we . . . found him."

"When you came down the driveway, did you see or hear anything unusual?"

"The driveway was awfully long, but other than that, no."

"Anybody coming the other way, leaving the house? Any shouting? Any sounds at all?"

"No."

"And when you parked, what did you see and hear?"

"As for hearing, not much of anything. We saw the camera over the door, the deadbolts. The car in the carport. Or we assumed it was his."

"Did you touch anything?"

I thought for a moment. "The door, when I knocked. Stephen knocked, too. And the door when I pushed it open."

"And when you found the body, how would you describe it?"

I hesitated, and my eyes started to water. "On the floor in front of the couch. Face up. There was so much blood. I'm sure it all still looks the same way, unless the crime scene people have moved something."

"What happened after that?"

"I checked his wrist for a pulse. Couldn't find one. Stephen called 911."

"Other than his wrist, did you move anything?"

"Not that I recall."

"Then what?"

"The paramedics showed up in the ambulance, then the two officers. Then we waited, mostly in our car." I paused, trying to remember. "A man from the medical examiner's office came . . . and a little after that, you arrived, and then the evidence technicians."

I looked at the house, now surrounded by yellow POLICE LINE DO NOT CROSS tape. One of the investigators, a woman wearing a dark blue, short-sleeved shirt and rubber gloves, was carrying out what appeared to be a Ziploc bag in each hand.

The pen clicked again. "And during that time, did you do anything in the house? Flip a light switch? Use the bathroom? Move any papers?"

"No."

He leaned forward even farther. "And you came to meet Mr. Tripp because . . . why?"

I sighed. It was all too complicated to explain. If only I had a synopsis or something, I could just—

Then I remembered... *USA Today*. The Life section was

still in the pocket of my jacket. I pulled it out and unfolded it to the "Willowgate" article.

"*This* is why," I said, handing it to him.

He looked at the headline. "Huh. Yeah, I heard something about this. From a guy at work." He looked up. "Somebody who spends a little too much time on the Internet, if you ask me." Something in his brown eyes said he wanted to smile, but he knew this wasn't the time or place.

"Stephen and I are editors at Pendleton House, the publisher of the book. We came to find out what Mr. Tripp knew about Willow Hayly's story."

He dropped his gaze and read silently for about a minute. I watched the somber bustle of technicians with cameras and tape measures and devices whose names I didn't know.

"Okay," he said when he was done. "Looks like the two of you are here to basically shut this guy down."

"I wouldn't put it that way. We just want to find out whether his charges are true, so we can decide what to do about the book."

"Uh-huh." Leaning forward farther than ever, he got up from the tree stump and rubbed his lower back. "I guess there's quite a bit of money at stake with something like this."

"Well . . . there could be, yes."

"Some people might think your employer wouldn't be too upset if this guy just disappeared."

I did a double take. Did he think we'd actually do something to get rid of Tripp?

"Now, wait a minute," I said. "We don't go around shooting people. If you—"

He raised his hands in a *Whoa* gesture. "Hey, I don't doubt that. It's not like you're working for a drug cartel or a chop shop or something."

"Thank you."

"You're in publishing, right? You work with lots of smart people. I mean, *really* smart."

I hesitated. "Well, not as many as I might like."

"But they're not morons, generally speaking. People who put out books are intelligent."

I didn't tell him I sometimes questioned that. This was no time to flaunt the publishing industry's dirty laundry.

"Look," he said. "You and I both know it'd be crazy to think such smart and talented people would be involved in something like this. But do you know of anybody *not* so smart and *not* so talented who might have wanted the victim to disappear?"

I shook my head. "I guess everyone who backs Willow's version of her story could have a grudge against Mr. Tripp. But I don't know anybody crazy enough to think murdering him would solve anything."

He nodded. "Like I said, too smart for that. I have a lot of respect for people in publishing."

"I'm sure a few of them actually deserve it."

He couldn't help smiling this time, a shy smile. The body language of interrogation softened. His head tilted to the side, almost like a toddler trying to charm a cookie from his mother right before dinner. I couldn't help smiling back.

"This has been . . . good," he said.

"I'm not much of a witness."

"No, no, you've been great." He clicked his pen once more, then stuck it back in his shirt pocket. "How much longer will you be in Atlanta?"

"I don't know. Why?"

He looked around as if for eavesdroppers. "I don't know whether I should bring this up. But speaking of publishing, I have a few aspirations in that area myself."

Uh-oh, I thought. My Editorial Pressure Indicator light went on.

"Yeah, I write what you might call cop novels. Or at least I'm trying. Finished one, and I'm halfway through the second."

My whole inner dashboard lit up.

I'd met too many would-be authors who'd tried at the worst possible times to get me to read their manuscripts. Like the one who followed me into the bathroom at a writers' conference and stood outside my stall, going on and on about her premise and protagonist. It was one reason I rarely attended such events anymore.

I tried to think of a diplomatic response. This was why God had created form rejection slips, but they wouldn't help me now.

I looked up at the leafy canopy over our heads. Maybe I needed to see this as a blessing in disguise. This wasn't a writers' conference. It was a murder investigation and we could end up caught in the middle, even on some kind of suspect list. It might be good to have a friend at the police department, even if it meant having to say a few nice things about his writing, which was probably unreadable.

"Maybe I can find time to take a look," I said.

"Hey, that would be fantastic." There was an awkward pause, as if he'd never expected to hear a yes. "I . . . well, I could make a copy and give it to you or something."

"Okay."

He cleared his throat, then reverted to something he must have read in the police academy manual. "Is there anything else you can tell me at this time that you think might be helpful?"

"Not that I know of."

He plucked a business card from his pocket. "Call me if you think of something," he said, handing it over. "I'll be in touch. There'll be more questions."

"I'm sure," I said.

"Now, I'm supposed to encourage you not to leave the Atlanta area. We can't say 'Don't leave town,' like they do on TV, and we can't make you stay. But things will go a lot smoother if you stick around for a while."

"We'll let you know when we're ready to go."

He smiled, this time a little less shyly. "Excellent. Would you mind asking Mr. Ames to come over so he and I can talk? The two of you could trade places."

"Of course."

I headed for the car, still seeing that grin. To my surprise, I hoped I'd see it again.

"Your turn," I told Stephen through the open window.

He raised his eyelids. "How did it go?" he asked sleepily.

"Can't tell you. Collusion, remember?"

"I saw that on—"

"You told me. Everything you know about crime-solving you learned from TV."

He cleared his throat. "And Wikipedia."

"We've been instructed to trade places."

He got out of the car, crunching the gravel, slightly unsteady. "Wish me luck," he said, and set off in Valenzuela's direction.

The Altima was an oven. Leaving the door open, I watched as Stephen shook the detective's hand. They ignored the stumps, kept standing, and seemed to get along famously.

Before long, though, the detective seemed antsy, frequently shifting his weight from one foot to the other. He looked like a man who needed a restroom, which unfortunately reminded me that I did, too. It led me to pray fervently that Stephen's interview would be short.

Closing my eyes, I settled back against the headrest.

Everything had changed. This morning had been bad enough, when the problem was vetting Willow's story to save her empire and the cash it produced for Pendleton House, not to mention my career.

Now we could be suspected of murder. I could see the headlines in *USA Today* and on CNN and NBC and every conspiracy-theory website in the world:

PUBLISHER SILENCES CRUSADING BLOGGER
Or
WILLOWGATE TURNS DEADLY SERIOUS
Or maybe just
ROGUE EDITORS KILL COURAGEOUS YOUNG
JOURNALIST

THE ONLY QUESTION was exactly how big a disaster Tripp's death would be for two hapless bystanders who'd been in the right place at the worst possible time.

I stared at the house's front door. Why did somebody have to shoot him? And couldn't someone else have discovered the body?

I shook my head. The young man was dead and I was ticked over the inconvenience. I'd probably just violated a couple hundred biblical commands. I told myself I was just tired, disoriented.

I was. But thank God nobody could read my mind.

~

JUST AS MY bladder was ready to burst our detainment ended. Stephen returned with a business card in his hand. I tried not to let on how desperate I was getting.

Taking my place behind the wheel, I backed the Altima away from the yellow tape, turned sharply, and headed slowly up the driveway. Stephen got out his phone. Every so often a faint sigh leaked out of him with no reason given and none requested.

Finally he cleared his throat. "Let's go to that doughnut place."

My mouth started watering again. "Well, if you insist," I said, trying to sound ambivalent. *Wow*, I thought. A restroom *and* doughnuts.

Ten minutes later we parked beneath the Valhalla logo, which consisted of a doughnut wearing a Viking helmet.

We walked in just as three giggling twentysomethings came out, none of whom looked as fleshy as I did. What was their secret? Youthful metabolism? Bulimia? Tapeworms?

Inside the shop it felt 30 degrees cooler. Heading straight for the ladies' room, I wanted to stay here forever.

Five minutes later we stood in front of the counter, over which loomed a mammoth menu picturing the reunion of every member of the doughnut family, living and dead. One wall was plastered with framed reviews from newspapers; another had shelves stacked with T-shirts and horned hats.

There were also a few tables, the nearest of which we claimed. I'd have to praise this place on Yelp when my social media fast was over.

"I'll have one of everything," I said.

Stephen shook his head. "Hunter won't pay for that."

I pretended not to hear. "They've got some healthy doughnuts. I'm sure Maple Bacon Cheddar has protein. Sweet Potato Cake's a vegetable. Fresh Strawberry and Cream is a fruit."

He snorted. "Yeah, like Pixy Stix."

I rubbed my eyes. "It's just that I need those carbs. I'm out of steam."

"Well, it's not every day you see somebody who's been shot."

"Thank God for that."

"What did you think of the detective?"

I hesitated. I wasn't about to tell him I thought the guy was cute. "He seemed . . . friendly."

"It was weird. I got the feeling he thought *we* might have done it. That's insane."

I nodded. "Unfortunately, I got the same feeling."

"So, what are we going to do?"

"I don't know. Let's order."

I got a Chocolate Wild Berry Fritter, a S'mores, and a strawberry iced herbal tea. Stephen got a custard-filled letter *A* for Atlanta, a Reduced Balsamic Vinegar Doughnut, and an iced coffee (hold the bug spray).

As we waited for our food to arrive, he looked me in the eye. "Do you really think we could become . . . suspects?"

"Hard to believe, but stranger things have happened."

"Should we be answering questions? Do we need a lawyer? What if they want our fingerprints or DNA or something?"

"I bet the Internet has plenty of advice on all those subjects."

"I'm too tired to look anything up now."

When our food came, I alternated tastes of both dough-nuts with sips of iced tea, trying to reach a more blissful plane of existence. Or at least wipe out the memory of what I'd seen on Hackberry Street.

Stephen, meanwhile, bit into the vinegar pastry and made a sour face. "Man, that's *artisanal*," he said, and choked it down with iced coffee. Then he moved on to the custard-filled *A*, which made me think of *The Scarlet Letter* until he'd rendered it unrecognizable.

When we were done, I looked around. "I may be working in a place like this pretty soon."

"Huh?"

"When the story of what happened gets out, I'll be on a fast track to oblivion. Or death row."

He looked down at what was left of his vinegar doughnut. "Are you gonna tell Hunter?"

"Probably don't need to. It'll be everywhere in a day or so. Maybe sooner."

"What do you think he'll do?"

"I don't know."

But I did. First, he'd put on his Ted Bundy face.

Then he'd ask Janice Pulaski to order some supplies, starting with a sign to post over my head in Rockefeller Center.

~

THAT NIGHT I HAD A DREAM.

I kept seeing the body lying on the floor.

It woke me up, then kept me awake. It was like the whole crime scene was burned on my brain.

I wondered whether I'd ever dream of anything else.

I prayed for Zane Tripp's parents, then drifted off about an hour later.

CHAPTER 7

NEXT MORNING, I DOZED PAST DAWN DESPITE THE RATTLING of the air conditioner. Stephen and I met downstairs for another Free Complimentary Breakfast, which seemed worse than usual after romping in the fields of Valhalla Doughnuts.

I didn't tell Stephen about the dream. I wondered whether he'd dreamed at all but didn't ask.

"We've got our work cut out for us," I said.

"No lie. What's our first move?"

"What do *you* think it should be?"

I waited, hoping he'd think I was using the Socratic method to squeeze out a great insight. I was just stalling until he answered his own question.

He picked a petrified raisin from his teeth and put it on his napkin. "The only way to prove we're innocent . . . is to prove someone else *isn't*."

"Exactly," I said, not sure what he meant.

"We need to figure out who had a reason to want Tripp dead," he said.

"And who might that be?"

"Besides us?"

"Well, yes."

He started counting on his fingers. "There's Willow . . . and Willow's cousin, the one who grew up with her, whose name I keep forgetting . . ."

"Maybe a roommate," I added. "Or a co-worker at the coffee shop. Or the 'repressed memories expert.'"

"Why him?"

"Tripp pretty much said he was a fake."

He shrugged. "Doesn't seem likely, but okay." He folded his arms across his chest. "Or it could be an enemy Tripp made with his 'indie journalism.'"

"That could be an awful lot of people," I said. "How do we narrow it down?"

I frowned. "*I'm* supposed to ask the questions."

"How should *I* know?" he asked. "I'm an editor, not Hercule Poirot."

He paused, leaning forward, reminding me of Detective Valenzuela's favorite posture. "Hercule Poirot," he said. "Maybe that's the key. The question is, 'What would Poirot do?'"

I shook my head. "I'd rather take my cues from people who actually exist."

He stirred the brown glop in his cereal bowl. "You don't mean who I think you mean, do you?"

"I think you know the answer to that."

He put down his spoon. "Are you a glutton for punishment, or what? Last time you took Marvin's advice, Pendleton almost got sued."

"That was before we found a body on the floor."

"But it's not like Marvin's been a policeman or a lawyer," he said. "He's a good true-crime writer, but that's hardly the same thing."

I fished my phone from my pocket. "*Good* doesn't do him justice. Besides, Marvin Ainsley Pitts is . . . special."

Stephen sighed. "It's because he's black, isn't it? All us white folks in Manhattan love to show off our 'friends of color.' Deep down we're afraid they could stab us at any moment."

I shook my head. "Whatever you say. I'm no expert on race. I grew up in Idaho."

I looked at my watch and picked up my phone. Same time in St. Petersburg, Florida as in Atlanta. Marvin was probably up by now.

His number rang and rang. Finally a voice came on the line. "Hello?"

It wasn't Marvin. It was his longsuffering wife.

"Tracy," I said. "This is Carolyn Neville."

"Sister Carolyn." Her voice was as soothing as a hot water bottle. "How are you, honey?"

I hesitated. There was no short answer to that question, not if I was honest. With Stephen sitting there, I decided to leave the personal stuff for another time.

"I'm in sort of a jam. But I always am when I call, aren't I?"

"'Man is born to trouble as the sparks fly upward.' Book of Job. What can I do for you?"

"Actually, I've got something to ask Marvin. Is he there?"

"No," she said, sounding a little less warm. "For all I know, he may not be anywhere. Not in this world, anyway."

"I'm not sure I follow you."

"He's jumping out of an airplane. Some place in Zephyrhills. At least that was his plan. He and his crackpot friend from the condo next door. They left yesterday. They're supposed to be back in two days."

"He's *skydiving*?"

She grunted. "Carolyn, the man is seventy-three years

old. He has less sense than the day I married him. 'Do not put the Lord your God to the test.' Book of Matthew."

"Has he done this before?"

"If you mean has he jumped out of a plane before, not that I know of. If you mean has he done anything stupid before, of course he has."

I made a sympathetic noise, not wanting to get in the middle of it.

"Says I'm not adventurous enough," she continued. "Says just because I was a bookkeeper all those years, I don't have to think like one. But you and I both know the truth is he won't take care of himself."

"Hmm," I said.

"Hardly ever turns his cell phone on. But if he survives and comes back in two days like he promised, I'll have him call you."

"If you talk to him before then, could you tell him it's urgent?"

"I will. Not that it'll do a lick of good."

"Thank you."

"God bless, honey," she said, then hung up.

I turned toward Stephen. "He's not there," I said. "I hope you're hap—"

"Shhh," he said, eyes on the TV. "We're missing something on CNN."

I looked and listened.

And groaned.

The anchorpersons were sitting in front of a photo of Willow. She looked as if she were laughing at a particularly hilarious joke, with WILLOWGATE hanging over her head and theirs.

In solemn tones they read what sounded like a paraphrase of the *USA Today* story, adding nothing except their impeccable hairdos. But then Willow's face was replaced with Zane Tripp's, the photo from his website, reflective and brooding and so young.

"And in a startling turn of events," the female anchor said, "Atlanta Police reported yesterday that the blogger who broke the Willowgate story was found dead of a gunshot wound at his home. Police are treating the death as a homicide."

I glanced around as if the other guests might guess our connection and turn on us with pitchforks. The woman on the screen said something about there being no comment yet from Willoworth International or Pendleton House Publishing. I tried to shrink in my chair.

Finally the show switched to a commercial, something about Medicare with jovial, white-haired baby boomers who wore fishing hats and did yoga. I wished I were 25 years older.

"Hope Hunter isn't watching," Stephen said.

"If he's not, you can be sure somebody who *is* will tell him all about it."

He crumpled up his napkin. "So, can Marvin help us?"

I shook my head. "He won't be back for a couple of days."

"Looks like we don't have that kind of time."

"Not anymore."

He considered the ceiling. "On the plus side, you were right. Not even a day's passed, and the story's out."

"I get tired of being right all the time," I mumbled.

"I can only imagine," he said.

WE KEPT STARING at the screen, even when the anchors turned chuckleheaded over viral videos about a lawn-mowing dog and a bank robber with a stuffed parrot on his shoulder. It was even less funny than it sounded.

Finally I turned to Stephen. "All right. Since Marvin isn't available, I'll ask the question. What *would* Poirot do?"

"First thing, he'd find a better motel to stay in. He was pretty picky, you know."

I rolled my eyes. "What next?"

"Oh, he'd probably do some other stuff eventually. But his top priority would be a more suitable place to park his little gray cells."

"This place was the best I could find. If you can do better, knock yourself out."

He held up his phone. "I already did last night, on airbnb.com. But somebody else has it for two more nights. We're trapped until then."

From my pocket came the tinny strains of the *1812 Overture*. I pulled out the phone and checked the screen. The area code ruled out Manhattan and, therefore, Hunter. It seemed to be from Atlanta, but the number was unfamiliar.

The smooth baritone of the caller, however, was not.

"Carolyn? Philip Minor." The baritone was not so smooth, actually. It was raspy at the edges.

"Philip. You sound a bit . . . apprehensive."

"Must be the connection. What would I have to be apprehensive about?"

"Nothing. Unless you watch CNN."

"Unfortunately, I do. Or rather Willow does. She is extremely upset, and understandably so."

"As are we," I said.

"She's distraught about all the 'Willowgate' references she's seeing there. And elsewhere."

"And by Zane Tripp's death, of course."

"Oh, that, too."

"Well, these things hap—"

"We want to strategize. This has to disappear. We need you here right away. Can you make a 10:30 meeting?"

I looked at my watch. "I suppose so."

"We'll see you then." He paused. "Oh, and Carolyn?"

"Yes?"

"Willow seems to have a great deal of faith in you. That makes one of us."

He hung up before I could thank him.

I turned to Stephen. "Well, that's a relief. We're about to make this whole problem go away."

"How?"

"By strategizing. In a meeting."

I got up, tossed the remains of my breakfast in the trash, and slung my purse over my shoulder.

"Time to go," I said.

"Where?"

"To the Department of Wishful Thinking."

WILLOW'S OFFICE hadn't changed since our last visit, except for the new bottle of antacid gummies on her desk. She sat on her throne, shook out a gummy, and started chewing.

Stephen and I positioned ourselves where we had the first time, as if it were a tradition. So did Minor, wearing a blank expression that probably masked a desire to have me fired, arrested, or skinned alive.

"I swear it's all collapsing," Willow said. "Absolutely out of control. Have you heard what they're saying? I can't turn on the TV without hearing about 'Willowgate.'"

"Same with the Internet," Stephen said, not making things better.

"And that photo!" Willow continued. "Where did they get *that*? Looking like I think the whole thing is a joke." She grabbed another gummy.

Minor put his fingertips together in one of those tent

shapes that are supposed to seem contemplative but just look pompous. "We can't control the images the media use. We could try to make sure the stock photo agencies have better shots to choose from. I'll look into it."

He took a stylus from his shirt pocket and scribbled something on the tablet in his lap. Probably the sort of meaningless doodling I did when I met with Hunter Thicke.

"And now the blogger," Willow said. "My God, it's unthinkable."

We all shook our heads for what seemed like a respectful period of time.

"I hear you found the body," Willow said.

I nodded.

"Oh, my dear," Willow said. "It must have been awful."

"It was. It also changes everything. Willowgate isn't just about a life story now. It's about a murder. We all stand to lose a lot more than we did two days ago."

Minor shot me a warning look, then turned back toward his boss. "Now, there's no need to panic. The police will find out who did this. People will see we and Pendleton aren't to blame. We're victims, not villains. Prey, not predators. Targets, not—"

"Unfortunately, alliteration won't save us," I said.

His eyes narrowed. "Nor will never-ending negativism."

"Ah," I said. "More alliteration. Nicely done."

Willow, looking out the window, seemed not to hear us. "This could wreck WorthTV," she said. "Not to mention all the ideas the Chronicle Merkel Media people have. Like turning the memoir into a feature film."

Minor raised his eyebrows. "Feature film? I hadn't heard *that*." He scribbled on his tablet again.

"Weren't you copied?" Willow asked.

"No," he said. "As usual."

"I'll have Melodee forward it to you."

He gave a mirthless chuckle. "A movie based on the memoir. Who's going to fact-check *that* script? Someone other than Carolyn, I imagine."

I felt my jaw clench. "If a certain co-writer had fact-checked Willow's memoir, we wouldn't be sitting here in our current predicament."

He smiled condescendingly. "A co-writer's role is to tell the subject's story, not to be an investigative reporter. I stand by my contributions to the book and I refuse to be the scapegoat. I can't help it if you were new to the job when the book came out and didn't know how to handle it."

The silence was deafening. In a figurative sense.

"All right," Willow said, her voice weary. "That's enough. The important thing is what we're going to do now."

I folded my hands in my lap. "We need to find out who *did* cause Mr. Tripp's death. Relying on the police wouldn't be wise, especially when Stephen and I seem to be among their most convenient suspects."

"Okay," Willow said, sounding dubious.

"We need to talk with other potentially guilty parties," I said. "Like the repressed memory retrieval specialist."

"Dr. Stanton Platte," Willow said. "Why would he be a suspect?"

"The blogger was essentially calling him a liar, saying the abuse was a sham. At least in theory, Platte had his reputation to protect." I paused. "Do you know where he is?"

Minor, not looking up, tapped his tablet. "We have an outdated address and phone on file. A Google search goes nowhere. You'd swear he vanished from the face of the earth about twenty-five years ago."

Stephen leaned toward Willow. "What about your cousin? Sorry, I can never remember his name."

"Gerald," Willow said, looking pained.

"Did he want to protect you?" he continued. "I know it

sounds extreme, but could he have killed the blogger to stop the attacks on your book?"

She gave the same unamused chuckle Minor had a minute before. "I can't imagine that. Gerald's never seemed very interested in my career, much less protective. I haven't heard from him since his mother died, probably because of what I said in the book. I'm sure he hates me. We know where he is, but he probably won't give you the time of day."

For a moment I saw that tense, haunted look in her eyes again, or thought I did.

"We'll have to try anyway," I said. "Where does he live?"

Minor tapped his tablet, balancing it on his thigh. "I have the address. He's still here in Atlanta. Has an auto repair business."

Willow shook her head sadly. "After all these years, I've never seen it," she said, as if it had just dawned on her.

"Well, we need to start somewhere," I said, "and right away."

I glanced around the office, hoping someone would argue with me.

Unfortunately, no one could.

CHAPTER 8

THE ADDRESS ON MINOR'S TABLET BROUGHT US TO A SMALL business park on the outskirts of Atlanta, one of those places where the word *park* had been stretched to include barren zones of steel warehouses, asphalt, and railroad tracks. It was the sort of place customers went only because they had to, searching for establishments with words like *parts* and *supply* and *collision* in their names.

And auto repair, which is why we found ourselves sitting in front of Gerry's Auto Works, a shop barely big enough to contain a single car. Next door on the left was Quality Trophy and Engraving; to the right was A Aardvark Furniture Refinishing, apparently angling to be listed first in the Yellow Pages, just in case anyone still cared.

I turned to Stephen, who'd spent the last half hour using his phone to vacuum up crumbs of Gerald's life from the Internet. "What did you say his last name is?" I asked.

"Sackett. Son of Annalynn Sackett, the aunt who raised Willow. His dad was a Sackett, but he and Gerald's mom divorced when Gerald was little."

"Okay. Let's go."

The tiny waiting room, lined with fake walnut paneling, was empty. A small oscillating fan whirred on the counter, not accomplishing much. Next to it sat an outdated computer, its yellowing beige case layered with enough grime to insulate it in a lightning storm.

In the corner sat a TV, the pre-digital kind with the heft of a diesel locomotive, producing no sound or picture. Three faded tan armchairs, looking as if they needed the immediate attention of A Aardvark Furniture Refinishing, faced the dead screen. From the other side of a wall came the wheeze and clack of some automotive thing.

A handwritten sign taped to the counter said RING BELL FOR SERVICE. There was no bell.

"Ding dong!" Stephen called.

We waited. Nothing happened.

He tried again.

Finally the door from the repair bay opened and something vast filled the opening. It was a man, a towering specimen whose physique might have been described as apelike by one less sensitive than myself. He stepped to the counter and stood there, his pale red hair nearly matching the tint of his freckled skin. The name embroidered over the chest pocket of his dark blue coveralls was GERRY.

"Help you folks?" The Georgia drawl was surprisingly soft, polite.

"Mr. Sackett?"

"That's me."

"I'm Carolyn Neville and this is Stephen Ames. We work for the company that publishes your cousin Willow's books."

The smile disappeared. "You don't say."

I glanced at Stephen, who glanced at me. I guessed we were thinking the same thing: *Uh-oh.*

"We . . . were hoping to talk with you about Willow's life story," I said. "Some questions have come up and we're trying to find out what really happened. You're one of the few people who might know."

He hesitated, looking as if he were trying to decide whether to chat with us or gut us with a hunting knife.

Finally he gave a sigh of resignation. "I guess I am." He waved at the chairs in his waiting room. "Have a seat."

"Care for some sweet tea?" he asked. "I've got about a gallon in the icebox."

"Uh, I'm good," Stephen said.

"How about you, Ms. Neville?"

"Oh, of course." He disappeared into a back room.

"Is sweet tea what it sounds like?" Stephen whispered.

I nodded. *Very* sweet."

"That's what I figured."

When Gerald emerged from the back room, there was a Mason jar in his oversized hand. "I'd join you, but my last one was about half an hour ago." He gave me the drink. "You folks have sweet tea where you're from?"

"Not in restaurants, not in Manhattan." I took a sip and smiled. "Now, that's the real thing. My great-aunt used to make it. She was from Tennessee."

He sat in the third chair, folding his huge, grease-stained hands in his lap as gently as a grandmother, albeit an enormous one. "So," he said quietly, "What would you folks like to know?"

I considered asking whether he could stop using the word *folks* for a minute or so but thought better of it. "I assume you've read *Worth It*," I said. "Willow's book about her life."

"Sure have. Long time ago."

"Are you aware that recently there have been some . . . doubts about it?"

He nodded sadly. "Heard a little about it on the news."

"And you know about Mr. Tripp's death."

"Mr. who?"

"The blogger who raised the doubts about Willow's story."

"He died?"

"Murdered," Stephen said.

Gerald's eyebrows rose. "Oh, my word. That's terrible."

"Mr. Sackett," I said, "This is an awkward question. But how did you feel about Willow's book?"

He looked down at the ugly vinyl floor, the color of which might best be described as Liverwurst Sunset. "I'm fifty-three now, Ms. Neville," he said. "Gone through some changes over the years. Truth is I used to take great offense at the things Willow said about my mother. Wasn't good for my blood pressure, I can tell you that."

He looked up again. "Usually had the radio on while I worked. Started listening to some of those shows where they try to work out some family's problems or answer questions people call in or whatnot. Never been much of a reader, so I wasn't gonna hunt for advice in a bunch of books." He looked sheepish. "You folks being publishers and all, I guess I should apologize."

I chuckled. "You're not exactly alone."

"Did read some of Willow's books, though," he continued. "Not just the first one. Didn't usually read them all the way through, but I could see she had some decent things to say. Like, 'If *anyone* can make you mad, *everyone* can,' and 'Revenge is a dish best served on an empty plate.'"

I nodded, not wanting to offend him by sticking a finger in my open mouth and making a gagging sound. I was all for forgiveness, but triteness was something else.

"Anyway, all that to say I learned to let it go. Wasn't that easy, but I kind of made peace with the past, if you know what I mean." He shrugged, looking a little embarrassed.

"Good for you," Stephen said.

I had my doubts.

I also had one more question but wasn't sure whether to ask it. A nerve might be hit. And he was, after all, a very large man.

I took a deep breath. "I . . . understand you and Willow haven't spoken in a long time. Why is that?"

He lifted his long arms and clasped his hands behind his head, his expression undecided. "Over the years I've thought about getting in touch with her," he said. "But there's a lot of water gone under that bridge. I figure she's too busy now, too famous to bother with the likes of me. Might be better to just let it lie. Go on with our lives."

He lowered his arms and folded his hands in his lap again. "Now I've got a question for you folks. Are you really trying to find the truth and get it out there?"

"Absolutely," I said.

"No matter where it might end up?"

"Yes."

"Well, I guess there's a favor you can do me. See, I know the truth about my mom. I was there. I can forgive, but I can't forget Mom."

He fell silent for a long moment. "Sorry." He cleared his throat. "Don't get me wrong. I don't blame Willow anymore. Maybe she got misled by that Dr. Platte or something when she wrote what she did. But right is right, and my mother does *not* deserve to be remembered as a child abuser. She had her problems, but there wasn't an evil bone in her body."

"Okay."

"That blogger, God rest his soul, had it right. There wasn't any abuse, even if Willow thought there was. If you can prove that and get the word out, I'd be much obliged."

"We'll do our best," Stephen volunteered.

I frowned. "Only if that's where the evidence leads," I said.

"Thanks," Gerald said. "Can't ask for more than that."

He stood up, which seemed to take several minutes, given

his resemblance to the Colossus of Rhodes. We got to our feet as well.

"Thanks for the sweet tea," I said.

"Yes, ma'am," he said. He shook his head. "I surely am sorry to hear about Mr. Tripp. What a world we live in."

"I take it the police haven't talked to you about the murder yet," I said.

"Well, no," he said, looking puzzled. "I'm not sure why they'd want to. I had no quarrel with Mr. Tripp. He was telling the truth about Mom. No quarrel with Willow, either. Nor anybody else, not anymore."

We let ourselves out. Dusk was gathering. Behind us the sounds of wheezing and clacking resumed as Gerald went back to whatever he was doing. We started toward the car.

"He reminds me of my mom," Stephen said. "She's a lot smaller, of course."

"I should hope so."

"I mean, she's so into this self-help stuff. Really believes it's changed her life."

"Maybe it has. I'm not so sure about Mr. Sackett, though."

He stopped. "You think he's faking it?"

"Hard to say. Seems a little strange that his big turnaround didn't motivate him to contact Willow."

"Maybe he thought *she* didn't want to talk to *him*."

I shrugged. "Either way, he won't be much help when it comes to Willow's memoir. He believes it's a lie, or at least a huge mistake."

I started walking again and Stephen followed. "Gerald doesn't seem to belong on the suspect list, either," I continued. "He *agreed* with Tripp, who said his mother wasn't an abuser. He had no reason to kill anybody."

"In other words, we need to find another tree to bark up."

"You have such a way with words," I said, and climbed into the car.

He got into the other side. "Does it seem strange to you?"

"Does *what* seem strange?"

"That we haven't heard anything from Hunter yet. I mean, surely he's gotten the news about Tripp from *somebody*, right?"

I frowned. "Yes, it does seem odd, now that you mention it."

I turned the key in the ignition, trying to ignore the wave of uneasiness that suddenly rolled through my midsection.

The wave passed, but then came another.

Not hearing had to mean something, and not something good.

It was never something good.

CHAPTER 9

THAT NIGHT I DIDN'T DREAM OF THE BODY ON THE FLOOR. MY sleep was sound... almost.

Toward morning, around 4:00 a.m., it was interrupted by a nightmare about being trapped alone in an elevator with Hunter Thicke.

It had a dreamlike quality, not surprisingly, but was utterly realistic in that nothing Hunter said made sense. He held up a photo of Harry Truman but dropped it. After bending to pick it up, he rose looking more like Ted Bundy than ever. He was brandishing a judge's gavel.

"The elevator stops here," he said.

When I woke up, not screaming but perspiring a little, the room was still dark. Watching the ruby numerals on the clock radio crawl from 4:08 to 4:17, I decided to seize the moment and take an early shower.

With no competition for the water heater, I discovered in the most inconvenient way that the shower was blazing— enough to sterilize surgical instruments, or at least parboil human flesh.

By the time I was dressed, it was still too early for breakfast.

I sat on the edge of the bed. Maybe there was a Gideon Bible in the nightstand drawer. I could muddle my way through a chapter of Ecclesiastes, which for some reason had been my favorite book since high school, perhaps because it was so refreshingly bleak. Dust in the wind, and all that.

Or I could pray. How long since I'd done that, other than blessing meals and occasionally requesting deliverance from an oncoming SUV or a snockered co-worker at a Christmas party?

I leaned against the pillows and sighed. My parents had warned me 20 years ago about going to New York, much less working at one of those "godless publishing houses." If I didn't stay close to the campfire, they said, I'd cool off and lose my faith. But somehow, I hadn't.

True, I'd met only four or five believers at Pendleton House over the years. It was no fun to sit through rants in Acquisitions meetings about Bible Belters who wanted to establish a deadly theocracy, complete with oppressed hand-maidens in red dresses and white bonnets. Yet most of the people were at least interesting, some of them even worth imitating. And there was a certain challenge in staying sharp enough to stay on the tightrope.

Thinking about that made me want to call Mikki. But she wouldn't be up yet.

I folded my arms. Well, there was always the Lord's Prayer. So I did that, wondering as usual whether I should use *trespasses* or *debts*, and opting for the latter because it seemed more down-to-earth. When I got to the part about daily bread, my stomach growled.

∽

I LOOKED AT THE CLOCK. Still too early.

Getting up, I went to the dresser where my phone had been charging. If we were ever going to find the elusive Dr. Stanton Platte, I might as well get started.

Thanks to his unusual first name, it took only 25 minutes to sort through a truckload of Stanton Plattes. The first was the one we sought, but his mentions were at least two decades old, before he'd disappeared. The others included a college basketball player from Alaska, a Pennsylvania metallurgist who'd plied his trade at the same steel company for the last 30 years, an eight-year-old Australian violin prodigy, an Indiana florist who was still arranging flowers at the age of 99, and the law firm of Stanton, Platte, Weinstein, & Curtiss. Not to mention all the long-dead Stanton Plattes, whose only relevance was as decorations on the branches of their descendants' family trees.

I tapped my phone to sleep, wishing I could do the same with my forehead.

Finally it was time for the earliest of birds at the Free Complimentary Breakfast. Stephen and I having made no plans to meet, I decided to go alone.

There were no surprises at the buffet. The same TV blathered in the corner. Mercifully, the word *Willowgate* wasn't seen or heard.

I was about to bus my own table when my phone rang.

I recoiled. *Hunter*. It had to be.

Talking to him was the last thing I wanted to do, probably because my most recent interaction with him had involved a deadly if imaginary weapon.

I checked caller ID. It was indeed Ted Bundy, Jr.

"Carolyn!" he said, his voice all smiles. "Long time no talk! Seems that way to me, anyhow." He didn't sound like the same man who'd so recently wanted to kill me in my sleep. "Been out of town. Two-day vacation in the Cayman Islands, courtesy of a hedge fund manager I went to school with. No e-mail; totally incognito."

Incognito? I pictured him in dark glasses and an orange polyester wig. *Ah*, I thought. He must have meant *incommunicado*. Seeing little benefit in correcting him, I didn't.

"Total relaxation," he went on. "Not officially a white-sand beach, but close to it. Massages. Umbrella drinks. You should try it sometime."

I rolled my eyes. "Next chance I get."

"So, I've just come back to an e-mail saying Our Friends in Legal have a great idea. They want to sue the blogger for the nuisance value. A shot across the bow to make him back off or spend the rest of his life in court."

To say that I experienced a sinking feeling might be unoriginal, but it fit. Hunter hadn't heard Zane Tripp was dead.

"Here, I'll read what it says," he continued. 'A phone poll of the Pendleton board has approved the plan, but only if there is sufficient evidence supporting Willow's story.'"

He paused with what I visualized as a look of triumph. "My question to you, Carolyn: What have you got that would make the blogger wet his pants?"

I closed my eyes. How was I supposed to break the news? When you got right down to it, there was no good way.

So, I opened my eyes and did the next best thing. "I'm afraid Mr. Tripp won't be performing any bodily functions for the foreseeable future."

"Why not?"

"He's been murdered. And Stephen and I seem to be persons of interest."

The pause that followed was so long I thought we'd been disconnected.

Finally he spoke, his voice barely above a whisper. "You . .

. didn't do it, did you? I mean, you were supposed to stop him, but not like *that*."

I looked ceilingward. "No, we didn't kill anybody. But the police apparently find it convenient to think we did."

"Oh," he said, sounding as if he were going into shock and needed a blanket.

I couldn't give him one, though. Not when I needed to terrify him into opening the corporate wallet to defend us.

"No doubt a man in your position realizes what all this means," I said.

"No doubt," he said faintly.

"I'm sure you can envision the headlines."

"I don't want to."

"Pendleton's stock will take a nosedive. The buck will stop at . . ." I paused dramatically. "Let's just say the board will blame you, too."

He must have been holding the phone next to his Adam's apple. I could hear the *glug* sound.

"That's why Stephen and I have to stay here and clear your name and ours."

The next pause was the longest of all.

It began with a strangled squeak, then silence. After a long stretch of quiet, however, it was clear something had changed.

The voice on the phone was suddenly firmer, more controlled. As if all those seminars on How to Fool Others into Thinking You're a Decisive Leader had finally kicked in.

"I'll give you forty-eight hours to find out who did it," the voice said flatly. "If you can't, you two will be on your own. You won't be Pendleton employees anymore. The company will hire an investigator who can get the job done."

The voice paused once more, but only for a couple of seconds. "We'll also hire a couple of editors who won't let this kind of thing happen again. Ever."

The line went dead.

Shoot, I thought. I'd been so close.

I FOUND Stephen in the lobby, having knocked on the door of his room and gotten no response. He sat on the shabby brown love seat, his fingers poking the screen of his phone. Three empty granola bar wrappers lay next to him, probably from the vending machine. He must have gotten tired of picking raisins from his teeth.

I told him about Hunter's ultimatum.

"He wants to get rid of *both* of us?"

"Looks that way. In my case, he can do it. But you're different. You could probably sue him for wrongful termination. I don't think he's cleared his idea with Our Friends in Legal."

He shook his head, then described Hunter in terms I can't even paraphrase. I couldn't condone his language, but I could certainly understand the sentiment.

"So," he added. "I've been thinking about our last conversation. We need to discover who, other than ourselves, might want to get rid of Zane Tripp."

"Right."

"So far, Gerald's out. Could be Stanton Platte, but nobody knows if he's still alive, much less where."

"I know. I already tried to find him."

"How about somebody Tripp put out of business? You brought that up."

"Yeah," I said. "But who?"

"It was in the *USA Today* article."

"The day care center?"

"Uh-huh."

"I can't believe a day care center would actually be shut

down just because it forgot to spray Lysol on its toys every single day."

"The Internet says the place is out of business," he said. "What if the owner blames that on Tripp?"

I shrugged. "Do you know where he is? The owner?"

"He's a she and she lives in Atlanta." He paused. "There's only one problem."

"What's that?"

"We'll have to hurry. She's almost dead."

CHAPTER 10

WHEN WE GOT INTO THE ALTIMA, STEPHEN LOOKED PRETTY proud of himself.

"In case you're wondering," he said, "I used the Internet to find Norma Sundstrom."

"Who?"

"Former owner of the Daybreak Early Learning Center. She's in a place called Peachtree Gardens. The website calls it a 'long-term care facility.'"

"So much warmer and fuzzier than 'nursing home,'" I said, and put the car in reverse.

"It'll take about forty minutes to get there," he said, and started rattling off directions.

As soon as we were on the highway, he turned to me again. "Okay. First, I looked up news stories about the toy-disinfecting thing. Found Norma's name and the name of her business, then looked to see whether it still exists. It doesn't."

"Nancy Drew would be proud."

"Then I—do you know what CaringBridge is?"

"Yes."

"Well, according to her family's latest report, Norma's

going downhill. The description's not very specific, but I get the feeling it's terminal."

"So, what's your plan?"

"We talk to her. Find out whether she's mad at Tripp."

"What? Excuse me. For a moment it sounded like you want to question an elderly, dying woman in a nursing home about whether she's shot anybody recently."

"I do," he said matter-of-factly.

Somehow, I managed not to raise my voice. "Regardless of how she felt about him, how is that even physically possible?"

"She could have had somebody else do it. What we need to find out is whether she blames Tripp for putting her out of business."

"What if she's asleep? Or busy?"

"Then we'll come back later."

I sighed, wishing I'd never brought the whole thing up.

"Do you have a better idea?" he asked.

"No."

He grinned. "Then relax and enjoy."

For some reason I couldn't do either.

"TURN RIGHT UP HERE," Stephen said about 35 minutes later.

We entered a residential area, a near-jungle of oaks and tiny, tan-painted brick bungalows that may have been considered charming during the Hoover Administration. The whole neighborhood seemed to doze in the heat.

Five minutes later we reached our destination.

Stephen pulled out his phone and tapped. "I downloaded this photo of Norma. She may not look like this now, though."

I looked it over. Wispy, white hair. Lantern jaw, prominent cheekbones, strained smile, intense gaze. She could have been Boris Karloff's sister.

We climbed out of the car, then walked past the sign, which was centered on a small lawn that might have been described as perfectly manicured if it weren't so full of dandelions. The place was mostly chalky white, with a porch swing out of *To Kill a Mockingbird*. The double-wide doorway, perfect for wheelchairs and ambulance gurneys, led to a small lobby decorated with artificial flowers, baskets of imitation fruit, and a fireplace as genuine as the ones next to Santa's throne at the mall. There was a musty smell, but none of the more objectionable odors so often associated with these places.

At the front desk sat a fiftyish woman in a flowered purple dress.

"We're here to see Norma Sundstrom," Stephen announced.

The lady scratched her chin. "I think she's in the courtyard. With her son."

I swallowed. "Her son?"

"Down the hall on your right," the woman said.

WE FOLLOWED HER DIRECTION. "This is getting complicated," I whispered to Stephen. "Her son is here."

"The more the merrier," he said. "I hope."

At the next opportunity, we turned right, passing through white French doors to a green expanse half the size of a Little League baseball diamond. In the far-right corner stood a fountain, a solemn concrete angel spewing water from its mouth. It looked like a cemetery decoration.

As with the front lawn, this one was flawless except for the weeds, one-fourth of which were being flattened under residents' wheelchairs and visitors' shoes. Since no one was doing anything more strenuous than a lethargic shuffle, it wasn't hard to examine the dozen or so individuals dotting the open space.

"There," Stephen said. "By the Angel of Regurgitation. In the wheelchair. With the guy in the blue suit."

Making our way to the corner, we parked ourselves near the old woman and the younger man. She was the one in the photo, only thinner, wearing a maroon bathrobe and tethered to an oxygen tank. It was clear she and the man were related, both resembling Karloff in a Scandinavian sort of way.

We stood silent in the sunshine for a moment. The temperate weather didn't seem to be helping the old lady's mood. Her frown was deeper than her son's, a tribute to the remaining power of her facial muscles.

"Sure seems like a nice place," Stephen said, as if he wanted nothing more than to stand there forever, listening to the angel gurgle.

"It's wonderful," the man replied, not sounding convinced or convincing.

There was a long pause, as if we were all hoping someone would put us out of our misery. Finally the old lady spoke, her wheeze just loud enough to hear.

"Eric, I know you have work to do. Feel free to go. I can get back to my room."

The man bounced his palms on the wheelchair handles. "I'll be happy to stay longer," he said, looking as if he wouldn't be happy no matter what he did.

Another long pause. The son seemed bent on prolonging the agony, maybe to prove his devotion. At last he bent down and kissed his mother on top of her head, a dutiful gesture at best. "See you Thursday," he said.

After he'd left, the old woman added a sigh to her wheezing. "He's a good son. Comes to visit when he can.

But he has to work so hard these days, even most weekends."

Stephen shook his head. "Yeah, I know what *that's* like."

I raised an eyebrow. As far as I knew, he hadn't worked a weekend in his life.

He nodded at me as if prompting me to say something. To start the conversation, even though this whole thing was his idea.

Making a mental note to discuss it later, I forged ahead. "Mrs. Sundstrom, I'm sorry to bother you. But we're here because we need to ask you about someone."

"Who?"

"Zane Tripp."

For a moment she looked blank. Then indignant, enough that she might need more oxygen than the tubes in her nose could supply. "Are you friends of his?"

"No, no. We're just trying to figure out what happened to him."

"I haven't heard of anything happening to him," Norma muttered.

I lowered my voice. "There's no delicate way to put this, I guess. But someone . . . shot him. And we need to find out why."

"Shot? With a gun?"

"I'm afraid so."

The old woman sat up straight, or as straight as she could. "That's news to me. Good news."

"I'm sure you don't mean that," I said.

"But I do." Her hands quivered on the arms of her chair. "Little parasite. Hiding behind his computer, ruining people's lives." Her voice rose. "He wrecked my business. If it weren't for him, I could have just paid the fine for breaking that one little nitpicking rule about disinfecting toys and that would have been the end of it."

Wheezing more loudly, she stopped for a few long breaths of air.

"So, you blame him for—"

Her voice grew more shrill. "Planted a seed of doubt in people's minds. Ruined my reputation. People stopped sending their kids to me."

More air in, more volume out. "Now Eric will never get to inherit the business. There *isn't* any business. Which is why ... he's working himself ... into an early grave."

She leaned back in the wheelchair, nearly panting. "So ... somebody shot Tripp? Is he ... dead?"

"Yes," Stephen said softly.

"I'm just sorry . . . I wasn't able . . . to pull the trigger myself."

I glanced around, wondering whether anyone else had heard. Several in our end of the courtyard were staring.

Just then a large green-and-white presence lumbered into my field of vision, carrying a clipboard and a vexed expression. It was a nurse with the jawline of a steam shovel.

"That's enough," she snapped. "Time for a rest, Mrs. Sundstrom." Grabbing the wheelchair grips, she unlocked the brake with her foot and backed away. She glared as if she'd caught us rummaging through the lady's purse for credit cards and power-of-attorney papers.

The hiss of the oxygen tank faded as Norma and the nurse rolled away.

"I think our work here is done," Stephen said.

"And not a moment too soon."

We quick-stepped through the French doors, winding our way past an array of poor souls in various states of disrepair. They could have wandered out of a Victor Hugo novel, except for the plaid shirts, walkers, and IV poles. I hoped I'd die before I got that way. It seemed biblical. To die is gain, right?

We passed the receptionist, then strode through the front door, skirting the porch swing.

The sun hovered higher in the sky, more insistent by the moment. A brown-shirted UPS driver with two parcels under his arm walked past us toward the building, blotting his forehead with a Subway napkin.

"Well, that was a good idea," I said.

"Thanks."

"I didn't mean it." I paused. "Stephen, do you believe in miracles?"

"Not really."

"Too bad."

"Why?"

"If this little exercise is any indication, a miracle may be our only hope."

"Then that would mean we have no hope at all."

"You're very perceptive," I said and set out down the sidewalk.

CHAPTER 11

THE CAR WAS A CREMATORIUM ON WHEELS. WE LEFT THE doors open until further notice.

It was silent as we sat there. Being surrounded by pitiful frailty, incurable disease, and the smell of death could do that to a person. But so could Cormac McCarthy and certain brands of cough syrup.

I knew how the writer of Ecclesiastes felt about the sufferings of old age. It was too depressing to think about.

"I don't want to get old," Stephen said.

I shrugged. "I hear it's not so bad. Thanks to the invention of the food processor, you get to have all the steak you can drink."

I twisted a few strands of hair around my finger, then let them drop. "I guess we answered the question of whether Norma Sundstrom blames Tripp for the loss of her business."

"You caught that, huh?"

"Not that it proves anything."

"Oh, I know she couldn't have killed anybody herself. But what if she hired someone to do it for her?"

I shook my head. "She's probably broke. And I can't picture her meeting with a hit man under that fountain."

"It's a stretch."

"If it makes you feel better, we can keep her on the list of suspects. Just not at the top, okay?"

I pulled my phone from my pocket, having rendered it unconscious, and roused it. Apparently, I'd missed a call. One of my favorite people, if I remembered that number correctly. Philip Minor was always full of good news. Or something.

I hit REDIAL and SPEAKER, then waited.

There were no formalities this time. The smarmy baritone was even more choked than during our previous conversation.

"The police were here," he said, as if such a thing were impossible, or at least illegal. "Questioning Willow. They wanted to know where she'd been during the last twenty-four hours. As if she killed the blogger!"

"I'm sure that's standard operating—"

"Willow's a basket case. Now she's a suspect, too. She doesn't even *own* a gun. She *hates* guns."

I didn't ask whether Willow's bodyguard was armed only with a list of empowering proverbs. Minor's mental state made him unlikely to appreciate the irony.

"The police also questioned *me*," he continued. "I hate guns as much as Willow does."

"Mmm," I said, knowing it didn't matter what sort of noise I made at this point.

"We've been huddling with our lawyers. Don't be surprised if we sue, Ms. Neville. Especially if we have to cancel Willow's national tour. Twenty-five cities. Over three million dollars in lost ticket sales."

"Sue for what, exactly?"

"I'm not saying any more, except that you've screwed

things up royally. Stay away from Willow and anybody connected with her, including me."

There was a click, then nothing. I turned to Stephen.

"I knew there was something I didn't like about that guy," I said.

~

"So . . . what are you going to do?" Stephen asked.

"Well, let's see. He wants me to stay away. And I can't stand to be within a mile of him. It's a tremendous sacrifice, but I'm going to grant his wish."

"And you'll stay away from Willow?"

"At least for now."

Just then the sound of the *1812 Overture* met my ears.

I looked at the phone's screen. Not Hunter Thicke, not Philip Minor.

It claimed to be Marvin Ainsley Pitts. I breathed a sigh of relief.

"Cranberry!" he said when I picked up.

He was the only one who called me that, thank goodness, but I didn't mind. He could call me anything as long as he kept letting me call him. Grandpas and granddaughters gave each other some pretty odd nicknames, and that was the kind of relationship we had, sort of.

"So," he said. "My stunning bride tells me you called. Unfortunately, that's about all she's told me since I got back. Guess she doesn't see the beauty in jumping out of an airplane at thirteen thousand feet."

I shook my head. "Did she mention how the devil tempted Jesus to jump off the Temple?"

"He didn't have a parachute. And a man's gotta do what he's gotta do. No offense, but I couldn't expect a sophisticated individual like you to understand."

"Good, because I don't. I'm just worried about you."

His voice softened. "I know." He paused. "Now, I don't think you called to talk about skydiving."

I wondered where to start. "Do you know who Willow Hayly is?"

"Sure. Have to keep up with my fellow Pendleton authors, don't I?"

"Well, she's been accused of—"

"Is this about the 'Willowgate' thing? Are you mixed up in that?"

I filled him in on the rest. The more I said, the quieter he got. When I told him about the murder, he let out a deep sigh.

"You're a suspect?"

"Apparently."

"Then you need to make the next move, honey. Talk to this memory doctor. He's got a motive."

"We've hit a brick wall there. According to Google, he's nowhere. Or dead or living off the grid in the woods."

"Well, if he's alive, maybe he doesn't want to be found. Could've changed his name."

I pondered that for a moment. "If he did, how are we supposed to guess what he changed his name *to*?"

He grunted, as he usually did when I didn't know something he thought was obvious. "You have a piece of paper?" he asked.

I rummaged in my pocket. "And a pen. I've learned to have them handy whenever I call you."

"If Platte has legally changed his name, there should be a public record. Go to the courthouse in the county where he changed it—if you know which one it was."

"I don't, but maybe I can find out."

"When a person changes his name, there's usually a public notice in the newspaper, which you could look up. But if the person asks the judge when he petitions for that name change, his new name can be left off the list. So that may not help you much."

I jotted as quickly as I could. As often happened at this point in my conversations with Marvin, I was beginning to get writer's cramp.

"If Platte's using a different name but didn't legally change it, that may be tougher," he continued. "If you can guess what he's doing for a living now, you might try tracking him down that way."

"How?"

"Let's say you think he's a plumber. You could search the Internet for pictures of plumbers and look for one that matches his photo."

I put down the pen. "Marvin, I can't look for a needle in eighty million haystacks. I'm younger than you are, but I won't live *that* long."

"Patience is a virtue, girl."

"Platte would be seventy-six. What if he does *nothing* for a living? He could be retired."

"In that case, good luck. Unless you can rent the AARP's mailing list. They're still sending me those membership cards, and I'm still ripping 'em up."

I closed my eyes. Too much information, but not enough to do any good.

"Hey," Marvin said. "You still there?"

"Yeah."

"Gotta go. My lady wants to take a stroll on the beach and I can't deprive her of my company. Not when she had to live without me the last few days."

I smirked. "I'm sure her agony was exceeded only by her ecstasy."

"Laugh all you want, Cranberry. But it never snows here in St. Petersburg. I'm not the one working fifty hours a week, getting myself accused in some murder for the sake of a bunch of suits who couldn't care less."

"Thanks for reminding me."

"Now, you try what I told you and let me know what happens, all right?"

"All right."

"Aloha."

The phone went quiet. I slipped it, along with the paper and pen, back into my pocket.

"Good news?" Stephen asked.

"Isn't it always?"

"Not when Marvin's involved."

"The good news is he's given us a lead," I said.

"And the bad news?"

"It's our *only* lead."

"So, if it leads nowhere . . ."

"Then we take a hint from Dr. Stanton Platte. Change our names and go off the grid. They'll never find us."

"Very funny," he said.

But neither of us mustered a smile.

CHAPTER 12

WE HAD LUNCH AT A CONVENIENCE STORE, HAVING PASSED NO restaurants by the time our stomachs were rumbling. After carefully choosing an assortment of grease-sweating hot dogs and other items known to the state of California to cause cancer, we ate in the car.

Stephen had bought a copy of *Entertainment Weekly*, which kept him occupied. He read bits of it aloud. To my surprise, it didn't contain a word about Willowgate or Tripp's murder.

By the time we were done, we'd decided to follow Marvin's advice about finding Stanton Platte.

It was increasingly torrid and muggy as we walked back to the car. Stephen downloaded directions and we drove to the Fulton County Courthouse in Atlanta. I could go into detail about what happened next, except that nothing did. As far as the county knew, Stanton Platte was a fictional character.

The same was true of Stephen's subsequent search of public notices from newspaper archives, which he conducted on the Internet. I was beginning to think Willow had invented the guy.

When we were finished, I pulled the Altima out of the pay-to-park lot across from the courthouse.

"Well, we learned something," I said.

"Don't listen to Marvin?"

"No. If Dr. Platte's alive and using a different name, he changed it in some other county. Or he didn't change it legally."

"So, what do we do? Check every county in Georgia? Every county in the country?"

I shook my head. "Time's not on our side. And it probably wouldn't help. My guess is the good doctor wasn't interested in red tape. He just wanted to disappear. If he's still breathing, he's doing it under an assumed name that's not on any court document."

"And did Marvin have any ideas on what to do about that?"

"Sort of." When I explained his suggestion, Stephen squeezed his eyes shut as if trying to work out the theory of relativity in his head.

"In other words," he said, "we're supposed to guess what Platte might be doing for a living now on the chance that he's upright and employed. Then match an old photo of him with a photo of somebody who does that kind of work."

"Exactly."

He opened his eyes. "So, we look up 'repressed memory retrievers'?"

"Nope. Not much call for them these days."

"How about . . . scam artist?"

"They don't advertise."

He folded his arms. "As I recall, he had a doctorate in 'interdisciplinary studies,' whatever that is. Probably from some diploma mill."

"Then the only real credential he ever earned was in something else."

"Hypnosis?"

"Correct."

"You think he's a hypnotist."

I lifted a hand from the steering wheel. "Why not? Hypnotist is an actual occupation. Unlike, say, publicity or marketing."

"Like hypnotizing people into losing weight, quitting smoking. Didn't think I'd ever say this, but that actually makes sense."

"I'll take that as a compliment," I said in the interest of time.

~

THE SWAN'S Corners Inn featured what a sign called the BUSINESS CENTER, apparently trying to match the amenities offered by real hotels. A large-windowed room, it was located halfway between the lobby and what another sign said was the FITNESS CENTER. Both places were well-stocked with inadequate equipment described by index cards as being OUT OF ORDER.

We discovered this room quite by accident, having taken a wrong turn after passing the front desk. When Stephen peered through the window, he tilted his head to one side as if getting an idea.

"Let's set up headquarters here. Nobody's around and it looks like nobody would ever want to be. That old Dell is probably still running Windows XP, and the ink light on the printer is blinking. Not too encouraging."

"Wouldn't you rather use smartphones in one of our rooms?"

He leaned against the glass. "If we've got to compare chin

warts and nostrils on a few thousand pictures, I'd rather do it on a decent-sized monitor. And we're closer to the vending machines."

"It'll be fun," I said, knowing I'd be ready to kill myself or him after the first hour or so.

I followed him into the room. The computer, an ancient spawn of Microsoft that probably had slumbered for eons, roused with a sequence of whirs and clicks when he pressed the POWER button. Slowly the monitor warmed to the task, crackling briefly. Eventually the screen arranged itself as if determined to prove its relevance to this century, but the blinking cursor nagged for a password.

"Oh, good," he said. "Before we can guess what Stanton Platte is doing, we have to guess the secret word."

"Let's just *ask*," I said.

The gentleman at the front desk appeared to be thirtyish and maybe Pakistani, which I hesitate to bring up because it's immaterial, but I happened to notice.

He smiled. "Yes?"

"Could you tell us the password for the computer in the Business Center?" Stephen asked.

The clerk plucked an imprinted Swan's Corners Inn pen from the imprinted Swan's Corners Inn mug on the counter and wrote something on a slip of paper. Then he folded the paper in half and gave it to Stephen.

"This is the password," he said in a portentous voice. "The Business Center closes at midnight."

"Just as well," Stephen said. "So do I."

"We have a deadline," I said as we padded down the worn Army green hallway carpet. "Twelve o'clock."

"We should be used to deadlines," he said. "We're editors."

"We need to come up with a system. That's how deadlines are met."

He strode down the hall like a general about to review the

troops. "We go online. We keep Platte's old portrait open in the background as a reference. We take turns looking for hypnotists who've posted pictures of themselves. Each time we find one, we both vote on whether it's a match. Thumbs up or down. In case of a tie . . ."

I could feel my eyes glazing over.

"In case of a tie," he continued, "the person who voted *yes* adds the web address for that photo to a written list, which we revisit at 11:45 p.m. if we haven't found a lookalike."

I may have dozed off at that point but shook myself awake.

"When the clock strikes midnight," he was saying, "we—"

"Are put under citizen's arrest by the desk clerk. An excellent plan."

"Thanks. It's what editors do."

Reaching the Business Center, we halted outside the door. After glancing around to make sure no one was watching, Stephen unfolded the paper in his hand and silently read the password. Then he handed it to me:

SWAN'S CORNERS INN

"TELL NO ONE," he whispered.

After typing in the code, he waited. Finally the aged browser launched, and we were online, more or less.

It didn't take long to find an old photo of Platte. The head was bald, shiny. He had a Roman nose and a soul patch under his lower lip. But his most striking feature was his eyes— piercing, all-seeing, nearly bulging. This was going to be like looking for Svengali's cleaner-shaven brother.

"Question," Stephen said. "Are we assuming Platte could

be anywhere in the world? Because if we are, this is going to take—"

"No. Let's limit the search to this country. Assuming he wants to stay off the grid, he probably wouldn't apply for a passport."

"Works for me." His fingers started to tickle the keyboard, then stopped. "Another question. Are we looking for hypnotists or hypnotherapists?"

I wasn't sure what the difference was. "What do *you* think?"

"Hypnotists. Shorter. Easier to type."

"Fine." I sat in the chair next to him.

He typed and hit RETURN.

A note appeared in the upper left corner of the screen. ABOUT 750,000 RESULTS, it said.

"Oh, crap," he cried.

"Don't panic. Just work your plan."

"But—"

"There can't be three quarters of a million hypnotists in this country. Have you ever met one?"

"Not that I know of."

"There you go."

Alas, I'd spoken too soon. There seemed to be far *more* than three quarters of a million. Apparently one of every two adults had chosen the field. All had long strings of letters after their names signifying mysterious degrees, calling their businesses things like Tranquility Clinic or dubbing themselves Amazing or Incredible if they fancied themselves entertainers.

Most had posted pictures. None of them looked anything like Dr. Stanton Platte.

For the next half hour, I stared at photo after photo, my eyeballs parching in their sockets. Before long, it was no longer necessary to consult Platte's old portrait, which had tattooed itself on what remained of my retinas.

I kept checking the time on the screen. Forty-five minutes passed, then an hour.

I kept blinking, trying to focus. Nothing matched. Too much hair. Nose too wide. Wrong race, wrong gender. The only thing they all had in common was possessing at least one ear.

Finally Stephen sighed and rubbed his eyes for the millionth time. "I hate to bring this up, but what if he got plastic surgery?"

I stroked my chin. Hadn't thought of that.

"If so, we've hit a dead end," I said. "But why would he do that? He wasn't a fugitive. Or in the witness protection program. Besides, we've got to work with what we have."

"Well, what we have isn't getting us anywhere. If I'm going to keep at it, I need some caffeine. And sugar."

"Fair enough," I said, getting stiffly to my feet.

Wobbling our way down the hall, we found two vending machines in an alcove next to an ice maker. A meager assortment of snacks dangled from the first machine's coils.

Stephen grunted. "All the good stuff's gone. The chocolate always goes first. Then the cookies. The last to go are the Wint-O-Green Life Savers and anything that says 'Natural' on it."

I looked at the second machine, which was devoted to soft drinks. "At least we've got some stimulants. That should keep us on our toes."

I searched my purse for all the quarters and singles I could find. Stephen did the same with his wallet and pockets. Five or six minutes later we trudged back to our posts with a malignant harvest of unsalted sunflower seeds, Red Hots, sour gummy worms, onion-flavored popcorn, and Mountain Dew. The machines had chewed up two extra dollar bills without yielding anything but in our diminished mental state it seemed like a fair trade.

I looked at my watch. "Ninety-seven minutes left," I said.

We ate and drank our purchases as if they were castor oil, only far less tasty. Our breath would have slain the Mongol hordes.

Unable to wait for our pick-me-ups to kick in, we turned our attention back to the parade of photos.

"Not him."

"Nice unibrow."

"Looks like that guy in Legal. I forget his name."

"When do we get our second wind?"

"My eyes are killing me."

Suddenly, at three minutes before midnight, Stephen jolted upright in his chair as if struck by lightning. At first, I thought his caffeine and sugar had taken effect before mine, catapulting him into Overdrive. But it was something else.

"Wait a minute," he said, his bloodshot eyeballs nearly as wide as Platte's. He pointed at the screen. "It's him."

Squinting, I leaned closer. The web page wasn't that of a therapist or a clinic. There were no degrees mentioned, no promises of pounds lost or acrophobia conquered.

It was an ad on Craigslist for a stage hypnotist who performed at private parties. Accompanying the three paragraphs of obviously unedited copy was an eerie, purplish, slightly blurry portrait of a man with a glossy pate and imperial nose. The soul patch was gray now. But there was no mistaking those eyes, the ones which, according to the ad, mastered audiences with a "mesmerizing gaze."

Dr. Stanton Platte was no more. He was now Szandor Mandini.

"The Silver Sandman" was his stage name and he practiced his exotic art in the town of Canyonville, Wyoming.

Stephen turned toward me. "*Wyoming?*"

"Maybe he likes elbow room."

"And *Szandor Mandini*? Where did *that* come from?"

"So, thumbs down for the name," I said. "But for the face, thumbs up."

Just then there was a rapping at the window. The clerk from the front desk had returned, this time with a ring of keys.

He stuck his head in. "So sorry," he said, sounding genuinely grieved. "The Business Center is closed."

I turned over the note containing the password and scribbled The Silver Sandman's name, location, and web address.

With a flurry of clicks, Stephen fled the browser and shut the old computer down. I gathered an armload of wrappers and cans and dumped it in the wastebasket.

"Thank you," the clerk said.

"Oh, thank *you*," I said.

So, this was the thrill of victory. I knew I'd better savor it while I could.

There'd be plenty of time later for the agony of defeat.

WHEN THE CAFFEINE and sugar locked onto my nervous system half an hour later, I knew it. My eyes sprang open. I went high-strung as a chihuahua in the Lincoln Tunnel at rush hour.

Unfortunately, I wasn't in the Lincoln Tunnel. I was lying in bed in my darkened room, the pillow moist with perspiration against my cheek, wanting to plummet into dreamland like an anvil into the Mariana Trench.

I fidgeted. Wakefulness was a long-time pattern with me. Apparently I lacked the genes to handle anything more stimulating than a Dostoevsky novel.

I rolled onto my back, then stared at what I knew but

couldn't see was a water-stained popcorn ceiling. The thrill of victory was fading.

Finding Stanton Platte was no unmixed triumph, after all. It meant we'd have to go to Wyoming. I'd never been there, but it seemed to be the world's largest producer of vast expanses of nothing.

The image of a sun-bleached cow skull floated in and out of my head. But then there was another picture. Yellowstone National Park. Old Faithful. I remembered it from a View-Master slide I'd seen in the fourth grade.

Perhaps it was unfair to see Wyoming as less than desirable. It was, after all, the state that had given us Dick Cheney, the dirigible headlight, and the remains of a great many dinosaurs.

Still, it was hard to believe anything Stephen and I might find there could exonerate us.

But it was worth hoping for.

Hope? I shook my head. What was I thinking?

It must have been the Mountain Dew talking.

CHAPTER 13

THE REST OF THE NIGHT WAS SHORTER THAN A HAIKU, AND even more unpleasant. The air conditioner provided long stretches of soothing white noise, the kind produced by Category 5 hurricanes.

By the time the caffeine and sugar released me from their grip, there was just enough time to fall asleep and snore myself awake again. I couldn't recall having done that before, but then I couldn't remember when I'd last dined on onion popcorn and a soft drink the color of urine.

After hauling myself out of bed, I stumbled toward the bathroom. Stephen and I had agreed to meet at 6:30, wanting to plan our visit to The Silver Sandman right away.

A tepid shower and half a bottle of mouthwash later, I was sitting in the breakfast room. After gathering my usual paltry fare, I turned to see Stephen sitting at a table on the half empty side of the room. He was doing something with his phone. I sat down across from him.

"I'm already working on getting a flight," he said. "Don't know why Platte has to live on another planet. There'll be some driving. Not even a direct flight to Laramie. You have to go through Denver. And it won't be cheap on such short notice. At least Pendleton will be paying for it."

I cleared my throat. "It could be the *last* thing Pendleton pays for."

He looked up. "You mean Hunter's ultimatum?"

I looked at my watch. "We've already used up half of our forty-eight hours."

"Piece of cake," he said.

I raised an eyebrow. "You think this is going to be easy?"

"No. I was just thinking I'd rather be eating a piece of cake than this Danish. What's this red stuff, transmission fluid?"

I stared at the misbegotten pastry in his hand. "As long as you're making reservations, we'll need a place in Wyoming for the night. Maybe you can find something with a little more class."

"It'd be hard to find something with less."

THAT NIGHT we found ourselves in Canyonville, Wyoming, population 2,613.

We were engaged in what appeared to be the two most common local pastimes: sitting in front of alcoholic beverages and perspiring like professional wrestlers.

We did both at a table in a place called the Starlite Lounge, which was really just a bar with a microphone stand in the middle of the room where the mechanical bull would have stood if this had been a movie from 1980.

I looked up at the lethargically revolving blades of the ceiling fan. Apparently, air conditioning had been judged too cowardly for the frontier spirit.

Weary after having spent the day searching for gates in

airports and jamming myself into seats on planes too small to be trusted with our carry-ons, let alone our lives, I peered through the beery haze. The brick walls were covered with neon signs and posters bearing the logos of brewers and distillers like Snake River, New Belgium, Coors, Wyoming Whiskey. They were also darkened by the tar and nicotine stains of Canyonville's third most common pastime, chain-smoking. At least half the patrons were enthusiastically poisoning the air and tapping cinders into their Budweiser ashtrays.

I was parked in front of a pint glass of something called Tommyknocker, a Colorado craft beer the menu touted as having hints of maple and brown sugar. I wasn't really a drinker, but figured I had to order. It tasted like something from the International House of Alcoholic Pancakes.

Stephen was on his third mug of Coors. It was hard to tell in the smoky gloom, but his face looked a little pink.

I checked my watch. "What time did you say The Silver Sandman is supposed to start?"

"About five minutes ago." He stifled a burp. "Things probably don't move on schedule around here. It's not exactly Las Vegas."

"It's not even Branson. And a hypnotist? Isn't this a place for people who sing about heartbreak and guns?"

He shrugged. "Maybe they're more sophisticated than you think." He looked around. "Or not."

I took a sip of beer, which was nearing the current room temperature of about 95 degrees. "I hope this won't turn out to be a waste of time. Not the best way to meet Dr. Platte. Or Szandor Mandini."

"Hey, what choice did I have? We couldn't show up at somebody's birthday party, like in the Craigslist ad. I was lucky to find a public place where he was booked."

I surveyed the room, trying in vain to spot a bald head with a soul patch.

I was about to refix my focus on Stephen when I noticed a trio of young men sitting a few tables away. One wore a tan cowboy hat fresh from the box; one sported a battered green cap with an oil company logo. The third was hatless, with a cigarette dangling from his lips. All three wore jeans and T-shirts and displayed the self-contented sluggishness of men who'd had too much to drink.

One of them, the guy with the green cap, was staring with heavy-lidded eyes in our direction. At me.

I looked away. His next step would be a leer, even if he had no idea what a leer was, which he probably didn't.

I was considering my options, the most attractive of which was pretending the guy didn't exist, when a loud *thump* sounded over the PA system. It was followed by a series of rustling noises.

"How's ever'body?" said a short, pudgy man at the microphone stand. The house lights dimmed, and a bluish spotlight snapped on, making his white vest and silver belt buckle sparkle. He held the mike in front of his grin, obscuring most of it.

"Now, most of you folks know the Starlite Lounge features some of the finest entertainment in southeastern Wyoming. Once a month we're privileged to have a change of pace from the ordinary. This month we're lucky to have one of our favorites, a fella who hails from right here in town. Calls himself The Silver Sandman. So, get ready to be amazed by an individual who's guaranteed to put you to sleep!"

He paused for laughter, which was unnecessary because there wasn't any.

"Well," he said. "That didn't come out right, did it? Ladies

and gents ..." He peered down at a slip of paper in his hand.
"... Mr. Szandor Mandini!"

Stephen and I applauded politely, joined by one or two of
the other spectators.

"Bring on the lap dancers!" said the guy with the
green cap.

"Shut your face!" yelled someone in the back.

And there he was, Dr. Stanton Platte, accepting the
microphone from the emcee, wearing a blue tuxedo that
looked as if it had been retired by a rental shop around 1975.
His head glinted in the spotlight, his soul patch was bright
white, and his eyes bulged like hard-boiled eggs.

He didn't share the emcee's smile. In fact, he looked a
little haughty, above the fray, even unaware of his surround-
ings. Maybe he'd hypnotized himself into believing he was
playing Carnegie Hall.

"Thank you so much," he said. His voice was melodramatic, gravelly, driven down by too much smoke, drink, age,
or all of the above.

His silver brows lowered ominously. "Welcome to the
world of the mind . . . a world where anything can happen."

A sneeze erupted somewhere. "Now, *that's* spooky,"
someone whispered loudly.

"To enter this world, I'll need the cooperation of a volunteer. An individual with courage."

The hatless young man at the nearby table elbowed the
one with the green cap. "Here's your big chance, Dwayne."

The one with the cap let loose with an impressive volley
of profanity and shoved his friend away.

The hypnotist ignored them. "Man or woman, young or
old."

There was a lengthy silence, then a loud belch from the
darkness. "Man, this is boring," a voice muttered.

Platte frowned. Raising a hand to shield his eyes from the spotlight, he turned toward me and seemed to perk up.

"How about you, Madam?" he asked. "You seem like a lady of intellect and grit."

I gulped.

"May I count on you?" he asked, sounding a little desperate.

"Yeah!" the Green Cap Guy called out. "Make her take her clothes off!"

Her companions snickered. "Show us what you got!" yelled the one in the cowboy hat.

I started to shake. Looking down at the beer in front of me, I got the urge to down it all at once. After praying, of course.

Suddenly Stephen got to his feet. "I'll do it. I'll volunteer."

Green Cap Guy groaned.

"Splendid!" Platte said, looking relieved. "Let's all thank our volunteer, shall we?"

He led the applause, which didn't take much leadership. I seemed to be the only one following.

Stephen made his way to the stage, wobbling slightly.

Platte pulled an empty chair from a nearby table, then motioned for him to sit. "And what is your name?"

"Stephen."

"Have you ever been hypnotized, Stephen?"

"Not that I know of."

"Are you willing to be hypnotized now?"

He sighed. "I guess so."

"Any heart trouble? Shoulder, neck, or back problems?"

His eyebrows rose. "Why?"

"Just a precaution. Don't worry. Hypnosis is one of the safest things in the world, like playing horseshoes."

"My uncle got hit in the head with a horseshoe once."

"Relax. Look up at that ceiling fan, going round and round, round and round. Can you see it?"

"Yeah."

"Peaceful, isn't it?" Platte knelt next to the chair and extended his hand. "Now, just push down on my hand and close your eyes."

He did so. Suddenly Platte yanked his hand away.

"Sleep!" he shouted. I jumped, along with half the audience.

Stephen's hand dropped into his lap, his head pitched forward, his shoulders sank.

I nearly sprang from my chair. He looked no more conscious than the average spaghetti squash.

Platte placed his palm on the crown of Stephen's head and rotated it a few times. "Limp as a rag doll. With every breath you relax more and more deeply."

Stephen's face was expressionless.

"How'd he do that?" someone asked behind me.

"It's a trick," the Green Cap Guy mumbled to his compatriots.

"Now, Stephen," Platte said gently, "I want you to imagine the number ninety-nine floating in the sky. Silently count backward from there and your mind will relax even more. Each number will fade into the clouds."

Stephen looked like he was in a coma—or worse, dead.

Platte got to his feet, but not without wincing. He was 76, after all.

"Very good, Stephen," he said, sounding a bit winded. "Now, let's—"

"He ain't asleep!" the Green Cap Guy called out. "He's fakin'."

Platte ignored the heckling. "Let's see whether our volunteer would make a good rancher. Stephen, can you give us your best impression of a cow?"

Eyes still closed; Stephen sat up. "Mmoooooo," he said, then worked his jaw as if chewing cud.

I blinked. He had to be in a trance. The Stephen I knew would rather face lethal injection than make noises like that. On the other hand, he'd been ding-donging pretty loudly at Gerald Sackett's repair shop.

"Excellent," Platte said. "How about clucking like a chicken?"

Slowly Stephen raised his elbows. "Buk-buk-*buk*," he said, flapping his arms. There were a few sniggers and a giggle.

Platte gave a tight smile and patted him on the shoulder. "Ladies and gentlemen, I think it's clear he knows his livestock. As a matter of fact—"

"You're not foolin' us, old man," hollered the guy with no headgear.

"Shut your face!" bellowed someone in the darkness.

"Shut *yours*!" echoed someone else.

Platte looked disgusted, but not surprised. I guessed this wasn't the first time he'd had to cut things short.

"Thus concludes our mystical journey of the mind!" he declared. "Many thanks to our volunteer!"

He spun to face Stephen. "And now I will count from one to five. When I say 'five,' you will open your eyes. You'll feel invigorated, rejuvenated. One . . . two . . . three . . . four . . . take a deep breath . . . and . . . *five!*"

Stephen's eyelids fluttered, then opened wide. A sappy grin spread across his face.

The pudgy emcee hustled into the spotlight, looking anxious and accepting the microphone from Platte. "Uh, ladies and gentlemen, the Silver Sandman!" he barked, and fumbled the mike back onto the stand.

No one applauded except Stephen and me. His eyes were as wide as Platte's, his grin somewhere between blissful and witless. I wondered whether he'd ever be able to edit again.

Someone punched a button on the jukebox and turned up the volume, probably hoping to tranquilize the crowd. Garth Brooks filled the room like carbon monoxide in a locked garage.

The spotlight winked out and the house lights surged back.

Picking up my purse, I threaded my way to the edge of the stage. Stephen rose to his feet, off balance but beaming. "Isn't this guy *great*? I haven't felt this good since . . . sometime."

"Quite a show, Dr. Platte!" I said, raising my voice to compete with the jukebox.

For a moment he looked startled, then went expressionless. "The name is Mandini."

"Of course it is. *My* name is Carolyn Neville. This is Stephen Ames. We work for Pendleton House."

"Never heard of it."

"The publisher of Willow Hayly's memoir. We'd like to talk with you about—"

"Absolutely not. I have no interest in discussing Ms. Hayly or her book. Or anything else."

I folded my arms. "A young man's been murdered, probably because of his connection with that memoir."

"Pardon my callousness, but it's not my concern."

I glanced around the room as if we might be under surveillance. "Would you rather talk to some reporter? Or the police? I don't think they'd care much about your privacy."

He snorted. "As if *you* do." He looked at Stephen, then at me. "There's a room in the back. I'll talk for a moment, but only because this young man came to my aid when I needed a volunteer."

"Thank you," Stephen said, still smiling like a brain-washed cult member.

"Lead the way," I said, ready to take whatever I could get.

~

"Is this your dressing room?" Stephen asked brightly.

We were sitting in a space not much bigger than a walk-in closet. The door was closed and locked. On the weathered barnwood wall was a mirror, topped with three light bulbs, two of which were burned out. A dozen or so autographed photos of people I didn't recognize were tacked to the back of the door.

Platte sat at a dark brown wooden table. On it were a dusty vase of plastic flowers and a Budweiser ashtray.

"Dressing room?" Platte repeated, then chased it with a bitter laugh. "Stars get dressing rooms. No stars in Canyonville, Wyoming. Not even at the Starlite Lounge."

Loosening the collar of his blue tuxedo, which looked considerably less resplendent than it had in the spotlight, he lowered his brows and waited. He seemed to be trying to intimidate me with his powerfully mesmerizing gaze, but finally gave up.

"How did you locate me?" he asked, obviously wishing we hadn't.

I explained our computer search.

"Very resourceful," he said, frowning at his watch. "What would you like to know?"

"Have you been following the Willowgate story?" I asked.

"As little as possible."

"You know about the blogger's allegations and his death."

"I suppose I do."

"Why haven't you come forward to defend Willow's story?" I asked.

"Because the past is the past."

"But surely you don't want people to think the memories you retrieved were . . . made up."

Another sardonic laugh. "I couldn't care less what people think. Most of them don't think at all."

"Is that why you disappeared? You wanted to be a hermit?"

"If I did, I picked a good place for it, wouldn't you say? Wyoming is the least populous state. Let's just say I value solitude."

I leaned forward. "It must be hard to have such a bleak view of humanity. Losing your career must have been devastating."

His expression turned sour. "If this is a therapy session, our time is up."

I shook my head. "I'm not trying to fix you. Just understand you."

He scowled at the ashtray. Finally he picked it up and moved it to a spot about three inches further away.

"My profession suffered a blow when repressed memories and past lives became . . . controversial. A few bad actors ruined it for everyone."

"You weren't one of them?"

He stiffened. "There may have been a few . . . misunderstandings about my credentials. But there's no denying I'm a qualified hypnotist, as Stephen just proved onstage."

As if a spell were wearing off, Stephen rubbed his eyes and cleared his throat. "He's right, Carolyn. I swear I don't remember any of it. One second, I was pushing on his hand and closing my eyes, and the next second I was blinking, and people were yelling. In between . . . blank."

Platte nodded. "Your confusion is understandable, Ms. Neville. My approach didn't fit the stereotype. No swinging watches, no endless pleas for the subject to fall asleep. Rapid

Induction Hypnosis. A relatively recent development, but remarkably effective."

"I suppose it works only on the highly suggestible," I said.

Stephen frowned. "What's that supposed to mean?"

"Actually," Platte said, "the opposite is true. It works especially well on the resistant. In the right hands, it works on nearly everyone. But enough about that. I refuse to give up trade secrets."

"You don't have to," Stephen said. "That stuff is all over the Internet."

"So I've heard," Platte said. He looked at his watch again.

"What are you doing now?" I asked. "Besides birthday parties and . . . entertaining?"

He sighed, placed a palm on his forehead, and ran it back over his shining head. "Primarily hypnotherapy—smoking cessation, weight loss, fear of flying. The stage act can be a train wreck, as you saw tonight. But I do what I have to."

Pausing, he seemed ready to stand. "I think we're done here."

"Just one more question," I said, forcing myself to look into those eyes. "Is there *anything* we can say to convince you to back up Willow's claim she was abused?"

"I haven't changed my story, Ms. Neville, nor will I. But it won't do Willow or your employer any good. I have no reason to step back into that scorpions' nest."

"But the police may come to consider you a suspect. Don't you want to stay off that list?"

He scoffed. "The idea that I might have killed the blogger is asinine. Why would I do that? It wouldn't save what's left of my career. It would only attract attention. Which, as you've probably guessed, is the last thing I want."

He looked down at the ashtray and toyed with it once more.

"What I did for Willow was perfectly valid. I helped her.

The memories were buried in her subconscious and I merely unearthed them."

He picked up the ashtray and set it down again, this time with a sharp *clack*. "Millions of people have experienced abuse of one kind or another. If a few leading questions are necessary to obtain the truth, so be it. Let the legal system sort it out."

I looked at Stephen. He looked at me. Clearly, we'd worn out our welcome.

"Now," Platte said, "I've answered your questions. In return, I trust you'll refrain from telling anyone my current name or whereabouts. Otherwise, I'll have to change them again. And I'm getting too old for this."

"I can't promise anything," I said. "We'll try."

He nodded toward the door. "If you want to avoid the unwashed multitudes, there's an exit at the end of the hall that goes directly to the parking lot."

He pulled the ashtray closer, then drew a pack of Marlboros and a chrome lighter from his pocket. Setting a cigarette between his lips, he began flicking the lighter with his thumb.

I raised an eyebrow. "I thought you said you can help people stop smoking."

Platte smirked. "That only works on people who want to live longer," he said.

We opened the door and found the exit. Outside, it was still hot. We could hear the jukebox.

"I didn't think it was possible," Stephen said, looking up at the stars.

"Didn't think *what* was possible?"

"To find anyone more cynical than I am," he said.

～

THERE WERE ONLY two motels in Canyonville, Wyoming. Ours was better, because the other was closed for remodeling.

Stephen had made reservations for us at the Saddleback Lodge, so named to obey what must have been a state law requiring all businesses to remind everyone of the Old West, tumbleweeds, or suicide.

We'd spent much of the ride from the Lounge to the Lodge in silence. Now, as I parked our rented white Ford Focus near the motel's main entrance, Stephen turned to me.

"What's your take on Platte?" he asked.

"Not sure. Noble victim or pathetic fraud, I guess. Right now, I'm too tired to know which."

"Me, too."

We trudged down the hall to our rooms, 208 and 210. We fished out our key cards and stood there.

I thought of what Stephen had done at the Starlite Lounge, when the three yokels at the nearby table had yelled about me. When I'd felt so vulnerable and he'd volunteered to take my place. He didn't have to do that.

"Thanks," I said. "For getting me out of a tough spot tonight, I mean."

He shrugged. "Maybe that 'love thy neighbor' stuff is starting to rub off on me. I sure hope not."

I gave a tired laugh, wishing he understood a little more about God than the story of the Good Samaritan. Not that I was an expert myself.

"Hope this place has more hot water than the last one," he said. He slid his key card into the lock, pulled it out, and went inside. I did the same with mine.

I switched on the overhead light, then the nightstand lamp. The latter had been fashioned by remarkably unskilled craftsmen to suggest a covered wagon.

There were no cockroaches, not that I could see. Maybe

they didn't have any in Wyoming. The air conditioning, apparently allowed in public lodging, was clattering away.

Taking out my phone, I proceeded to plug it into the charger. I flopped on the bed, undid my watchband, then checked the time.

It had been 48 hours since Hunter Thicke's ultimatum.

The ax was about to fall.

CHAPTER 14

THE FOLLOWING MORNING, WE WALKED NEXT DOOR TO THE Chuckwagon Café. Its sun-bleached sign hailed from the days of red Texaco gasoline pumps and featured a bigger attempt at a Conestoga wagon.

"Must be where the locals go," Stephen said as we steered ourselves onto the puffy green vinyl seats of a corner booth.

I studied the menu, whose cover depicted a cartoon cowboy scorching the hide of a bawling calf with a branding iron—a sight bound to whet the appetite of any diner.

"Only one drawback to eating where the locals eat," he said.

"What's that?"

"The locals."

"Oh, come on," I said. "It's a *family* restaurant."

He looked around. "Gotta admit it's everything the Free Complimentary Breakfast isn't. By that I mean the food looks edible."

A waitress came to take our order. To my surprise, she wasn't very colorful. No gum-popping, no calling us "Honey," no telling us how she'd just gotten out of prison for setting drizzle it on my pancakes. "We should keep the receipts, just in case."

He took a bite of his omelet, the cheesy, bell-peppery oozing of which suddenly looked unaffordable.

"I wonder what we'll do for money," I said, "now that we're stuck in Wyoming without jobs or lawyers."

He poked a forkful of eggs into his mouth and somehow enunciated around it. "Beats me."

"Me, too," I said, recklessly tucking into my flapjacks. "I can hardly wait to find out."

THE PLANE from Laramie to Denver was a puddle jumper, about the size of a German Shepherd and owned by one of those regional airlines not even the Federal Aviation Administration has heard of. The pilot bore a passing resemblance to Sully Sullenberger, only much ruddier due to what looked like the effects of chronic alcohol consumption.

Fortunately, the Denver to Atlanta flight was more promising. According to the safety instructions in the seat pocket, the plane was an Airbus 320—a major improvement even though the French were better at producing things like chocolates and snobbery.

The pilot, all sharp pleats and clear eyes, delivered his opening remarks without a trace of inebriation. Comforted, I sank into the seat, closed my eyes, and contemplated 172 minutes of blessed isolation.

I was off by 171 minutes and 36 seconds.

"We need to talk," Stephen said.

I sighed. To my knowledge, those words had never preceded a pleasant experience. What did he want to talk about? Had he decided to blame me for the loss of his job?

The plane gathered speed, hurtling down the runway,

thumping and whining in a way that made me wonder whether its French designers had overlooked something crucial while distracted by a Jerry Lewis movie.

The landing gear retracted with a *thunk*. We slipped the surly bonds of earth. As to whether we were about to touch the face of God, only He could say.

"What do we need to talk about?" I asked.

"Strategy. How we're going to resolve this little problem of surviving. Stuff like paying bills and finding murderers. I figured this would be a good time, since we're stuck in an airplane with nothing else to do."

Relieved, I sank back against the seat. "By all means." Having dodged a bullet, I was willing to discuss anything, except monster trucks and Japanese anime.

"Okay," he said. "If we leave Georgia and go back to Manhattan, we can't mount much of a defense."

"Agreed."

"Most of the players, except for Platte, are in Atlanta. If we stay there, we have access to information. Like from Detective Valenzuela. As long as we're on his good side."

I thought for a moment. "Oh, yeah," I said. "Did I tell you how we're going to do that?"

"No."

"He's got literary aspirations. Wants to write 'cop novels.'"

"Uh-oh."

"I told him we'd look at his manuscript, help him get it published."

"*We?*"

"Hey, we're in this together." I paused, thinking again. "But now we can't say his book will be considered at Pendleton. We don't even work there anymore."

"Yeah, that's a problem."

I looked out the window. We were still rising, those Gallic

engines laboring as if they could burn themselves out at any moment.

"So," I said. "Here's an idea. We can say we're not bound to Pendleton anymore. We've decided to be literary agents."

"We have?"

"For the time being. All you need to be an agent is a website and a business card, right? We can get those later."

"Okay."

"We'll tell him we can help him make his book good enough to submit anywhere."

He shrugged. "I guess an empty promise is better than none."

"As for affording a lawyer, maybe we don't need one. We haven't been charged with anything."

"Not yet," he said. "And we'll have to cut expenses, starting with housing. The airbnb place I reserved on the Internet would be great, but now the price is too steep. I'll try to find something closer to Atlanta—a budget place, but a little more tolerable than the Swan's Corners Inn."

"I didn't think such luxury was possible."

"Maybe we can downgrade the rental car. To a bicycle."

He leaned back in his seat. "So glad we could have this little talk." Sticking his earbuds in his ears, he proceeded to fiddle with his iPod and closed his eyes.

I shut mine, too, and returned to a state of blissful isolation, 151 minutes of which remained.

I must have fallen asleep and woke when the captain announced our descent and Atlanta's time and temperature. Unable to find a tissue in my purse, I wiped the drool from the corner of my mouth with the back of my hand and hoped no one would notice.

The moment the Airbus touched the tarmac, Stephen grabbed his phone and started tapping. It seemed to take another 151 minutes for the plane to halt and the rows in front of us to empty.

By the time we stepped into the terminal, he'd made reservations elsewhere. The place even advertised a Free *Continental* Breakfast, which was at least grammatically correct. We were also downgraded to a tiny Kia Rio.

"Still going to be expensive," he said as we fast-walked our way down the concourse. "Gives us another reason to hurry up and find out who the real killer is."

"Right," I said, panting.

As if we needed one.

～

CHECKING into the Southern Suites Motel was painful. I had to use my own credit card now.

A brief walk-through revealed that this place was indeed a step up from the Swan's Corners Inn, or at least a half-step. There was an indoor pool not much larger than a Ping-Pong table, which we'd probably never use, and a conference room not much bigger, which Stephen seemed to think we might.

A white board was bolted to the wall of the conference room, with three black erasable markers in its tray. He uncapped the first and tested it with a scribble. Dry. The second was no better. The third was the charm, sort of, producing a pale gray line that was nearly readable.

"Perfect," he said.

"For what?"

"A list of suspects. It's like the white board they had on *House*. The doctors would list all the diseases a patient might have, then try to eliminate them one by one. Only we eliminate suspects."

He ran off to reserve the room. I picked up the marker and made a list:

WILLOW HAYLY
PHILLIP MINOR
GERALD SACKETT
STANTON PLATTE
NORMA SUNDSTROM
UNKNOWN CO-WORKER

UNFORTUNATELY, the marker chose to give up the ghost after SUNDSTRO. Close enough.

"Okay," Stephen said when he returned. "Let's start with Willow."

I folded my arms. "Hard to imagine her shooting anybody. But her motive for having someone *else* kill Tripp would be to silence him and save her empire."

Stephen shook his head. "Can't see it. She'd know killing Tripp wouldn't make Willowgate go away. It would just make it a bigger story than ever."

"Maybe you haven't noticed, but people sometimes do boneheaded things."

"Like the guy who invented Marmite. Have you ever tasted that stuff?"

"Speaking of boneheaded, how about Phillip Minor?"

"Hard to imagine him killing anybody, either. If he did, it would be out of loyalty to her. Or to preserve his job by preserving hers."

"Except he'd also know it would make things worse," he said. "As a PR guy, he'd know that better than most."

He paused. "Then there's Gerald Sackett. Why would *he* do it? He wanted Tripp to be proven *right*. He asked us to show everybody the abuse charge against his mom was a lie."

I picked up the marker and tapped it on the table. "Whether or not Gerald's as forgiving as he claims to be, he's got no motive. At least not an obvious one."

"Stanton Platte," Stephen said.

"You heard him. Resented the idea that the retrieved memories were a sham. But killing Tripp would have gotten the police involved, making it tougher for him to disappear again. Platte may be a fake, but he's not an idiot."

"Now *there's* a ringing endorsement." He looked at the board. "What about Norma . . . *Sundstro?*"

"Motive, maybe. But means and opportunity? Practically impossible. Same with the idea that she hired someone to do it."

"That leaves Unknown Employee."

"Need to follow that up," I said. "Would have to be something personal, I guess, not related to Willowgate."

Scratching his chin, he looked at the board. "That's everybody. So, nobody did it."

"Something's wrong here. Lots of people may have disliked Tripp, but none of them really would have benefited from his death."

He took a felt eraser from the tray and began to scour away the list of names. "Hope you've got this memorized. No point in confusing the next people who use this room."

I tossed the dehydrated markers into a wastebasket in the corner. "The best we can do is find a piece of evidence that points to somebody on the list. Or that points away from us."

"Evidence . . . as in physical?"

"The kind the police would know. For instance, when did Tripp die? What kind of gun was it? Were there fingerprints?"

"We can't get any of that stuff."

"I know. It's time to start making the literary dreams of Sergeant Luis Valenzuela come true."

CHAPTER 15

Next morning, we ate our first Free Continental Breakfast.

Actually, I'd encountered my first on The Continent itself at the Paris Book Fair of 2006. My hotel offered baskets of croissants, jam, espresso, and packets of instant cocoa. There were no waiters, saving me the trouble of having to communicate with still another French *patriote* who refused to speak English without sneering.

The breakfast at the Southern Suites Motel, on the other hand, was nothing to write home about—unless one came from a household that enjoyed hearing about cinnamon toast, coffee, tea, two kinds of juice, and a few greenish bananas.

After breakfast we navigated the Kia to downtown Atlanta. Our destination: Zone 5 of the Atlanta Police Department, specifically the precinct office on Spring Street. Our mission: to see Detective Sergeant Luis Valenzuela.

We found him sitting in a gray-walled cubicle, scribbling on a yellow legal pad with his famously clickable pen, at arm's length from an overflowing wire in-basket and an ineffectual oscillating fan. A child's crayon drawing was taped next to the entrance of his workspace—a humanoid figure with red curlicues sprouting from its head, its mismatched green and purple eyes protruding like those of a condemned man in the midst of electrocution.

"I see you have an artist at home," I said.

He smiled. His teeth were still perfect as his hair, not that I noticed.

"Not at *my* home," he said. "My nephew drew that. The kid's a firecracker. My sister says he takes after me."

He came around the front of his desk to lift stacks of papers from the two visitor chairs, both of which were as dusty and purple as his own. "Have a seat."

We did. He started tapping his keyboard. "From what you said on the phone, I take it you have some information for me."

I smiled. Maybe over-smiled. "We like to think of it as good news. We've been . . . well, fired. Seems our employer fails to appreciate all the attention we've brought the company lately."

He stopped tapping and sat up straight. "How is that good news?"

"It means we're free to . . . take on our own projects now. We're going to be literary agents."

"Oh," he said, probably not knowing the difference between an agent and an eggplant. Come to think of it, that difference was often vanishingly small.

"Since we're in Atlanta for the duration, we need to make the most of our time. That means acquiring an author or two we can represent. We're always on the lookout for up-and-coming writers, and we'd love to see your novel."

He grinned. Reaching down, he rolled out his lower left desk drawer, pulled out a blue shoebox, and plopped it next to his mouse pad.

"Sometimes I work on it over lunch. About a year ago I sent the first draft to this guy, a friend of a relative of a friend, you know? Some kind of producer in Los Angeles. Never heard anything back."

He paused for a moment, his brow furrowing. "Nothing personal," he said. "But how do I know you won't steal my ideas? Not that you would, see, but—"

"We'd never do such a thing," I said gently.

The furrows didn't leave his brow.

Fortunately, Stephen chose that moment to play Good Editor, Bad Editor.

He started with a shrug. "That's fine. We understand if you don't feel comfortable showing us your manuscript. We'll find another author. There are so many, you know."

The detective's eyes widened. "Well, now, wait. I don't mean—"

"You can trust us," I said softly.

"No, no," Stephen countered. "We don't want to pressure the man. We'll just—"

"Okay, sure, okay," Valenzuela said quickly, raising his palms in surrender. "If I can't trust you, who can I trust, right?"

"Wonderful," I said. "We can hardly wait to read it."

"Yes," Stephen added. "Hardly."

"Um . . . before I forget," I said, "We've been wondering how the investigation is going. Were there any fingerprints at the crime scene? And that surveillance camera. Did it get any video?"

The detective looked pained. "I . . . don't think I can talk about that."

Stephen shook his head. "That *is* too bad. It'll take so long to track that information down ourselves; we probably won't have time to read your manuscript after all."

Suddenly Luis bore a strong resemblance to a man who'd

painted himself into a corner. During an earthquake. In a burning building.

"Alright, yes, okay. I guess under the circumstances . . ." His eyes darted toward the entrance of his cubicle, but just for a second.

He slipped a file folder from the cabinet behind him. From my pocket I fished the pen and paper I'd used to take notes on my chat with Marvin Ainsley Pitts.

The detective lowered his voice. "We don't have a lot of information yet. Tentative time of death was three to six hours before Tripp's body was found. Bullet was thirty-eight caliber; gun wasn't located. Only one shot hit the body. Entered the chest without an exit wound. Haven't found any strays."

I wrote as quickly and as small as I could. He didn't pause, apparently wanting to get this over with.

"Nobody in the neighborhood heard a shot. No other noise, no unfamiliar person or vehicle. No recording from the camera. Not that it was busted or that the killer disabled it. The thing was just a dummy, a cheap way to scare burglars off. No fingerprints so far, other than Tripp's—and a few from the two of you, but only at the entrance."

I put the pen down and flexed my fingers. "Did he leave anything that could be traced back to his source on the Willow book?"

Valenzuela shook his head. "His files looked like they'd been messed with. Hard to tell, though, since the guy wasn't exactly a master of organization. We haven't found anything about Ms. Hayly. We're looking at his hard drive, but so far, nothing."

"What about a roommate?" Stephen asked.

The detective flipped some pages in the file. "Didn't have one. Sounds like his parents in Nebraska were sending him money to help with the rent. Like they thought he was about to be the next—what's his name, that Wikileaks guy."

"You talked to his parents?" she asked.

"Yeah, on the phone. They're pretty broken up, naturally. I asked if the kid had enemies. They said that if he did, they didn't know about it."

"Speaking of enemies," I said, "have you talked with Norma Sundstrom?"

"Who?"

"That answers *that* question. Never mind."

He closed the folder. "That's all I got." He glanced toward the entrance of his cubicle again.

"Thank you," I said.

There was an awkward pause. I picked up the shoebox. "May we borrow this?"

"Oh, yeah, sure."

"We'll take good care of it. We'll read it as soon as possible."

He smiled that shy smile. "Hope you like it."

I doubted I would.

But I had to admit the author was kind of interesting.

WE DROVE BACK to the motel, trying to make out the Atlanta skyline in the smog. Stephen seemed to be frowning more than usual.

"Something wrong?" I asked.

"About this division of labor," he said. "We don't *both* have to read the manuscript."

"You want to have it all to yourself?"

"I don't want to have it at all."

"Well, what else are you going to be doing?"

He held up his phone. "Somebody has to do something

with that information dump we just got. As in looking all that stuff up and trying to figure out what to do with it. Like the caliber of the gun. Does that tell us anything? Or the time of death? Valenzuela gave us so much you got writer's cramp making a list."

"So why can't *I* look it up?"

"With all due respect, when it comes to Google, would you say you're a power user? We both know I'm going to be doing the heavy lifting."

I tried to come up with a response, but his logic was bulletproof.

"Okay. My job is to start reading."

"Good luck. Just remember, it was your idea."

Twenty minutes later, alone in my room, I lifted the lid of the blue shoebox.

What I saw next is hard to describe. I'll err on the side of caution.

The title page said *HARD BARGAIN*. In the upper right corner, it said 200,000 WORDS, which might have worked as one of those massive doorstops by Stephen King or James Michener, but not for any normal human being.

Reluctantly I turned the page and started reading.

The protagonist was named Humberto "Hard Guy" Herrera. It soon became clear that he was, shall we say, reminiscent of a certain three-digit secret agent and a certain Atlanta police detective.

He was a man's man. A woman's man. In the first chapter he managed to crack a coconut with his thumbs, mix a piña colada in his shoe, defuse an improvised roadside device with his eyes shut, and rescue a Siamese cat from a tree. The latter earned him the favor of the animal's owner, an impossibly shapely woman with a strange accent, sort of Irish-Bulgarian or something.

And don't get me started on the adjectives.

I set the manuscript on the bed and closed my eyes. My gorge was rising, something it did only on special occasions such as eating poisonous blowfish.

Call it an abomination, an excrescence, an assault on the English language. There was only one thing to do with it. The thing had to be buried at sea.

Unfortunately, I was nowhere near the ocean. Opening my eyes, I picked the pages up again and tried to press on. But no. About halfway through Chapter Two, my brain began to reject the words like a bad kidney transplant.

I dropped the whole thing into the shoebox, wishing I had some hand sanitizer. Picking up my phone, I dialed Stephen's room.

"How is your unbelievably difficult search going?" I asked.

He sighed. "Slowly. This is a very long list, you know."

"Well, this is a very bad book."

"I'm afraid I can't help you there."

"If I read any more, I may need medical attention."

"Sorry," he said. "Got to hang up. Miles to go before I sleep."

The line went silent.

I took a deep breath and counted to 40, since 10 was insufficient at the moment. Then I dialed a different number.

It was time to take matters into my own hands.

"I HOPE THIS IS IMPORTANT," said Marvin Ainsley Pitts's voice on the phone.

"Isn't it always?" I asked.

"I mean important as in hanging by your fingernails from the edge of a cliff in the middle of a hurricane, Cranberry."

"It's more of a literary crisis," I said.

"No such thing, except for missing a deadline. That what this is about?"

"It's about me spending the rest of my life in jail."

"Okay," he said. "You got my attention."

"Here's the situation. We found the memory doctor, but he wasn't very cooperative. We got some stuff from the police department, though. I was hoping you could help us figure out what it means."

"What kind of stuff?"

I told him about the detective's reluctant report—what I could recall of it, anyway. Stephen had the list.

When I was done, he grunted. "You'll need another piece of paper."

Reaching for the nightstand, I seized the Southern Suites official pad and pen. "Ready."

"Nothing unusual about the handgun. They make thirty-eight caliber service revolvers for police and military. Specials, too. Pretty reliable, good for self-defense. So, unless you find a suspect who owns one, that isn't much of a clue."

"I see."

"The single shot could mean the killer was an experienced shooter. Probably pretty close range, though, which wouldn't take much marksmanship. It's not like the victim was hit between the eyes, right? So that's not a great lead, either."

I tapped the pen on the pad. Not exactly what I wanted to hear.

"Time of death tells you when your suspects need alibis. Including you. Also lets you know when somebody in the neighborhood might have heard something. But since nobody seems to have heard anything . . ."

I sighed.

"You say the surveillance camera was a dummy?" he asked.

"Yes."

"The killer didn't disable it? Pull the wires out?"

"Apparently not."

"Might mean the shooter could tell it was a fake by looking at it. Could indicate a certain technical expertise. Or maybe not." He paused. "The door was unlocked, right?"

"Uh-huh."

"Forced open?"

I tried to remember. "I'm not sure. The detective didn't mention it."

"Could be important. If it wasn't jimmied, maybe Tripp knew the killer. But not necessarily."

"You seem awfully indecisive today," I said.

"I report, you decide."

I slumped in the chair. "Marvin, it's just that I don't know what to do." I felt my throat tighten. "Maybe I'm not cut out for this. I guess nobody is."

He paused. "You feeling alone again?"

I didn't want to answer. Of course I was feeling alone. There was Marvin and Tracy and God, Mikki and a couple of other friends, Stephen and a few sympathetic co-workers, my family two thousand miles away. But nobody else. Not anymore. I'd been engaged once. He'd gotten cold feet. Nothing since.

"We've talked about this before, Carolyn. You go to a big church. You said there's a singles group."

"Hasn't worked out." I didn't want to get into that again. Besides, that was the kind of conversation I preferred to have with Mikki Flaherty. I made a mental note to try calling her in the morning.

"Well, I'm no expert on that sort of thing. With Tracy and me, I prayed for somebody and eventually she showed up. Worst decision she ever made."

I'd heard that story, too. I just wanted one of my own to tell.

"Well, I know you're busy, so I'll let you go. I'll see what I can make of these clues."

"Oh, one more thing," he said. "About Mr. Tripp. I'm guessing that being a rookie reporter on the Internet doesn't bring in a lot of cash. What did he really do for a living?"

"Worked in a coffeehouse. Got help from his parents."

"Well, if I were you I'd talk to some of his fellow employees to find out whether they know anything. I don't figure these latte types are a real competitive bunch, but you never know."

"That's our plan."

"Anything else?"

"I guess not."

"Call anytime, honey."

The line went silent.

I picked up my notes, not wanting to think about the last part of our conversation. Not now, anyway.

The more I read of Marvin's advice, the clearer it was that nothing was clear. Most of the clues seemed to lead in two directions at once, or nowhere at all.

Looking over at the blue shoebox, I shuddered.

Perhaps we'd made a poor trade with Luis. In exchange for 200,000 words apparently banged out by a roomful of monkeys with typewriters, we'd gotten a mess of pottage.

One thing was sure, though.

If I had to read the rest of that book, my gorge wouldn't be falling anytime soon.

CHAPTER 16

IN THE MORNING, HAVING SPENT ANOTHER HOUR SKIMMING enough of *Hard Bargain* to make me wish for a severe case of macular degeneration, I tried calling Mikki Flaherty. I got nothing, not even a message. I sent her an e-mail and hoped for the best.

About 7:30 I met Stephen downstairs. I couldn't eat much breakfast, due to the quality of the food, the rising of my gorge, and the peppiness of his opening question.

"What do you think of the manuscript?"

"Still very bad."

"Yeah, but I expect a more detailed review from you."

I sipped my apple juice. "In the words of Dorothy Parker, 'This is not a novel to be tossed aside lightly. It should be thrown with great force.'"

He shook his head. "Are you going to tell the detective that?"

"I'll tone it down. Maybe say it should be placed carefully on the railroad tracks."

"I thought you wanted him on our side. To give us information."

"So far it's not worth much. Or so I learned from Marvin."

He rolled his eyes. "You called him *again?*"

"He said most of what the detective told us won't help our case. He had a few other suggestions, like finding out whether Tripp's door had been forced open."

"Which we'll need to ask the detective, right? All the more reason to keep him happy." He shrugged. "Personally, I don't give a rip. You're the schmoozer around here."

I stared into the depths of my apple juice like a dispirited drunk. "I'll give him a ring to make sure he's around. May as well get it over with."

When I called, he was there. Unfortunately.

After I hung up, I looked at my watch. I had one hour to figure out what to say.

MR. VALENZUELA, *I have never seen a book quite like this.*

Nope. Every editor and his brother had used that one. Not to mention the fact it was so obviously condescending.

I can see you've put a great deal of effort into it.

No. Same reason.

I'd appreciate it if you'd kill yourself immediately.

Too true. Well, no. I kind of liked him. The problem was that he didn't know his limits.

I sighed. This wasn't working. Finding something positive to say about the contents of that shoebox was impossible.

I'd been rehearsing lines in my head since leaving the motel. Now we were entering downtown Atlanta again, watching the skyline crawl by. The fog had thinned to the consistency of petroleum jelly. Despite the air conditioning, I was starting to sweat.

"I can't do it," I said suddenly.

"Sure you can," Stephen said. "We do it all the time. Flattering authors who know somebody important. Buttering them up before we ask them to make fifty pages of revisions."

"He doesn't know anybody important. He only knows us."

"Besides, we're not editors now. We're agents. Stretching the truth is our job."

I fell silent. He had me there.

I stayed quiet for the rest of the drive, still trying to string the right words together. Nothing was materializing, even as we parked and entered the building and walked down the gray hall. Not even as we stepped past the grotesque crayon drawing outside Valenzuela's cubicle and sat down.

"I've looked at the manuscript," I announced, trying to sound sunny as a library storyteller on amphetamines.

He grinned. "Yeah, you said that on the phone." He leaned forward on his invisible racehorse. "What did you think?"

And then the answer came. I'd probably heard it somewhere but couldn't remember where.

I cleared my throat. "Mr. Valenzuela, there is no question you've been inspired by the greats."

Stephen clamped his hand over his mouth.

"I *thought* you might like it!" the detective exclaimed. "And call me Luis, okay?"

"Okay, Luis."

"So, what's the next step?" he asked.

I tapped the top of my purse. "Well, I'm sure you realize no manuscript is perfect. There are a number of changes to be made, of course."

His brows lowered. "What number are we talking about?"

"A pretty large one, I'd say. Nothing to be concerned about, though. Quite routine."

He shook his head. "Problem," he said.

"Excuse me?"

"I can't make a lot of changes. I've worked too hard on it already. And everybody I've shown it to loves it the way it is."

I closed my eyes. "Your friends and family?"

"Yeah."

I rubbed my temples with my fingers, contemplating how I might respond in an alternate universe. Probably something like, "Perhaps you should ask *them* to be your agents. And to buy your book."

In this universe, though, my reply was different. "I'm sure we can work something out. Maybe we can make the changes *for* you."

I opened my eyes. Stephen was looking at me as if I'd lost my mind.

"Mr. Valenzuela, could you excuse us for a moment?" he asked.

"Uh, sure."

He nodded toward the hallway outside the cubicle. Slowly I got to my feet and followed him out—past the crayon drawing, past a poster of a polar bear on a melting ice floe.

He turned to face me. "Are you sure you want to do this?"

"I know it's not fixable," I said. "I know what it really needs is about ten seconds with a flamethrower."

"Then why did you say *we'd* make the changes?"

I put my hands on my hips. "We can't lose our friendly insider. If we need a favor, he'll tell us to go pound sand."

"Okay. But *I'm* not making the changes."

I took a deep breath and let it seep out slowly. This time he'd pushed the envelope too far. No one, not even one of the best editors I'd ever met, could be allowed to show his boss this kind of disrespect.

"Mr. Ames," I said. "As your supervisor . . ."

"My what?"

I paused.

Then I remembered. I wasn't his boss anymore. He could say or do whatever he pleased.

It was the opposite of an epiphany.

"Never mind," I mumbled.

I trudged back to the cubicle, Stephen trailing me. We sat down.

"*I'll* be making the changes," I said.

"I guess that's okay," Luis said. "As long as I get to approve them."

I gave him a four-watt smile. "Perfect."

There was an awkward moment, no doubt the first of many.

Stephen turned to me. "We were going to ask a question, weren't we? Something our . . . friend brought up?"

"Oh," I said. "About Mr. Tripp's door. Was it forced open?"

Luis rummaged around for the manila folder, then looked over the report. "Doesn't say it was. Why?"

"If it wasn't, we thought it might mean he knew the killer."

He scratched his chin. "Maybe not. See, it's possible the killer disguised himself to *look* like somebody Tripp knew. I used that trick in the book. You must not be to that part yet."

I sighed. "I must not be."

There was another awkward moment.

"Well," I said, "we have to follow up on another suggestion."

"What's that?"

"The coffeehouse. We want to talk to Tripp's co-workers."

He shrugged. "Well, the powers that be think it's better to concentrate on the Willowgate thing. But let me know what you find out."

I patted the top of my purse. Nothing like doing the police department's job. And I wasn't even a resident of Georgia.

Heading down the long, gray hallway, I wondered what it was like to be a winner.

~

THE NAME of the place was Bean Thinking.

The bad pun was no surprise, considering what some people called their coffeehouses and hair styling salons. Remarkably, though, the Bean in the logo appeared to be of the kidney or pinto variety, not the brewable kind. Whoever had painted the picture over the door had depicted Rodin's *Thinker* with a large legume where his head should have been.

Entering beneath him, I felt out of my element. I tried to avoid trendy, overpriced places unless they sold clothes or shoes. But desperate times called for desperate measures.

Stephen, of course, looked right at home. He'd always spent an inordinate amount of the working day with his laptop at Starbuck's, pretending to edit while he probably went to Snapchat and Buzzfeed.

The interior was hardly worth describing—the smells of mocha and caramel and cinnamon, the signs saying things like FAIR TRADE and FREE WI-FI, the studiously arranged shelves of hardcovers no one ever opened, the couches, the patrons staring at their MacBooks through eyeglasses with fashionably outdated frames. There was also the requisite unreadable menu on the wall, printed to look as if it had been scrawled in chalk. I peered at it, knowing we'd have to buy something to justify our presence.

There was no line, probably because the morning rush of caffeine addicts was over, and the lunchtime crowd had yet to materialize. A girl about Stephen's age, a brunette with a wide face and long lashes, stood behind the counter.

"Hi," she said, brushing crumbs from her rubberized apron. "What can I get you?"

"Mocha latte, tall," Stephen said.

Checking its price on the wall, I flinched. "Iced Caramel Contemplation, short." I'd never seen one, but it sounded appropriate for 90-degree weather and I could pronounce it.

The young lady went off to do something with a stainless-steel machine that hissed and spat like a testy feline. Another barista, this one male and morose and sparsely goateed, stepped up to the battalion of pump bottles next to the register. Choosing one, he pounded two squirts of syrup into a cardboard cup and disappeared into the back.

The girl returned, carrying our drinks. She told us the price, somewhere between that of a mass market paperback and a Mercedes-Benz. I paid it, though not gladly.

"I remember the days before coffee became an art form," I said. "Or a major investment."

She smiled. "Yeah, I know. My dad says, like, the same thing. Guess he's right."

Stephen raised his eyebrows. "He's *right*? Were you home-schooled? Beaten with a wooden spoon?"

She chuckled. "No. Just kind of, like, traditional."

I took a sip of my drink. It was fine if one enjoyed that sort of thing. Which I did if it was Free Iced Coffee Day. Which it wasn't.

"We understand a guy named Zane Tripp used to work here," I said.

She sighed. "Yeah. Did you know him?"

"Not exactly. But I'm trying to get acquainted with him through some people who did."

"Are you, like, from the police?"

"No. But we've met more than once with the detective assigned to the case."

She seemed satisfied with that explanation, though I wasn't sure why.

"What do you need to know?" she asked.

"Did Mr. Tripp have any enemies?"

She shrugged. "I didn't, like, know him well enough to say for sure. He wasn't, like, mean or nasty or anything. But . . ."

I waited for her to finish. She left the thought hanging.

"But what?" I asked.

"What's that old saying? Like, not speaking ill of the dead? I don't want to do that. But he wasn't, like, everybody's best friend."

"Why not?"

She looked at the row of syrup bottles and picked at a label with her fingernail. "I guess he could be, like, irritating sometimes. He seemed to want everybody to know he didn't belong here. That he was, like . . . meant for better things."

Suddenly the guy with the goatee returned to the counter. He leaned toward Stephen. "As if ninety percent of us didn't feel the same way about ourselves," he said.

"Speak for yourself, man," Stephen said.

The girl gave Mr. Goatee a sideward glance but continued. "Everybody was, like, shocked when Zane died. Some of them talked about how he always seemed so worried something terrible was going to happen to him."

"And then it did," said the young man with a snicker.

"Jeremy, it's not funny," she said.

"Maybe not. But he *was* irritating. All his stories about reporters who disappeared for telling the truth in Russia or somewhere. Dude thought he was in the same league, but he really wasn't."

A middle-aged couple stepped up to the register. Mr. Goatee flashed a final Sardonicus smile in our direction, then went to wait on them.

The girl shook her head, then turned to me with a

confiding look. "When Zane died, some people were sorry they'd said harsh things about him behind his back. Jeremy never seemed very sorry, though."

Another customer approached the counter. The girl adjusted her apron. "Anyway, Zane wasn't all that popular. But it was, like, a personality thing. Nobody wanted to kill him or anything—at least nobody here."

"I can see you have to get back to work," I said. "You've been a big help."

"Good luck," she said. "Zane wasn't perfect, but he didn't, like, deserve what happened to him, you know?"

She hustled away.

Stephen shook his head. "She used that word *twelve times*."

"What word?"

"*Like*. She's giving millennials a bad name."

"Could have been worse," I said. "I felt like thanking her."

Sitting at a table near the counter, we sipped our drinks.

"What do you suppose made Mr. Tripp so nervous?" I asked.

"No clue."

I looked around, trying to imagine the scene when that young man, full of ideals and himself, was still upright and moving through it.

Something had made him so anxious that in the night he probably wished he were home in Nebraska, where towns were smaller, and the darkness was safer. I knew what that was like.

In his case, though, someone had made his worst nightmare come true. It wasn't fair or right or decent.

He could have been Stephen, or my little brother. I couldn't leave his parents never knowing what had happened.

Not if it was up to me, anyway.

CHAPTER 17

It took half an hour to get back to the Southern Suites. Carrying the detective's blue shoebox under my arm, I went to my room. Stephen went to his.

I sat on the bed for a long time, staring at a print on the wall, a watercolor vaseful of pink flowers. My mind was elsewhere, painting oils of Luis and Tripp.

And Stephen. It felt a little dangerous to know I had no influence over him anymore. Our only common goal was trying to stay out of debt and prison. And, judging from past conversations, public readings of the *Twilight* books.

Even if we achieved those objectives, we'd go our separate ways. There'd never be a Neville & Ames Literary Agency and he'd never report to me again. One way or another, everything would change.

Rising from the bed, I caught a glimpse of myself in the mirror over the dresser. Who'd hire this woman, an alarmingly religious nitpicker who'd just been fired for incompetence and embarrassing her employer by being a murder suspect?

The lady in the mirror tried to look hopeful. Maybe, she

thought, there'd be an opening at Wal-Mart for a greeter who really knew her intransitive verbs.

I swallowed. I needed to talk with somebody. Somebody who really knew me.

I'd never heard back from Mikki Flaherty, not even in e-mail. I got out my phone and tried again. Nothing.

A knock at the door interrupted my reverie. It always seemed reveries existed only to be interrupted, which made me wonder why they existed at all.

Crossing toward the sound, I proceeded to peer through the peephole. There stood a short, balding man in Hawaiian print shirt and sunglasses, holding a large, white envelope.

Engaging the chain lock, I opened the door about three inches.

"Carolyn Neville?" the man asked.

"Yes."

"Package for you."

He poked the envelope through the gap and waited.

Not knowing what else to do, I took it.

He turned and walked down the hall. I heard the elevator clunk open, then closed.

Returning to the bed, I opened the envelope with my thumb and read:

United States District Court
For the Northern District of Georgia

Willoworth International Corp.
Plaintiff
V.
Carolyn J. Neville
Defendant

Civil Action No. 3076412

Notice of a Lawsuit and Request to Waive Service of a
Summons
To: Carolyn J. Neville

A LAWSUIT HAS BEEN FILED against you, or the entity you represent, in this court under the number shown above. A copy of the complaint is attached.

This is not a summons, or an official notice from the court. It is a request that, to avoid expenses, you waive formal service of a summons by signing and returning the enclosed waiver. To avoid these expenses, you must return the signed waiver within 30 days from the date shown below, which is the date this notice was sent. Two copies of the waiver form are enclosed, along with a stamped, self-addressed envelope or other prepaid means for returning one copy. You may keep the other copy.

I'VE BEEN SERVED, I thought.

Willow was suing me. Or at least her organization was.

But Philip Minor had warned me, hadn't he?

I kept reading. There was something about how, if I returned the waiver, I'd have 60 days to answer the complaint. Otherwise I'd have to pay the expenses of making service, whatever that meant. It was signed by Robert Vidic, attorney at law.

Taking a deep breath, I flipped to the complaint.

It was all legal voodoo, like the e-mail from Hunter. Pages of nonsense about how I, through my negligence and dereliction of duty, had damaged the reputation of Willoworth

International Corp. and Willow Hayly in particular. I had thereby devalued the plaintiffs' brands and impeded their ability to recoup their investment in the upcoming tour. Restraint of trade. Slander. They were shooting all their slings and arrows at the wall and hoping something would stick.

I scanned the rest to see how much this might cost.

Ah, there it was.

PLAINTIFFS SEEK *judgment in the amount of one million dollars.*

WELL, why not? I had deep pockets, didn't I?

They knew I didn't. They knew they couldn't win. They weren't even bothering to sue Pendleton House or Chronicle Merkel.

It was personal. Minor wanted me to twist slowly in the wind until I was as miserable as possible. It was a classic nuisance lawsuit, the kind Our Friends in Legal had wanted to file against Zane Tripp.

I crammed the forms into the envelope. All at once, without really thinking about it, I heaved the whole thing at the door.

BAM!

It sounded good, that fat wad of paper whacking the steel.

So good, in fact, that I picked it up and did it again.

I stood there, my heart pounding.

If only I'd never accepted the delivery. But no matter. From what I'd heard, it would have been enough for the process server to toss it into the room.

Besides, it was a good distraction. It had taken my mind off Tripp and Stephen and Luis.

But probably not for long.

I WAITED for my heart to ease its hammering and to see whether some irate guest down the hall or an officious manager might complain about the racket. There was nothing.

At length I picked up the envelope and lobbed it onto the bed, then sat next to it.

No.

I wouldn't let myself get bogged down in some specious lawsuit, not now. Philip Minor might think it was all a game, but he had lawyers and all the time in the world.

I went back to staring at the painting with the pink flowers. They probably had nothing to do with it, but this time I felt an idea taking shape.

Willow. Have to talk to Willow.

Surely she'd see the craziness of it all. She wasn't like Minor, who held a bus-sized grudge against me for implying he couldn't do his job. This wasn't her vendetta. Somehow he'd talked her and a team of ambulance chasers into doing this, wasting everyone's time and money. Especially mine.

I got up and started pacing.

Talking to Willow wouldn't be easy. Minor had warned me to stay away from her. I'd have to do an end run around him, and the rest of her inner circle.

Worse, I had no leverage. Pendleton House had severed all ties with me, so I had no official relationship with Willow anymore. If she wanted to ignore me, she could keep working with my former employer as though I'd never existed.

I quit pacing and looked at my phone on the nightstand. My only option was to call Willow's cell and let the chips fall.

I picked up my phone, hit the numbers, and her voice mail answered. It was a lovely greeting, full of what Minor had called her trademark intensity, warmly welcoming my communication and empowering me to leave a message after the tone.

"Willow," I said, "Carolyn Neville. I hope you don't mind my calling you like this. I think we've got a misunderstanding here. Can we talk about it? Alone? Please let me know. Thanks."

I set my phone on the nightstand, leaving it on in case she returned my call.

By the time I went to bed, it had made no sound.

But I could hear the chips falling already.

CHAPTER 18

THE ALARM ON MY PHONE WOULD HAVE GONE OFF AT 7:30 a.m., but my ringtone beat it to the punch. My eyes fluttered open. I grabbed the phone.

"Hello, Ms. Neville," said Willow. She sounded polite but wary.

"Morning," I said, doing my best to sound alert. "Thanks for returning my call."

"I understand you'd like to have a chat."

"Yes."

"Well, I'm looking at my schedule and it's not exactly full of holes. But I'd like to make time for you. Mostly because you want to see me alone. I'm tired of always having handlers and lawyers around, telling me what to do."

"I can imagine," I said, sitting up.

"Say, ten o'clock?"

"That works."

"There's a little county park about halfway between Atlanta and Swan's Corners. Buttonbush Trails. Not much to it. Hardly anybody goes there. I use it every so often just to get away from the office. And people in general."

"I'll Google it for directions."

"Good. See you there."

She hung up.

I put the phone down. *So far, so good.*

Not that *so far* was a long way.

I started staring at the picture of the pink flowers again, wondering how I'd convince her to drop the lawsuit.

Nothing came to mind.

I shook my head. Thanks to Minor, this might be my last chance to convince Willow of anything.

I got out of bed and stared harder.

IT WAS a red-letter day at the Free Continental Breakfast. The cinnamon toast had raisins in it, the low-impact kind.

Stephen and I met there half an hour later. He sipped his orange juice, a half-smile on his face. He seemed to be watching the TV newscast over my shoulder.

I took a long drink of coffee. "I just talked to Willow."

He paused in mid-sip. "Weren't you going to stay away from her?"

I told him about the lawsuit and the meeting at the park.

"Willoworth is *suing* you?" He made a disgusted noise.

I shrugged. "Not Willow's fault. It's the merciless Mr. Minor." I looked down at my coffee. "You seem to under-stand Willow pretty well. What can I say that might get her to drop the lawsuit?"

He frowned at the crumbs on his plate, then lifted his gaze again.

"I have no idea," he said helpfully.

I checked my watch. "Well, *I'd* better come up with one."

"You always do." He paused. "How about the rest of your day?"

I sighed. "Guess I'd better get going on that manuscript. Maybe get together with Luis and tell him what changes I'll have to make."

He shook his head. "I can't believe that guy. Why are the worst authors always the most uncooperative?"

"He may not be what you'd call a writer, but he's . . . unique. And, in his own way, bright."

"So's a platypus if you set it on fire."

"Glad you won't be dealing with him. I'll be breaking it to him a little more gently."

"I'd help, of course, but—"

"No need to explain. I'm sure you've got plenty of Googling to do."

"Actually, I'm planning something else. Thought I'd go back to the coffee shop and talk to a couple more people. Like that Jeremy guy with the goatee. Strange dude. Obviously didn't think much of Tripp."

I raised an eyebrow. "You think *he* might be behind this?"

"Don't know. But the coffee was pretty good."

I thought for a moment. "Okay. So, I'll meet Willow, then come back, and we can both go downtown. I'll call Luis to find out when he'll be around."

"Why bother? He's always around. Doesn't the guy have any detecting to do?"

I picked up my phone. "He certainly does. And so do we."

I GOT to Buttonbush Trails County Park first.

By *first*, I mean I was literally the only one there. The small gravel lot was empty. Which was understandable, given that the place didn't offer much more than two dilapidated picnic tables off the highway in the middle of nowhere. There was a sign with the county seal at the bottom and another displaying a trail map the sun had faded to a light green shadow of its former self. A trash can sat chained to a post, as if a gang of garbage thieves might be on the prowl. A concrete-block restroom was locked and labeled with still another sign that said OUT OF ORDER.

I assumed there were also buttonbushes, whatever they were. There were plenty of oaks and pines. It was easy to see why Willow chose this place to be alone. Everything past the parking lot was a wall of leaves and needles.

But the silence was unnerving. I was just about to get back in the Kia and wait when I heard a rumbling behind me from the highway. Turning, I saw a bright green sportscar, small and sleek, maneuvering into the parking lot. I didn't know any more about cars than I did buttonbushes but could tell it wasn't American or affordable.

Willow was at the wheel. Empowerment had its perks, it seemed.

"What kind is that?" I called as she emerged from the glimmering vehicle.

"A Jaguar. Don't know much about automobiles. I just think it's pretty."

"So do I." *Good*, I thought. *Common ground.* But I'd have to do more than that to win her over.

She looked around. "I love this place. Not much chance of being recognized or bothered. Safe. I usually don't even feel the need to bring my bodyguard."

"Mr. Yates," I said, remembering.

"Yes." She pointed at the wall of foliage. "Let's walk, shall we?"

We made our way down a hill into the woods. A sweet fragrance filled the air. Maybe it was buttonbush or just her perfume. Trees soared over our heads like the flying buttresses of Notre Dame. The silence no longer seemed unnerving.

Suddenly she stopped in the middle of the path and gazed up at the treetops. "I like you, Carolyn," she said. "You speak your mind. I can tell there's always something going on in there."

"Looks can be deceiving."

She chuckled. "You'd make a terrible yes-person. I should know. I've got plenty of those around."

She nudged a leaf on the ground with her dark blue Michael Kors wedge sandal. An odd choice for hiking, I thought, but she seemed used to it. "So what did you want to talk to me about?"

I cleared my throat. "I know you're busy, so I'll get to the point. Stephen and I have been . . . let go."

"I know. Your old boss called and told me they'd be hiring someone to replace the two of you. But I haven't heard a thing from him since."

She started walking again, slowly. "I'm sure you can understand why you've slipped off our list of favorite folks at Willoworth these days. You've sort of complicated our lives."

I followed a few steps behind, hoping it would be taken as contrition. "Not intentionally," I said.

"I know. And I sympathize, I really do. But I'm afraid I can't control what Pendleton House does with its employees." She stopped again and stared into the distance, all at once looking very tired. "Sometimes it seems I can't control much of anything."

She turned toward me. "This is really about the lawsuit, isn't it?"

I tapped my cheek as if I'd never considered the possibility. "I suppose you could say that."

"I know the whole thing is silly. But the lawyers don't see it that way. Philip certainly doesn't. He actually hired a private investigator to find out which motel you were in so the court papers could be served."

"I should feel honored."

She stopped and turned toward me. "So, I have misgivings. But I have to rely on my staff."

"Of course."

"I'm not a CEO. Or a writer, or a legal expert. I'm just somebody with a story. And a way of telling it that helps people believe in themselves."

I nodded, my mind racing to get things on track.

"Sometimes that means letting people like Philip and the lawyers have their way," she said, "even if I don't want to. Philip's been with me for a long time, maybe too long. But he and the others have gotten me this far. I can't do it without folks like that."

She looked down the trail. "Carolyn, have you ever had to turn a blind eye to things you didn't approve of, in order to survive?"

I thought of the questionable deals I'd seen at work, the office politics, the affairs kept quiet from spouses. A pang of guilt squeezed my middle like a cramp.

"Sometimes you have to ignore things, even hide them," she continued. "Terrible things. Sometimes you don't really have a choice."

She hesitated, looking as though she feared having said too much. Two seconds later, the look was gone.

She gave a rueful smile. "Guess I don't sound very empowered, do I?"

"But you are," I said. "There's a reason your street is named after you."

She looked me in the eye for a long moment, then sighed. "You're right. It's not fair to you or Stephen for me to plug my ears and ignore the lawsuit. I'll see what I can do."

"Thank you," I said.

She checked her watch, the pawning of which probably could have fed a family of five for a year. "Looks like I'm running late. Time for me to get back to the office. Even though I'd rather not."

We climbed back up the hill to where our cars were parked. "Take care, Carolyn," she said. "Give my best to Mr. Ames."

She got into the Jaguar, and the engine rumbled to life.

I watched her drive away.

Words like *reasonable* and *cordial* and *polite* came to mind. But so did *guarded* and *concealed* and *secret*.

There'd been only one moment without the mask, with that fearful, furtive look. When she talked about having to hide things.

Was she just talking about the lawsuit?

No, it was too much like the other time, in her office. When she'd had that tense, haunted aura.

She knew more than she was saying.

And something very scary was keeping her from saying it.

CHAPTER 19

I GOT BACK TO THE SOUTHERN SUITES JUST IN TIME TO PICK
Stephen up. Luis had told me on the phone he'd be gone
most of the day, but we had a one-hour window that would
open in about 45 minutes. I already had the blue shoebox in
the back seat.

"Cutting it a little close, aren't you?" Stephen asked,
standing in the lobby and sticking his phone in his pocket.

"We had so much to discuss." I headed for the car, and he
followed.

"Yeah? How did it go? Did she agree to drop the lawsuit?"

"There was sort of a pledge to help," I said, climbing into
the car. "But I'm getting the impression that with Willow,
things are never as they seem."

"Are you saying she's not telling the truth?"

"Not necessarily." I started the engine. "By the way, she
says hi."

"Uh-huh."

I pulled onto the street. "Did you know she has a Jaguar?"

"Cool. I don't think my mom knows that. If she did, she
might wonder who's really getting empowered here."

When we reached the highway, I squinted at the hazy skyline and the dashboard clock. *Uh-oh*, I thought, and pressed the accelerator.

"Maybe I did cut things a bit close," I said. "We'll make it, though."

"Not at this rate." He pulled out his phone and started tapping. "This app's supposed to give you current traffic conditions. I'll see if it can get us there in time."

At first things looked promising. On The App's advice we took an exit we hadn't taken before, and it seemed we might shave 20 minutes from our arrival time. But then we saw the orange DETOUR signs.

Downtown Atlanta was under construction, and The App had not been notified.

Squinting at the phone, he frowned. "Try turning right onto Spring Street." But when we reached that intersection, all we found were City of Atlanta Department of Public Works barricades.

"Oh, man," he said.

I shook my head. "If memory serves, we're close to the police station. There must be a right we can take somewhere along here."

"There better be," he said. "We're lost."

"I'm aware of that."

"Don't kill the messenger."

"Don't tempt me."

Just then I saw my opportunity. Jerking the wheel to the right, I lurched onto a side street. Another driver paid tribute to my ingenuity with what was obviously a honk of praise.

Stephen poked his phone, but it went dark. He turned to me. "You're flying solo."

I glanced left and right, breathing faster. "Watch for a parking garage coming up any minute."

"I don't see any—"

"There it is." I jerked right again, careening to an abrupt halt halfway inside the entrance to a concrete hive of automobiles. After pulling ahead, we paused before a yellow-and-black-striped arm as the machine spat out a ticket.

Heartbeat drumming in my ears, I watched the arm ascend.

"I think we're just a few blocks from Luis's office," I said.

"I'll take your word for it."

The Kia began to struggle up the spiral of the parking structure as if it were a bicycle on Mount Everest. I punched off the air conditioning, hoping to give the engine more power. The fan under the hood kicked in.

We passed a giant numeral 1 painted in white on a concrete pillar. Then another, and a third. Level 1 was full.

The same happened on Level 2.

I looked at the dashboard clock. In 11 minutes, we'd be late.

After passing two giant numerals on Level 3 and finding no spaces, I skipped to Level 4. *Ah*, I thought. Here the cars were few and far between.

"Finally," I said.

"We're supposed to be there in seven minutes."

"We will." I parked, and we got out of the car. The engine fan kept running.

"We can't possibly make it," he said.

I hauled out the blue shoebox and slammed my door. "Of course, we can," I said.

I was wrong.

That was when bad things started to happen.

WE HEADED FOR THE ELEVATOR, which had another white numeral 4 painted on its steel door. A fire extinguisher stood guard next to it, along with a security floodlight. Our footsteps echoed, quick and clipped.

Suddenly there was another sound, a much louder one. A kind of pop. At first I didn't recognize it.

Then came another. With a piercing *KISSHHHH* the window of the fire extinguisher cabinet exploded in front of us. Glass shattered and splashed to the floor.

A gun. There was a gun somewhere.

God, help.

Someone was pointing it in our direction and pulling the trigger.

"Get down!" I called to Stephen.

The concrete floor was gritty, oily against my palms. Stephen was about six feet away, slightly behind me.

Crawling on hands and knees, we managed to get closer to the elevator. I pushed the blue shoebox before me as if it were actually worth preserving.

The shooting stopped. If my heartbeat had been drumming in my ears before, it was thundering like a marching band now.

"He must not be able to see us when we're down," I whispered.

"He or she."

"Yes, he or she. But we have to push the elevator button."

"I know."

It was clear he didn't plan to volunteer.

With a grunt I sprang up just long enough to hit the DOWN arrow. Pain flashed in my thighs, no doubt as I yanked some crucial tendon. Another pop burst from somewhere behind us, and a zing sounded as a bullet ricocheted from the door.

"Thanks," he whispered. "I owe you one."

We listened for the hum and click of an elevator car in the shaft. There was nothing.

Just then the shooting started again. One sharp report, then another.

"Where do you think it's coming from?" he whispered.

"I can't tell. But it seems to be getting louder. Which probably means closer."

Finally there was a click and hum from somewhere below.

We waited and listened again. I stuck the blue shoebox under my arm, which was shaking.

At last the doors parted. The car was empty, thank God.

Still on hands and knees, we crawled inside. Lying on the floor in opposite corners, we waited once more, this time for the doors to close.

A bullet pinged against the back wall between us, then must have bounced out somewhere. At last the doors rolled back together.

Another pause. Why weren't we moving? I held my breath, straining to hear whatever might be happening outside the door, or beneath us, or anywhere.

Suddenly, somewhere on the other side of the door, the squeal of tires echoed. A vehicle was burning rubber, peeling out, speeding away. The sound faded. The shooter was gone.

The elevator swayed slightly. A motor in the shaft began to hum, and our descent began.

Exhaling, I melted into the floor. A wordless prayer of thanks floated through the back of my mind like the smell of ozone after rain.

Slowly Stephen sat up and propped his back against the wall. He closed his eyes.

The elevator slowed, then halted. Level 1.

The door slid open. We were still on the floor.

About half a dozen people stood outside the door. A portly businessman with a laptop case. A couple with a baby. A teenage girl with a shopping bag. They all stared at us as if we'd grown fur between the fourth level and the first. Except for the baby, who was looking off in some other direction entirely.

Wobbling, I got to my feet. I was lightheaded. Stephen rose, too, looking a little off balance.

Listing one way and then another, we made it to the sidewalk and leaned against the building. The concrete felt pebbly against my back.

"Are you . . . all right?" I asked.

"No," he said faintly. "Are you?"

"Not that I know of," I said.

CHAPTER 20

FROM NOW ON, TIME WOULD BE DIVIDED INTO TWO ERAS: Before the Shots, and After.

This was After.

We kept leaning against the building, holding it up. Or vice versa. At the moment we were in no condition to tell the difference.

"Should we dial 911?" Stephen asked. Except he pronounced it *nine eleven* instead of *nine one one*, a clear indication of his state of mind.

I shook my head, which made me feel dizzier. "The police station's right around here. At least I think it is. Walking there would be faster."

"Okay," he said, sounding doubtful.

I gazed at the passersby, too shell-shocked to tell whether anyone was pointing a gun at us. "This way. I think."

We walked as fast as we could, weaving our way around oblivious Atlantans who presumably were leading normal lives. We paused impatiently at crosswalks, checking over our shoulders for anyone who could be following, not even knowing what that might look like.

When we finally reached the Zone Five police station, my watch claimed it had taken us only 14 minutes. Obviously, it was broken.

Luis was waiting for us by the front desk, sitting in a chair with another shoebox, this one tan, balanced on his thighs. I'd forgotten we were supposed to go to lunch and talk about his book. It felt as if we'd discussed it on the phone a month ago.

"Sorry we're late," I said, sounding deflated.

He set the box on the floor and stood up. "You look terrible," he said. "I mean, you look like something terrible *happened*."

"Somebody just tried to kill us," I said.

I knew it sounded melodramatic. But under the circumstances, I lacked the brainpower to be more subtle or original.

"We were in the parking garage," Stephen said. "He had a gun."

"*What?*"

I explained as well as I could what had happened. Considering what had happened.

"Gotta get over there," Luis said. "Are you sure the shooter's gone?"

"He drove away," Stephen said. "He or she."

"Well, it's still a crime scene. If nothing else, there could be shell casings or spent bullets to collect. Tire tracks, maybe."

He turned to the desk sergeant, a jowly African-American fellow whose race I didn't notice. He seemed unfazed by our conversation.

"I guess we'll need a couple officers to secure the elevators and the fourth floor of the garage," Luis told him. "And as many evidence people as you can get. Murphy and Robinson if they're around. We'll meet them there."

The desk sergeant picked up the phone. "Anything else?"

Luis reached down and snagged his shoebox. "Hold on to this for me, will you?"

"Yeah, sure."

Motioning for us to follow, the detective headed toward the door. He led the way to his unmarked car, a black Ford compact with the words WASH ME fingered in the dust on the trunk lid.

"I can't believe you just walked away from a crime scene," he said as Stephen and I got in the back seat. "You could have dialed 911." He pronounced it correctly, not having been shot at recently.

Stephen's response, while not quite dripping with sarcasm, was at least moist. "Forgive us. We missed that day at police academy."

Luis raised a conciliatory hand. "Hey, it's just that I can't let the scene get compromised. Can't catch bad guys without evidence, right?"

"Right," I said, suddenly feeling like I might pass out. I leaned back and closed my eyes.

"Are you sure you're okay?" Luis asked.

"I'll be all right."

I left out the part about how it would happen in the next life, not this one.

BY THE TIME we arrived at the parking structure, two officers had locked the elevators and cordoned off most of Level 4 with POLICE LINE DO NOT CROSS tape. Grouchy-looking civilians were still getting to their cars on Levels 2 and 3 by climbing the stairs and cursing the heat.

Stephen, Luis, and I followed them, but continued one

floor higher. Soon we stood next to the scatter of glass shards under the fire extinguisher.

"Walk me through what happened," Luis said.

Turning toward the space where the Kia was parked, Stephen ducked under the yellow plastic ribbon. "When we first got here—"

"Whoa, whoa," Luis said, putting a hand on his shoulder. "Come on out."

"But I thought you said—"

"I don't mean *literally* walk me through it. You'll need to stay on this side of the tape."

"I know why," I volunteered, then wished I hadn't. It made me sound like the teacher's pet.

"Tell me why," Luis said.

"Even though we've already been in there, you have to keep us from adding new fingerprints or hair or fibers."

He broke into a grin. "Smart lady. You saw it on *CSI*, right?"

"I think it was a P.D. James novel."

"A book? Should have known. Anyway, you've got the basic idea." He paused. "Okay, Mr. Ames, go ahead."

Stephen stuck his hands in his pockets, frowning at the glass fragments on the asphalt. "I think I'll let Carolyn take it from here. She seems to know a lot about this subject, not to mention the . . . *rapport* she's developed with the Atlanta Police Department."

I rolled my eyes. Maybe the brain wasn't fully developed at Stephen's age, but the male ego seemed to be thriving.

I launched into a description of what had happened. I tried not to take all the credit for our escape, not even mentioning my heroic and dangerous hop to press the elevator button. My thighs were still sore.

Luis took notes, nodding and knitting his brow and saying "Mmm-hmm" every 15 seconds or so. There was no idle pen-clicking, which I took to indicate he was really listening.

When I was done, I looked past the yellow tape into no-man's land, where three evidence technicians in blue uniforms, two women and a man, were scrutinizing the floor. They placed small, numbered signs on spots that caught their fancy. Once in a while a camera would flash.

Luis looked where I was looking. "Hey, Murphy," he called. "You guys found anything yet?"

One of the women, a redhead, tall and slender as a fire hydrant, tiptoed over. She held her rubber-gloved hands up in front of her like a surgeon. "Three bullets so far. Four casings. Getting photos of the dents in the elevator doors."

"Tire tracks?"

"Takes time, Sergeant. Too much traffic to tell one mark from another. We'll do what we can."

"Thanks," he said.

The woman tiptoed back to work. I couldn't help wondering whether being so close to the ground helped in her profession.

"Murphy's good," the detective said. "She once took a—"

"Sergeant Valenzuela?" came a voice from the top of the stairs. It was a uniformed officer, the younger of the two men we'd seen guarding the door to Level 1. "We've got a few folks down here who parked on this floor. They'd really like to get their vehicles."

With a grunt the detective looked at his watch. He hesitated, then nodded. "Yeah, all right. But get their names and contact info in case we need to talk to them later."

"Will do," the officer said, and left.

Luis stood there for a long moment, tapping his notepad against his leg. "She's right, you know."

"Who?" I asked.

"Murphy. There's just too much traffic here to match a

tread pattern or a gum wrapper to an individual or a time. Other than bullets and shell casings, I'm afraid they won't find much that would hold up in court."

"But somebody was *shooting* at us," I protested.

"I don't question that. But certain people might. In fact, it may be impossible to prove the whole thing even happened."

"That's crazy," Stephen said.

Luis shrugged. "No witnesses as far as we know. Some might even say you staged the whole thing to get the attention off yourselves."

I shook my head in disbelief. "We shot at ourselves?"

"They'd say you shot at an elevator. But of course, they don't know you like I do."

"But we're the *good* guys here," Stephen said. "We've been fired. We're running out of money. And now somebody's trying to off us."

Luis closed his eyes and rubbed his forehead. "There isn't a whole lot I can do, much as I might like to." He glanced around as if making sure no one could overhear. "See, you're both persons of interest in a murder investigation. Which basically means the police are looking for enough evidence to charge you. My job is to find it."

He paused. "I can try to convince my boss that what happened here actually happened. But thanks to the whole Willowgate thing, there's been a lot of publicity about Tripp's murder. That means pressure on him to make an arrest."

"And we're the most guilty-looking people you can find?"

"You didn't hear it from me."

Stephen shook his head. "That's nuts."

"Of course, that doesn't mean I can't keep an eye out for people who seem to be at risk," Luis said. "Especially people I care about."

He smiled at me again. "Maybe I can look in on you. You

know, unofficially. Trying to keep the bad guys away until somebody figures out who the heck they are."

He looked at his watch again. "You're probably a lot more tired than I am. Let's talk about the book another time, okay?"

I sighed. He'd get no argument from me there.

"But give me your phone numbers and the license number of your rental car," he added. "And room numbers where you're staying. So I can check on you later."

He handed me his notepad, on which I dutifully scribbled.

Stephen cleared his throat as I returned the pad and pen. "At least there's a silver lining in all this," he said.

Luis raised an eyebrow. "Yeah?"

"There's only one thing we have to do to get people to believe our story."

"What's that?"

"Die," he said.

It was very dramatic.

And, I had to admit, quite true.

CHAPTER 21

BACK AT THE MOTEL, STEPHEN AND I HID IN HIS ROOM.

We could have chosen mine instead, but two determined-looking plumbers were banging away on a tangle of pipes right outside my window. The clanging reminded me of the bells in *The Hunchback of Notre-Dame*, except that Quasimodo was a better musician.

Stephen sat at the desk, reading *The Atlanta Journal-Constitution*. I sat in the other chair, reading more of *Hard Bargain* and trying not to scream. I read so hard and fast, in fact, that my gorge rose to new heights.

Despite my queasiness, at 5:00 p.m. we took a vote on what to do about dinner, settling on ordering Chinese from a place called Peking Palace, which promised 30-minute delivery. Then we waited.

The longer we waited, the less we talked. The less we talked, the more we thought. The more we thought, the more we thought the unthinkable.

Finally Stephen said it out loud.

"He could be anywhere."

"Who?"

"The person who shot at us. He—or she—could be aiming at us through the window." He got up and pulled the curtains closed.

"That should do it," I said. "Those bulletproof drapes are amazing."

He picked up the newspaper. "The killer could pretend to be from the Chinese restaurant. When we open the door, *blam.*"

I squeezed one eye shut. "How would he know we ordered Chinese food?"

"Maybe he bugged our phone. Or he's been hiding in the hallway all this time, listening."

"You know," I said, "it *is* possible to read too much Dean Koontz."

There was a knock at the door.

"Be sure to look through the peephole," he whispered.

I headed for the door, thinking about the fiasco with the process server. Maybe this would turn out just as well.

Putting my eye to the tiny porthole, I saw an Asian-looking teenager in a polo shirt and jeans. He held a white paper bag in his hand. It had the words PEKING PALACE printed on the side under a dragon.

I opened the door. "Neville?" he asked.

"That's me."

"Just a minute," Stephen said, coming over. "I have a couple questions, if you don't mind. Nothing personal. What's in the bag?"

The delivery man read the black-marker scrawl near the top of the sack. "Sweet and sour chicken, egg fu yung, fried rice, steamed rice."

"That's cheating," Stephen said. "Answer this one. What are the ingredients in moo goo gai—"

"Thank you," I said, pressing a $10 bill into the hand of

the baffled-looking young man. "He's harmless, really. Keep the change."

He nodded. I closed the door.

"Harmless?" Stephen said. "For all we know, that food could be poisoned."

"No need for you to eat it, then. I'll let you know how it was."

After I'd eaten half the egg fu yung and steamed rice without doubling over in pain, he grudgingly agreed to join me. The meal turned out to earn my Not Lethal rating of two and a half stars.

When the time came for fortune cookies, Stephen paused before opening his. "You know," he said, "if this were a bad novel, our fortunes would help us solve the crime."

"How convenient."

"So, let's see what happens."

I popped open the cellophane, cracked the cookie, withdrew the thin strip of paper, and read:

NOTHING SUCCEEDS LIKE SUCCESS.

HE WRINKLED HIS NOSE. "That's not even a fortune. When did these things stop predicting the future?"

I flicked the slip of paper into one of the cardboard cartons. "Might as well say, 'Nothing smells like a nose,' or 'Nothing looks like an eye.'"

"Actually, those would be better. At least they're puns."

His snapped open his own crispy oracle and read:

THE JOURNY OF A HUNDRED MILES BEGINS WITH

A SINGLE STEP.

"That has a typo," he said. "Which makes it a tiny bit interesting."

"Neither of these gets us a single step closer to solving the murder. Does that mean we're not in a bad novel?"

"I'll let history be the judge of that."

We took a moment to gnaw at our cookies, which were only slightly more edible than the messages themselves.

"Speaking of bad novels," he said, "how's the one in the shoebox going?"

I threw up my hands. "Okay, it's awful. But we have to follow the plan. We need Luis's help more than ever."

We fell silent again. The silence grew longer. I got up, gathered the cartons and wrappers and packets of soy sauce, and stuffed them in the bag. I was out of things to do.

"Maybe I should go," I said. "The pipe-pounding next door might be over."

We listened. No clanging. It had been replaced by what sounded like a chainsaw.

Stephen shook his head. "You may as well stay for now. Sorry we can't afford a quieter place, thanks to Hunter." He paused. "Still can't believe that e-mail he sent. You replied to it, right?"

I bit my lip, trying to remember. "Did I?"

"You never copied me on it."

Getting out my phone, I called up my SENT list.

"Uh-oh."

"You *forgot*?"

"Hey, things have been busy."

"Well, we can't leave him hanging," he said. "*Your* job may be toast, but he's probably wondering if I'm coming back to beg for mine. Let's come up with a reply."

I sighed. "Nothing crude, okay?"

"Of course not."

He picked up his Southern Suites pad and pen. "Let's start with the salutation. 'My dearest Hunter,'" he began, then looked at me. "Are you comfortable with that? This will go over your signature, remember."

"Maybe something a little less intimate."

"'To whom it may concern'?"

"Not intimate enough. We can come back to that part later."

"Very well." He paused, thinking. "How's this? 'Thank you for your . . . informative missive. I only wish it were possible to . . . convey my deep appreciation for . . . the many hours we have spent together . . . laboring . . . no, endeavoring . . . to make the world a better place.'"

"Oh, I like that. If only it were true."

"Of course it isn't. The important thing is that—"

There was another knock at the door.

Stephen froze.

"I'll get it," I said, not really wanting to.

"Remember the peephole," he whispered.

I squinted through the circle. "It's a man with a bag in his hand," I said.

"Again?"

"Well, not exactly. This one looks like Luis. Do you want me to ask him questions to see whether he's just *disguised* as someone we know?"

"Very funny."

I opened the door. Luis was still in his suit, but his tie was loosened. "Ms. Neville," he said, smiling. "Just thought I'd check in."

"Please do. And call me Carolyn."

I didn't think his smile could get any bigger, but it did. "Carolyn, I see you've had dinner. I brought a little something for dessert." Opening the bag, he took out a half-gallon of ice cream, a trio of plastic bowls, three spoons, and a scoop.

"Pomegranate Dark Chocolate Swirl!" I said. "My favorite flavor! How did you know?"

"I'm a detective."

"So, we've heard," Stephen mumbled.

"Also, there's Facebook." He filled three bowls, sat with his share on the remaining chair, and leaned forward in steeple chasing position. "You have good taste," he said.

"It's health food," I said. "Pomegranates. Dark chocolate. Antioxidants."

"Ah," he said, then glanced at Stephen, who didn't seem to be eating. "Not a fan?" he asked.

"A little too sweet for me," Stephen muttered. It was pretty clear he wasn't talking about the ice cream.

Luis and I returned to our conversation. I didn't bring up his book, which would have canceled my ice cream high. It was bad enough talking about the afternoon's events.

By 8:00 we'd run out of ice cream and things to say. I was feeling a little outnumbered by men and a little too interested in the one who cared about my favorite flavor.

I faked a yawn. "Well, you'll have to excuse me. It's been a long day."

"But they're still making that racket," Luis said.

"I have earplugs."

He shrugged. "Okay." He stood up. "Guess I'll move along, too."

Stephen went back to reading the paper or pretending to.

"I'll stay in touch," Luis said. "Unofficially."

I slipped out, not wanting an awkward goodbye in the hallway.

Two minutes later I lay on my bed, staring at the shoebox. The earplugs were, of course, completely ineffective. I could hear every whine and shriek of the saw, or whatever the thing was.

On the positive side, I had a good excuse to quit reading.

~

THE SAWING finally stopped at 8:47 p.m.

I took out the earplugs. I was tired, but not enough to fall asleep. Deciding to finish the e-mail to Hunter, I reached for my pad and pen.

After five minutes of staring at the blank page, it was plain the fun had gone out of that enterprise.

I doodled a series of squiggles on the paper. Not diverting.

What else could I do with this pad? Last time I'd picked it up, it was to write down Marvin's advice.

I tapped pen on paper. *Marvin.*

Actually, calling him now wouldn't be the worst idea in the world. As far as I knew, he was still staying up late enough to watch the opening monologue of at least one talk show.

I found my phone, awakened it, and dialed.

Marvin picked up and apparently regretted doing so.

"Man, I need to change my number," he said.

"Am I interrupting anything?"

"Of course not, Cranberry. What's happening?"

"Things are different here now. It's not just a murder investigation anymore."

"How so?"

"Someone tried to shoot us today."

There was a pause. "Are you all right?"

"We lived through it." I told him about The Shots. Every

time I got to a new turn in the story, he gave a concerned "Oooh," or "Lord, have mercy."

When I was done, he sighed. "You all right now, girl?" he asked gently.

"A little shaken up. Well, no, a lot. Mostly we want to find out who did it."

"'Course you do."

"The police found a few bullets and shell casings. But they're not likely to find more. As far as they're concerned, we might have staged the whole thing."

"They don't know you like I do."

"No, I guess not. But if you have any suggestions, my notepad's ready."

He exhaled slowly, noisily. "The police aren't going to strain themselves trying to get you off the suspect list. But that doesn't mean you're stuck with what they find out. You and Stephen may know some things they don't, even if you don't realize it."

I put the pen down. "I'm sure that means something, but I seem to have lost my decoder ring."

"I'm talking about stuff you noticed at the scene where the blogger died, or in the parking garage. But not consciously. They didn't make enough of an impression. They're stuck in your head, along with all that other junk like every license plate number and McDonald's commercial you've ever seen."

"How do we get them out?"

"Well, you could ask yourselves some questions. Try to visualize those places, kind of like watching a slo-mo replay in your head. Or . . . maybe you should get that hypnotist guy to retrieve those memories."

"Stanton Platte?"

"Yeah."

"Really?"

"No, not really. He's a fake, right?"

"Probably. But at least he can hypnotize people. Stephen in particular. He proved that in his act. Maybe it's not such a bad idea." I started writing again.

"But—"

"It might even give us a chance to see whether he's the type who plants false memories. In case he did that with Willow."

Marvin grunted. "You realize testimony obtained by hypnosis isn't admissible in court."

"I do now."

"On the other hand, if that testimony helped you find corroborating physical evidence, that physical evidence *would* be admissible."

I wrote that down and gave the pen a click. "Any other ideas?"

Another pause. "I think that's all I got." He lowered his voice. "This is serious stuff, lady," he said. "If somebody's really taking potshots . . ."

"It sure seems that way."

"You have any kind of protection? Not that I don't take the idea of guardian angels seriously."

"The detective's looking in on us from time to time."

"Stay safe, Cranberry. Don't take any unnecessary chances. And let me know what happens."

"Don't worry, Marvin. That's my department."

He seemed to linger on the line longer than usual, as if he wanted to say more. But in the end, he hung up first

~

ALL WAS QUIET AGAIN.

I sat on the bed, staring at the painting with the pink flowers.

There were so many things not to think about.

Somebody with a gun. Having to go to Wyoming. What I was going to feel like in the morning, after having been unable to stop thinking about these things.

I looked at the nightstand. Was there really a Gideon Bible in there?

I pulled out the drawer. Sure enough, there it was.

I read Psalm 23, which I knew by heart, but it looked more legally binding in print. Then the story of Paul and Silas breaking out of jail during an earthquake. Which didn't have much to do with my present situation. Or maybe it did, if we couldn't prove our innocence.

I knew there were a bunch of psalms or proverbs about protection against violent men but couldn't find them.

Finally I pulled on my pajamas and got under the covers. The second my head hit the pillow; I was wide awake.

I got to sleep eventually, of course.

I think it was a little after 2:15 a.m.

CHAPTER 22

HAVING BEEN REFRESHED BY SUCH PROFOUND REST, IT WAS NO problem when I was jolted awake by a call on the motel phone at 6:49.

Stephen was on the line, sounding fully charged. "Ready for breakfast?"

I grunted.

"Seen the sunrise?"

"Many times."

"I mean this morning."

"No. If you've seen one, you've seen 'em all. Kind of like Danielle Steel."

"Meet you downstairs in half an hour."

"But I need—"

He hung up. As a matter of principle, I didn't look out the window.

But I dragged myself out of bed and through the shower. Surrounded by so much steam I almost couldn't find the soap, I kept telling myself the previous day had all been a dream.

I pulled my tweedy editor's blazer from its hanger in the

closet, wishing for something more substantial. A Kevlar vest, maybe body armor or a Popemobile.

But there was really no way to protect myself. All I could do was keep my eyes open, whatever that meant.

I put one of those eyes to the peephole in the door. The hallway was empty, or so it appeared. As I opened my door and stepped over the threshold, I could hear my own breathing.

Moments later I waited in front of the elevator, checking repeatedly over my shoulder to make sure I was alone. No numeral 4 was painted on the door, but it brought back more than enough memories of yesterday.

At last the door slid open. No one got out. No popping noises behind me. The fire extinguisher down the hall remained intact.

Stepping into the box, I heard the door roll shut.

Just one floor to descend, but it felt like 20.

"WIPE THAT GRIN OFF YOUR FACE."

It was one of many things I didn't say to Stephen when I slipped into the chair across from him in the Continental Breakfast room. The temptation was hard to resist, though.

I was about to get up and start foraging for comfort food when my ringtone sounded. It was Luis.

"Hope I didn't wake you up," he said.

"No, that honor goes to someone else." I rubbed my eyelids with my fingers.

"Just got to work and wanted to make sure you were okay." He paused. "Can't concentrate 'til I know."

"We're okay. About to have breakfast." I looked at Stephen, whose smile was fading.

"What are your plans for today?"

I opened my mouth to tell him about Marvin's advice to go to Wyoming but closed it. Luis would probably think it was a terrible idea.

"We haven't discussed that yet," I said.

"Well, keep me in the loop. We'll talk later."

"Thanks for calling. Bye."

I turned to Stephen. "That was Luis."

"No, really?"

"Checking in on us. Isn't that nice?"

"He's a sweetie, alright."

"Wishes he could do more, of course."

"I'll bet he does."

I put the phone back in my purse. "But since he can't, there's something we can do for ourselves."

"Oh?"

"I called Marvin last night. During our conversation, it became clear that we should go to Wyoming. To see Dr. Platte."

"*What?*"

"Marvin thinks we may have seen more clues at the two crime scenes than we realize. Platte might be able to get them out with hypnosis."

"That's the worst idea I've ever heard. Especially the part about going to Wyoming."

"Now, listen to—"

"If we have to get hypnotized, there must be plenty of hypnotists in Atlanta."

I nodded. "But they haven't hypnotized *you*. Or Willow."

He leaned forward and lowered his voice. "This is not exactly the best time to be wandering around in public. May I remind you somebody's trying to kill us?"

"But that somebody is in Atlanta, not Canyonville. We just have to be careful we're not followed. We'll be safer there than we are here."

He shook his head. "If we leave town, Luis won't be able to check on us."

"Sure he will. We'll have our phones."

Turning away, he stared at the CNN newscast, daring me to try again.

We watched the screen in silence. After a string of commercials, there was a story about a Philadelphia prisoner convicted of murder 23 years before. Now, thanks to new DNA evidence, his conviction had been overturned.

File footage showed the poor guy standing in a courtroom at his original trial, wearing a jumpsuit as orange as campfire coals. His hands were shackled. He stared at the floor.

I got an idea. This could be an object lesson. A teachable moment.

"Twenty-three years," I said. "This is what happens to people who don't prove their innocence."

Stephen didn't move or speak.

"Sometimes the justice system makes mistakes."

He cleared his throat but still said nothing.

"I don't look good in orange," I added. "Do you?"

He gave an exasperated growl. "You can stop now. I get it, okay?"

"I knew you would." I paused. "I'll start looking at flights."

He grunted. "The sooner the better. Remember my motto."

"Which one?"

"'Life: Let's get it over with.'"

~

THREE HOURS later I tried to keep that orange jumpsuit in mind as we power-walked our way through Hartsfield-Jackson International Airport, our carry-ons jouncing from our shoulders. I was out of breath already. Stephen, right behind me, sounded like he might reach that point any time.

"I still think this is a terrible idea," he said, panting. "Just for the record."

"You may be right," I said, not getting enough oxygen to argue.

"Last-minute flights are way too expensive."

"We should feel grateful to get anything. Aren't many flights to Laramie. And it's a pain to go through Denver."

We stopped talking but kept rushing. My head swiveled back and forth like a telemetry dish, seeking strangers who might be tailing us.

"We should have worn disguises or something," he said.

"Couldn't have gotten through security. Had to match our ID photos."

"Oh, yeah."

I hoisted my bag higher on my shoulder, but it was just as heavy and kept bouncing.

"Feels like we've walked halfway to Wyoming already," he said.

"Almost there."

When we reached B34, the flight was boarding. No time to sit down, no time to do anything but surrender our passes to the woman at the Delta desk and head down the jetway.

The cabin was solid with unfamiliar faces. After wedging our carry-ons in the overhead bin, we collapsed into seats 21A and B.

"We're safe now," I said, closing my eyes.

"How do you know?" Stephen asked. "*Anybody* could be on this flight."

I looked out the window. The sky was smoggy. "I called Luis to tell him where we were going. He thought it was a crazy idea, too, but said he couldn't stop us."

"That's reassuring."

"He also said evidence given under hypnosis is inadmissible in court. But I already knew that. According to Marvin, it might lead to other evidence that *could* be admitted."

Stephen looked around one more time, then fastened his seat belt. "More likely this is just a wild goose chase that gets us killed."

I fastened my own belt. "As C.S. Lewis once said, 'Has this world been so kind to you that you should leave with regret? There are better things ahead than any we leave behind.'"

He stared at me. "Is that supposed to make me feel better? I'm not exactly religious."

"It's not about religion. It's about—"

"I know. It's about a relationship. But let's not go there today, okay?" Shutting his eyes, he sagged back into his seat.

The intercom clicked, then crackled.

"Flight attendants prepare for takeoff," the pilot said, sounding bored.

The engines began their customary scream. The aircraft began to budge, then roll, then barrel down the runway.

I looked over at Stephen. It probably had nothing to do with our conversation, but he was squeezing the armrests of his seat, his hands locked in a white-knuckled grip.

CHAPTER 23

BY THE TIME WE LANDED IN LARAMIE, STEPHEN HAD MANAGED to pry his fingers from the armrests and pretended to examine his copy of *Delta Sky* magazine. Scrunching deep in his seat, he never raised his head except to whisper the word "Sprite" when the attendant came by with the beverage cart.

Our walk to the connecting flight was mercifully short. As was the 40-minute hop to Laramie, during which he buried his head in the same magazine, apparently having brought it as a good-luck charm. He studied its ads for executive dating services and legendary steakhouses with disturbing intensity.

In Laramie the rental car was another white Ford Focus. I hoped the color would reflect the sun, which was cruel as ever. Retracing our path to Canyonville, we drove as quickly as the laws of physics, if not the laws of the state of Wyoming, allowed.

Things hadn't changed since our first visit. All the qualities that had endeared The Cowboy State to us—searing heat, endless vistas of motionless desolation, hazardous-looking roadside fireworks stands—were still there. The

ENTERING CANYONVILLE sign indicated that the population held steady at 2,613.

What *had* changed, of course, was that we now checked our rearview mirrors every few minutes for people who might want to kill us.

Passing the ENTERING CANYONVILLE sign seemed to lift a weight from my shoulders. Fishing my phone from my purse, I placed a call to Luis. Or his voice mail.

"Luis? Carolyn. Just wanted to let you know we made it to Wyoming. All the way to Canyonville. Maybe we'll get a chance to talk later. Bye."

I turned toward Stephen. "Left a message for Luis."

"Thanks for clearing that up."

I dropped the phone in my purse. "I'm ready."

"For what?"

"To do what we came for. It *does* feel better here. Maybe because there aren't any crowds. Not enough stuff to hide behind."

"That's what they'd like you to believe."

We checked into the Saddleback Lodge, whose covered-wagon nightstand lamps I'd hoped never to see again. And there was the Chuckwagon Café, its kitschy sign beckoning weary travelers home. For a few seconds I was overwhelmed with nostalgia, or maybe it was just jet lag.

Then on to the main event: Holistic Hypnosis.

I'd found it on the Internet. It was the business address of Dr. Stanton Platte or Szandor Mandini. The Starlite Lounge was only the glamorous tip of his occupational iceberg. Holistic Hypnosis was his bread and butter.

It was also a dump.

The shabby Sagebrush Center strip mall on Arroyo Street housed half a dozen storefronts, two of them vacant and the others looking one unprofitable month away from the same fate. We parked in front of an establishment called East

Meets West which offered a unique combination of Vietnamese Pedicures and Five-Alarm Chili. Sadly, we didn't have time to learn more.

The windows of Holistic Hypnosis were blocked by white metal blinds and painted with a simple green logo, a palm tree that couldn't have survived a Wyoming winter but belonged in Dubai or Beverly Hills. The only other item on the glass was a faded high school football schedule for the previous season of the Canyonville Vultures, a team whose cheerleaders I could only imagine.

A brass bell over the door didn't quite ring as we entered but clicked. The smells of tobacco, hot vinyl, and dusty upholstery filled the waiting room. The unattended desk and trio of empty chairs were watched over by a large artificial fern in a clay pot of excelsior.

"Looks like business is booming," I said.

The only sound was something like the distant drone of an outboard motor, except that it rose and fell.

"Hear that?" I asked.

"Sounds like snoring."

It came from a doorway to the back, through a plastic-bead curtain that may have had a mate in the Vietnamese Pedicure shop next door. Pushing our way through the cascade of glittery blue and green teardrops, we entered.

There was an office of sorts, with two chairs as decrepit as the ones in the waiting room facing each other. And a futon in the corner, on which lay the body of Dr. Stanton Platte who, fortunately, wasn't dead.

"Probably up late at the Starlite Lounge," Stephen whispered.

I coughed, hoping to wake him without having to take the blame. The snoring continued undeterred.

"Excuse me," I said. "Dr. Platte?"

The snoring paused. He mumbled something unintelligible, grunted, then slowly pushed himself to a sitting position. He looked different in jeans and a denim shirt, without his shiny blue tuxedo. Older, maybe, or just less magical.

He blinked and looked at us.

"Good grief," he said. "Not you again."

I tried to look harmless. "We have a request."

He ran his hand over his soul patch, as if checking for naptime drool. "So do I. Get out of here and leave me alone."

I took a hesitant step forward. "You didn't want us to tell people about you and we haven't."

"Good. Please see that it stays that way."

"But we have something to tell *you*."

His frown was apparently perpetual. "Is it a matter of life and death?"

"Actually, yes."

"Yours or mine?"

"Ours."

"Not interested. Feel free to exit the way you came."

Sighing dramatically, I looked around the room. "Apparently I was mistaken. I was the one who suggested we come here. Stephen pointed out there were plenty of hypnotists in Atlanta. But I believed we needed *your* expertise."

Platte raised an eyebrow. I couldn't tell whether he was skeptical, curious, or both. "Is that a fact?"

"If I can explain—"

"Thirty seconds," he said, and looked at his watch.

I told him about the parking garage, the police, and the notion that we might know more than we thought. It took longer than 30 seconds, but he let me finish anyway.

"So, we need your help," I added. "You've already proven you can hypnotize at least one of us."

He paused, then shook his head. "No. Your perseverance is laudable, but I believe you know the way out."

My jaw clenched, keeping me from delivering a final, irrefutable argument I didn't have.

Stephen stuck his hands in his pockets. "Okay, Doctor. Did we mention there's something in it for you?"

"Really."

"If this case isn't solved, the police will go looking for other suspects. They'll probably wonder whether you got rid of the blogger for calling you a fake. You don't want that kind of attention, do you?"

He fell silent for a moment. "No," he said finally.

"Well, if you can suck a few clues out of our heads, maybe you can get us all off the 'persons of interest' list."

Platte looked up at the ceiling. "I'm afraid you'd have to make it worth my while. I'm not running a charity here."

I bit my lip. "Please keep in mind that we're on a budget."

He snorted. "So am I, Ms. Neville." He patted the blanket on the futon. "This office is where I live. Bathroom and kitchenette in the next room. I can't afford to work *pro bono*."

"Very well," I said. "How much are we talking about?"

"Let's say . . . a thousand dollars."

My mouth dropped open. "A thousand—"

"Plus, your word that I'll never have to speak to either of you again for the rest of my life."

I tried not to moan out loud. It was one thing when the money came from Our Friends in Legal. Now it was personal, like the removal of a pancreas.

"Take it or leave it," he said.

"We'll take it," Stephen said.

I turned in his direction. "Is that the *editorial* we?"

"No, it's the editorial *you*. This was your idea, remember?"

I closed my eyes. For a thousand dollars I could get an autographed letter from Maxwell Perkins on Charles Scribner's Sons Publishers stationery. *Two* of them. With enough left for a copy of *The Elements of Style* and a whole box of Skinny Cow chocolates.

On the other hand, I really didn't look good in orange.

Opening my eyes again, I found myself looking at the overflowing ashtray on the floor, next to the futon. Raising my chin, I faced Platte's expression of studied indifference.

"For that price, I expect your best effort," I said.

He climbed off the futon and stood in his stocking feet. "I never give anything less," he said, and bowed as deeply as he might have at the Starlite Lounge itself.

STEPHEN WENT FIRST.

He and Platte sat in the two chairs, their knees almost touching. I sat on the futon, poised with pad and pen.

The hypnotist had put on his shoes. "Well, Stephen, you're an old hand at this by now." His voice was less stagey, quieter, more calming.

"Not sure that helps."

"You have every reason to be relaxed, young man. No spotlight, no crowd, no catcalls. But we do still have a ceiling fan. Nice, don't you think?"

"Outstanding."

"So peaceful. Watch it move round and round and round. That's the way." He paused. "Now, just press down on my hand and close your eyes."

The instant he did, Platte pulled his hand away. "Sleep!"

Just as it had at the Starlite Lounge, Stephen's hand fell into his lap. His head dipped forward, his shoulders sagging.

I shook my head. Even without the element of surprise, somehow it still worked. Platte was frighteningly good at this. Or Stephen was. Or both.

"It's nice to be so at ease, isn't it? Every breath you take relaxes you more and more."

"Yeah."

They went through the part about the number 99 in the sky, counting backward, etcetera, etcetera. More relaxation, floating into the blue, no tension, lots of peace.

Stephen's eyes stayed closed, his muscles slack. He looked as oblivious as last time, but now there was no patter about mooing or clucking. Things had gotten much more complicated.

Platte paused, glancing at my pad. He ran a hand back over his gleaming head. Then, with a slight nod, he pushed ahead.

"Stephen, let's take a little walk. Down a beautiful path. It leads to Mr. Tripp's house. It's the day you went to visit him."

There was a pause. "I see it," he said.

"What else do you see?"

"Long driveway. A car parked. Camera watching us."

He described the car, the camera, the door, the doorbell. So far there was nothing I hadn't heard before.

"Then what happens?" Platte asked.

"The door's open."

"What do you see?"

Suddenly his brow furrowed. He shook himself, as if trying to get rid of something.

"Don't want to look."

Platte's voice was quiet. "How do you feel, Stephen?"

"Sick to my stomach. But I can't let Carolyn know."

My eyes started to water.

"The guy's practically my age. I don't want to die."

"Of course, you don't. But it's all right. You're safe here. We'll be done soon, but try to tell me what you see."

He went on to describe the position of the body, the

papers strewn on the floor, the blood. I wrote it all down. But none of it sounded new.

Platte looked at me. I shrugged.

He turned back toward Stephen. "Take just one more look. Is there anything else that bothers you about what you see in that living room?"

There was a long silence.

"The old blue couch," he said finally.

Platte looked puzzled. "It bothers you that the couch is old? Or that it's blue?"

"The cushions . . . don't match."

"How?"

"Three cushions. All with zippers. One's unzipped."

I wrote it down. Probably insignificant, but at least it sounded new and inspirational. Attention to detail was a hallmark of all great editors. That was why they got on everyone else's nerves.

After checking his watch, Platte kept going. He asked Stephen whether anything looked different as we left Tripp's neighborhood. He also asked about the parking garage.

I kept writing, but none of it seemed fresh or important.

Finally Platte turned and leaned toward me. "Any other questions?" he whispered.

I shook my head.

He pivoted to face Stephen. "You've been very helpful. Now I'll count from one to five. When I reach 'five,' you can open your eyes. You'll feel better than you have in a long time."

The count commenced. On "five," Stephen's eyelids parted.

For a moment he looked confused, but then seemed to realize where he was and why. He appeared energized, but then he usually did anyway.

He leaned forward. "Okay. What did I say?"

I flipped my notes back to the first page and ticked off the highlights. I left out the part about being afraid to look, and not wanting me to know.

When I got to his observation about the couch, he laughed. "I have no idea where *that* came from."

"Your subconscious, apparently," Platte said. "You did well. Nearly forty minutes in a hypnotic state. Clear answers. Very cooperative."

"Thanks."

There was a long pause.

Platte looked at Stephen.

Stephen looked at me.

I looked at my feet.

I tried to swallow, but my mouth was suddenly as dehydrated as the landscape outside.

For the last 24 hours I'd been in denial about what was to happen next. It had been my idea but getting hypnotized wasn't my thing. I'd never done it and had never wanted to.

As Platte uttered the words I least wanted to hear, there was no silencing them.

"I believe it's your turn," he said.

WE TRADED PLACES.

Stephen sat on the futon and pulled out his own pad and pen. I sat in the chair, which may as well have been located on death row and wired to a million volts of electricity.

"Ever undergone hypnosis, Ms. Neville?" Platte asked.

"No."

He sat back in his chair, which seemed considerably less threatening than my own. "You seem a bit tense. Any concerns? Heart condition? Shoulder, neck, or back trouble?"

"No."

"As I tell all my clients, there's nothing to worry about. Hypnosis is safer than walking down the street. Certainly safer than being shot at in a parking garage, which I understand you've already survived."

"Good to know."

"So, you have every reason to relax." His smile exuded confidence, but a hint of doubt flickered briefly in his eyes. He scratched his soul patch. "Let's see. I asked Stephen to concentrate on the ceiling fan, but maybe you'd be comfortable focusing on something more tranquil. See that print on the wall behind me?"

"The Secunda?"

"Ah, you're a connoisseur," he said. "The layers of color look like sunset over a mountain to me, but perhaps you see something else. I find it brings me serenity, harmony, and balance no matter what's going on around me. I'd like you to enjoy it for a few moments."

"I'll try."

"No need to try. Simply let the colors infuse you."

Whatever that means, I thought.

I stared at the picture. I took a deep breath and exhaled slowly.

"Excellent. You're more relaxed with every moment. As you relax, simply press down on my hand and close your eyes."

As soon as I did, he jerked his hand away. "Sleep!" he exclaimed.

But my hand didn't drop into my lap. My head didn't tilt forward. My shoulders didn't descend.

"Ow," I said.

He frowned. "What's the matter?"

"When you pulled away, you scratched my hand with your fingernail. Ruined the mood, I guess."

He closed his eyes and rubbed the spot between his

eyebrows. "My apologies," he said, sounding more impatient than repentant. "Let's give it another go, shall we?"

"Of course. Sorry."

He went through the routine again, his voice still soothing but not quite so untroubled. I stared at the picture, which was looking less and less like a mountain sunset and more and more like an uncontained forest fire.

When the time came to jerk his hand away, I did my best to help by dropping my hand and pitching forward. When he tried rotating my head, I tried to assist by swiveling it myself. Unfortunately, I did it in the wrong direction.

He removed his hand from my head. "Ms. Neville," he said gently, "I do appreciate your efforts. But in this instance, trying is counterproductive."

"Oh."

He sat back in his chair and folded his hands. "Not everyone is susceptible to hypnosis. Some resist it, especially those who are skeptical. Or who fear losing control."

Stephen looked at the ceiling. "Heaven knows that doesn't describe anyone in this room."

Platte looked me in the eye. "When I asked whether you'd ever been under hypnosis, you said no. But we all have. When you're engrossed in a daydream or a book or a hobby to the exclusion of everything else, you're in a kind of trance. You've done this before, with no ill effects whatsoever."

"But—"

"Technically, it's not even falling asleep. And you needn't fear losing control, because you won't. No hypnotist can force you to do anything."

"If you say so."

"Trust me. You want your money's worth, don't you?"

Ouch. Suddenly I was highly motivated.

He stood up and went to a metal file cabinet in the corner. "I sense you're a person who values tradition." After sliding out the bottom drawer, he rummaged around, took something in his fist, and pushed the drawer closed.

"This belonged to my grandfather," he said, returning to his seat.

Opening his hand, he revealed a gold pocket watch on a chain. The image of a steam locomotive on its lid was worn nearly smooth. "They gave him this when he retired from the railroad. The watch doesn't run anymore, but it's fine for swinging back and forth in front of those who prefer it. Especially when combined with the phrase, 'You are getting sleepy.'"

"Ah," I said.

He grasped the end of the chain and dangled the watch before my eyes. "Third time's the charm," he said, and started it sailing like a pendulum. "Back and forth . . . back and forth . . ."

Once more he murmured his way through the preliminaries, the watch describing its arc again and again, its rhythm changeless, my eyes following. I felt my lips part slightly and stay there. I didn't mind how they might look. I didn't seem to mind anything.

Maybe it helped that I imagined a thousand $1 bills suspended in the sky, and was counting them backward, relaxing more deeply as each one didn't float into the blue. There was no tension left, only peace and restfulness.

I felt myself starting to drift.

Then I felt myself drift back.

I was blinking.

Stephen was grinning.

Platte was rubbing that spot between his eyebrows, his lids squeezed shut.

I groaned. "I almost did it. But I must have come back before I could get all the way under."

Stephen laughed. "Not quite."

"Not quite what?"

"I mean that's not quite what happened. You did great."

"I did?"

He picked up the pad and pen. "I have almost ten pages of notes."

"You're kidding. Did I say anything new?"

"Not a lot. But you remembered something about the sound of whatever peeled out of the parking garage." He flipped a page. "You said it was big and loud."

I frowned. "Not very specific."

He flipped another page. "You also recalled something you saw parked in Tripp's neighborhood. You didn't know anything about the car, but you could picture the bumper sticker. It said, 'I'd rather be Fishin'—with only 'fishin" capitalized."

"Not much of a clue."

"Maybe not. But it shows your attention to detail. The hallmark of all great editors."

"Did I teach you that?"

"No. My idea entirely."

There was a prolonged silence.

"Ten pages," I said. "Sounds like I wouldn't shut up."

"I would never put it that way," Platte replied wearily.

"Did I . . . say anything . . . embarrassing?"

Stephen looked away. "Of course not." But then he looked at Platte and smirked.

I frowned. What was *that* supposed to mean?

Better not to know, said a voice in my head.

I turned to the hypnotist. "Am I supposed to feel refreshed now, like Stephen?"

"Yes," he said, still rubbing his forehead.

"Well, I don't."

"That makes two of us." He paused. "But I'm certain I'll feel better when I receive the compensation we discussed."

I wished I could say the same.

I glanced at the pad in Stephen's hand, full of words that might ultimately prove worthless.

This could be the smartest thousand I'd ever spent.

Or the biggest waste of money since the two thousand I'd spent to get here.

CHAPTER 24

IT WAS EASY TO SEE WHY SOME PEOPLE MIGHT WANT TO GET out of Laramie.

Or at least to get out of the Laramie Regional Airport.

I tried to distract myself with this thought the next morning, sitting three seats away from Stephen in the tiny, half-empty, brick-shaped terminal. We were still looking over our shoulders for anyone who might be following us.

At the moment, no one seemed to be.

"This place does have its good points," Stephen was saying. "Short security lines. Free long-term parking. Great high-altitude views through the windows."

"Which also describes heaven, if you think about it."

He groaned. I wasn't sure whether it was because of the subject or the quality of the humor.

"But heaven couldn't possibly be this dull," I added. "Even the vending machines are boring."

I thought nostalgically of our breakfast at the Chuck-wagon Café, a hearty, down-home meal involving way too much cholesterol, white flour, gravy, and bacon. Now, instead of being a wanton luxury, it looked like a wise investment that would carry us through this food desert.

Scanning the room for the two hundredth time, I once again noted a poster on the opposite wall. LAS VEGAS, it said in huge neon-tube type, with a photo of a roulette wheel below.

"I take it you can fly to Vegas from here."

"Yeah. I looked it up."

"I can see the attraction. Even Newark seems appealing right now."

"Maybe you should have brought the Manuscript from Hades."

There was a long moment of silence. Then my ringtone broke it.

"Hello? Luis?"

"We were just talking about you," Stephen mumbled.

"Carolyn, what's going on?"

"We're okay. The airport's so little and boring I feel safe. At least compared to the way I'll probably feel in Atlanta."

"Did you do your thing with the hypnotist?"

"Yeah. Very weird, but maybe helpful. We'll have a lot to talk about when we get back."

"Good. I've been worried about you. Both of you."

I thought for a moment. "Before we get there, can you do me a favor?"

"Name it."

"When we found Zane Tripp, did any of your people look inside the cushions on his sofa?"

When I heard no reply, I could imagine the expression on his face. It did sound like an odd thing to ask.

"Cushions?"

"Yes."

"I'd . . . have to look at the report again. Off the top of my head, I don't think so. Why?"

"According to Stephen, they had zippers on them. At least one was open."

"Is that . . . important?"

"I don't know."

Another pause. He was probably squinting at his phone as if it had malfunctioned.

"I'll look into it," he said.

"Thanks. See you before too long. I'll help you with your manuscript, I promise."

"That's why I can't let anything happen to you," he said, and I could almost see that shy smile.

After I put the phone in my purse, I went back to staring at the Las Vegas poster.

"Feeling lucky?" Stephen asked.

"Not yet," I said.

ATLANTA SEEMED unaware we'd been gone. No one was waiting for us at the airport, which was probably a good thing.

When we finally made it back to the Southern Suites, the sun was well past its zenith. We'd stopped for lunch at a Bojangles' Famous Chicken 'n Biscuits, which only made me more lethargic but had launched Stephen into Overdrive.

"Twenty minutes," he declared when we arrived at the motel. "Then we reconvene in the room with the white board."

"If it's empty," I said.

"If it's not now, it will be." He took off down the hallway without further explanation.

Twenty-four minutes later, after trying unsuccessfully to reanimate myself by drinking and eliminating equal amounts of water, I walked into the conference room. Stephen was already writing on the board.

"You're late," he said, not turning around.

Seating myself, I looked around for signs of struggle. "Did you have to drive anyone out?"

"You don't want to know." He capped the marker and sat across from me, then made a sweeping motion toward the board. "These are some things we remembered yesterday. And some questions."

I looked over his head and read.

- VEHICLE AT THE PARKING GARAGE "BIG AND LOUD"
- PICKUP TRUCK? JEEP? OTHER LARGE VEHICLE?
- ANY SUSPECTS HAVE PICKUP TRUCKS OR JEEPS?
- OR ACCESS TO SOMEONE ELSE'S?
- ETC.

"I especially like the last one," I said.

"Thanks."

"Platte hasn't got a large vehicle. There was a little blue car parked in front of his office with a magnetic sign on the side that said, 'Holistic Hypnosis.'"

"Good eye."

"Of course, he wouldn't have to *drive* to Atlanta," I said. "He could have flown here and rented something."

"True. Anyone could have rented something big and loud. Or borrowed it."

I folded my arms. "Which makes discussing this kind of pointless, doesn't it?"

He shook his head. "Let's assume people don't rent cars to go shoot other people. It'd be just as traceable as using their own."

"Well, then, there's Willow," I said. "She has a Jaguar."

"Are they big and loud?"

"Not big. And it depends on your definition of loud."

"Well, you're the one who said it was loud."

"That was my subconscious talking. I don't know what my subconscious thinks is loud."

He sighed. "This is going well."

I was about to suggest moving on to another question when my ringtone interrupted. Luis again.

"Thanks for checking, but we're okay," I said. "We're at the motel."

"You were wondering about the couch cushions," he said.

The words sounded even more bizarre now than they had then. "Yeah, that was me."

"I asked Murphy to take another look. She found something."

My eyebrows went up.

"The others hadn't looked. So she did, and found three manila envelopes stashed away."

"Anything in them?"

"You bet. Stuff about Willowgate. From Tripp's source, whoever that was. I guess sticking things in the couch cushions was Tripp's version of a safe deposit box." He paused. "I think you should take a look at what she found."

"Now?"

"If you're available."

I looked at Stephen, assuming he wouldn't mind. "We'll be there as soon as we can."

I put the phone away. "Huh," I said.

"Problem?"

"Not exactly." I told him what had happened.

"Wow," he said, and started erasing the board. "You said you weren't sure whether you were feeling lucky. This could be our lucky day."

"Actually, I don't believe in luck. I'd like to think this is divine intervention."

Rubbing away the last of the *ETC.* on the list, he shook his head. "Maybe. But if there's a God, He has a lot of explaining to do."

~

Dear Mr. Tripp:

I've seen your blog, and its quite informative. It could reach a much bigger audience, I think—with a little help. And I would like to give you that help—with a story that many people would be interested to hear. And deserve to hear, as the one they've been told is a lie from beginning to end. . . .

I WAS SITTING in Luis's cubicle, reading from three photo-copied pages. He'd explained that the originals were among about two dozen in the manila envelopes. The whole thing was in some lab down the hall and analysis would start tomorrow. It would take time, he said. Since Stephen and I didn't seem to have a lot of that, he wanted to get a head start.

Chances are you've heard of Willow Hayly. Everyone's heard of the great Willow. Her followers are in the millions, all over the

world. Their fools, but its not their fault. They give her power over
their lives, the kind of power nobody should have—especially a
woman who's built her empire on fake acusations that make her
look good and trash the lives of everybody else. They also give her
their money—more than anybody could make honestly. . . .

STEPHEN WAS SITTING NEXT to me, reading a few pages of his own. Luis was in his chair, leaning forward, watching.

She has built everything on the backs of others. Her followers think
she cares so much about them. However, nothing could be further
from the truth. Everything revolves around Willow and what she
wants. She's a theif, a user of people. She will keep on using them
unless she is stopped. . . .

WHEN WE REACHED the ends of our pages, we traded and kept reading. We were done within half a minute of each other.

"I don't suppose the author signed his or her name to these documents," I said.

"Afraid not," Luis said.

"That certainly would have simplified things."

He took the pen from his pocket and clicked it. "You're word people. Can you tell anything from the way this person writes?"

"A bit florid."

His head nodded, but his eyes indicated he hadn't been stretching his vocabulary lately.

"Over-the-top," I said.

He scribbled in his notebook.

"Pretty awful grammar and spelling, of course. And the author has a tendency to use too many em dashes. And starts sentences with *and* and *however*."

Luis chuckled. "Not crimes, last I checked."

"They ought to be."

"Right."

I shrugged. "These could have come from anybody who isn't much of a writer. But that describes most of the Western world. Probably Eastern, too."

Stephen put his pages on the desk. "I think we can narrow it down a little more than *that*. It's somebody who hates Willow and probably has for a long time." He paused. "No wonder she's got a bodyguard."

"Which is more than we've got."

Luis put down his pen. "I don't think Tripp's source wants to kill Willow. He or she could have done that long before now. Whoever wrote this wants to bring her down, though, no question about it."

Settling back in his chair, he looked at me and sighed. "Unfortunately, whoever killed Tripp, and apparently wants to do the same to you two, is a whole different animal."

"That's comforting," I said.

He bent forward again and spoke quietly. "We're doing everything we can. So far, we haven't found anything that would help us trace this guy. Or woman. No prints on the envelopes, no handwriting, no odd typefaces. Just plain old laserprinting on plain old multipurpose paper."

Stephen scratched his chin. "Speaking of which, seems strange that this person used hard copies. Kind of old-fashioned."

"Not strange at all. Probably wanted to mail them from a big-city post office or drop them off in a prearranged spot. E-mail attachments are way too easy to trace."

There was a pause. It turned into a lull, which became an awkward silence.

Luis looked at his watch. "Hey, it's been a long day. You folks were still in Wyoming this morning."

He gathered up the photocopies. "Let me know if you come up with any other ideas," he said. "We'll wait to hear from the lab. You never know. A stray fingerprint on a page, a hair—sometimes even the most careful bad guys make a mistake."

He held up the sheets with one hand. "Especially the angry ones."

~

WHEN STEPHEN and I finally emerged from the police station, it was dinnertime. We ended up going to some restaurant so generic, so forgettable, I can't remember its name. We ordered some kind of food, the nature of which I can't recall either.

I was so fatigued, in fact, that I failed to put more than a cursory effort into spotting people who might murder us.

Fortunately, I found none.

On our way back to the motel, I somehow managed not to fall asleep at the wheel. When we arrived, it took three tries to steer my room key card into its slot.

Finally sheltered under the covers, I was about to drift away when the ungentle strains of the *1812 Overture* intervened. I fumbled my phone from the nightstand, which took only two attempts, and did my best to focus on the screen.

It was Willow's number.

"Carolyn?" she said when I picked up. Her voice sounded strained. "I'm so sorry. I heard you and Stephen had . . . an incident. In a parking garage."

"We did."

"God knows I didn't want anyone to get hurt. But I can't let this go on. I should have stopped it a long time ago. Guess I didn't have the guts."

I sank back against the headboard. "I'm not sure I understand what—"

"I can't say any more on the phone. It's not safe. Can you and Stephen meet me in the morning? Around 10:30? At the county park where you and I met before?"

"Well, I suppose we—"

"Remember how to get there?"

"Yes, but—"

"I have to go. I'll see you then."

The line went dead.

Dazed, I put the phone down on the bed.

What was she talking about? Why the apology? What was all that about guts?

I looked around the room, trying to get my bearings. Had I dreamed the whole conversation?

I checked the log on my phone. It was Willow's number, alright.

Whatever the reason behind her call, I wasn't keen on meeting anyone in the middle of nowhere when someone was trying to kill me.

I hope she brings her bodyguard this time.

It sounded like we all could use one now.

CHAPTER 25

THE NEXT DAY DAWNED FULL OF PROMISE AND POTENTIAL.

Or perhaps I'm thinking of a different day entirely, which would explain why I spent the first 20 minutes of this one paralyzed in bed. The memory of Willow's cryptic phone call seemed to open up a whole world of possibilities, none of them good.

When I told Stephen over breakfast about meeting Willow in the park, he rubbed the side of his face. "Maybe it's a trap."

I scoffed. "You think *Willow* is out to get us?"

"Hey, it's possible. I saw this thing on *Dateline NBC* where—"

"Come on. We're just about the only thing standing between Willow and whoever's out to get *her*."

"Maybe."

"On the other hand, *somebody's* got our worst interests in mind. I should at least let Luis know where we're going."

"Luis," he said, not quite inaudible. "My hero."

I speed-dialed into voice mail. "This is Carolyn. Remember the messages I left to let you know we were okay in Wyoming? This is like that, only the opposite." I proceeded to explain why, where, and when we were going.

"Hope you hear that before we go, Luis. If you can get away from work, we really need you."

I kept one eye on my phone as we ate breakfast. Back in the room, I did the same.

But when the time came to leave for the park, there had been no reply.

∼

"MAYBE HE'LL MEET US THERE," I said as we drove toward Buttonbush Trails.

But that wasn't to be, either. When we pulled up to the tiny lot and the restroom with the OUT OF ORDER sign, we were the first.

"Maybe he's on his way," I said.

We waited. And waited.

The longer we did, the more sinister the wall of trees in front of us looked. We stayed in the car.

"I still think it's a trap," Stephen said. "Maybe it wasn't really Willow you talked to."

"An imposter? Like the delivery guy from the Chinese restaurant?"

He looked out the side window. "Sometimes you can't be too careful."

"*Which* times?"

"I don't know. That's just it."

Just then there was a noise behind us, the drone of an engine and the pop of gravel under tires. Checking the rearview mirror, I saw a shiny green Jaguar pulling up.

"Doesn't sound so loud to me," I said.

"Huh?"

"Willow's car. We wondered whether it could have been the one in the parking garage."

"So, we should take her off the suspect list?"

"Let's figure that out later."

I opened the door and faced the sportscar. Willow was rising from the driver's side. Her bodyguard, the square-jawed Philip Minor had called "the steadfast Mr. Yates," rose from the other.

Willow approached, her arms out. "Oh, girl," she said, suddenly walking faster and giving me a hug. "I hope you can forgive me."

Stephen got no hug, but she put a hand on his forearm. "Same to you."

I'd never been this close to Willow before. As she stepped back, I was stunned. She looked as if she'd aged 10 years since I'd seen her last. The circles under her eyes were nearly dark as bruises. She'd been wrestling with something, that was certain.

The bodyguard stayed next to the Jaguar, his head turning slowly as he scanned the foliage. He didn't wear sunglasses or a wired earpiece, but they wouldn't have been out of place.

Willow looked down at the gravel. "I have a confession to make."

It seemed like a good time to sit at one of the picnic tables, but no one suggested it. The splinters and bird droppings were obvious.

"I should have said something when the blogger died," Willow said. "I'm embarrassed to say I didn't. Then the police detective told me almost a week ago what happened to the two of you. Ever since, I've been agonizing over what to do."

She lifted her chin and looked at me. "Carolyn, maybe you remember something I said last time we were here. About the terrible things people hide to survive."

I nodded.

"I wasn't speaking hypothetically. There's something very specific I haven't told anyone, ever. For at least forty years. Now it's killed an innocent person and wants to kill the two of you. I have to stop this. I have to tell the truth."

She looked down at the gravel again. "It's about my cousin, Gerald."

I waited for the rest, but it seemed permanently stuck in her throat. "What about him?"

She shook her head. "I'm . . . afraid he must have shot Mr. Tripp. And now he's trying to do the same to you."

I took a step forward. "With all due respect, how is that possible? We met Gerald. We talked to him. He's big, yes. But soft-spoken. Thoughtful. I don't see how he could kill anybody."

She nodded. "Oh, I know. It's always been that way. Even when we were kids, he seemed normal to practically everybody. Saintly, even. The whole 'gentle giant' thing. Only Aunt Annalynn and I knew what he was really like."

We waited again. She seemed to be trying to decide how to phrase it.

"The things he did," she said finally. "Flying into a rage for no reason. The way he treated animals . . ."

She trailed off, stuck again.

"How did he treat them?" I asked.

"Torture, really. Frogs he found. A cat. I remember the neighbor's hamster . . ." She shuddered. "Never mind. The point is it took me years and a lot of reading, but I finally figured it out. Gerald is a sociopath—a high-functioning one, but a sociopath, nonetheless. No empathy, no conscience. And the ability to hide it whenever it suits him."

"But why keep it a secret for all that time?"

She looked up, where the sun flashed through the tree-tops. "When I was nine, Gerald was twelve. One day I found him behind the garage with a penknife and what was left of a pigeon. It wasn't the first time I'd seen something like that. He said if I ever told on him, he'd kill me. I always assumed he'd do it. I was never brave enough to find out."

Stephen raised a hand. "I'm confused. Why would Gerald kill the blogger? He wanted Tripp to succeed, to let the world know his mother was no child abuser."

Willow shook her head. "He never cared about Aunt Annalynn. He hated her; said she was weak. He put up with us because we were his ticket to my folks' estate, such as it was. Playing the devoted son is part of his act."

"So . . ." Stephen trailed off, still looking puzzled.

She put her palms together. "Here's what I'm saying. I think Gerald killed Mr. Tripp because he kept trying to dig up more dirt about 'Willowgate.'"

"He was looking into your background, your family," I said.

"Right. Gerald must have been afraid Tripp would find out what he was like and would let everybody know."

"Okay," Stephen said slowly. "But how do *we* fit in?"

"Now he's trying to keep *you* from discovering he killed Tripp."

"Makes sense. I think."

I folded my arms. "I'm not so sure. But you have to let the police know. Are you willing to tell Luis—the detective— what you just told us?"

"I don't want to," she said. "But I have to. People's lives are at stake."

"Then I guess we need to go to the police station so you can make a statement or something."

"If that's what it takes."

"Do you want to bring your car and meet us there, or—"

A loud squeal, a screech of brakes burst like fireworks from somewhere behind us. From the highway, maybe, a vehicle avoiding a crash. Or coming to a halt just inside the entrance to the park.

Whatever it was, it was big, and loud.

We all whirled toward the sound. I swallowed. The bodyguard's hand flew toward his sports jacket and hovered near his waist. Over a concealed weapon, I guessed.

"What if that's Gerald?" Stephen whispered.

Gravel sputtered under someone's shoes. Trees rustled.

About 50 feet away a bush, maybe a buttonbush, leaned to the side. Slowly a face rose above it.

"Luis!" I cried. "Thank God."

His gaze went from me to Stephen to Willow to the bodyguard. The latter lowered his hand.

With a grunt and a snap of underbrush, Luis stood up. He was out of breath, tieless, his white sleeves rolled, his hair disarranged. His gun rode in a hip holster and a badge was clipped to his belt.

"Sorry I'm late," he said. "Did I miss anything?"

HE WALKED TOWARD US. "Got here as quick as I could. Came as soon as I heard the voice message."

I exhaled, feeling as if I'd held my breath for the last three minutes. "Willow has some things she needs to tell you."

"Oh?" He pulled a small pad and pen from his shirt pocket. "Nice to finally meet you in person, Ms. Hayly. Fire away."

She told her story, slightly condensed and lacking her trademark intensity. It was too real for playacting.

Luis wrote as fast as he could, raising his eyebrows frequently.

When she was done, he clicked his pen several times. "So," he said. "Your cousin isn't the person he seems to be."

She shook her head.

"You believe he's capable of murder. And in fact, has already committed it."

"I do."

"Well, that changes everything, if it's true," he said.

She put her hands on her hips. "Of *course*, it's true."

He put the pen and pad away. "Ms. Hayly, you say Gerald promised to kill you if you ever told anyone what you've just told us, correct?"

"Correct."

He looked around at the woods. "Do you know where Gerald is right now?"

"No," she said.

"Well, neither do I."

The rest of us began to look nervously at the trees.

He tapped the notepad against his thigh. "Maybe we'd all feel a little more comfortable in a place we know Gerald *isn't*. I'd like to cordially invite you folks downtown so Ms. Hayly can make a formal statement. It's pretty darn safe there with all those cops around."

No objections being heard, the motion was carried.

Smoothing his hair with his hand, he ambled toward me. "Carolyn," he said, "would you do me the honor of riding in my car again? I figure it might give you more of a feel for how us law enforcement types operate. So, you can get that into the book."

I gulped and didn't know why. Except that of course I did.

"Can . . . Stephen come along?"

"Oh. Yeah, sure."

Stephen rolled his eyes.

We followed Luis toward the parking lot. A pair of handcuffs dangled from his belt. I realized I'd never seen handcuffs before, except on TV and in the movies.

There were a lot of things I'd never seen.

I had a feeling I was about to see a lot more.

~

WE WERE in a different part of the precinct office this time, a part that smelled of sweat and French fries, but mostly ammonia. The vinyl flooring looked a little too shiny, as though it had to be washed every 15 minutes after some drunk had retched on it.

Stephen and the bodyguard and I sat on a long bench, waiting for Luis to take Willow's statement down the hall. The bench was hard as it looked which didn't seem to bother the bodyguard, who didn't seem bothered by anything.

Stephen was bothering me, though.

"That was quite a ride," he said. "Too bad it was an unmarked car. I'm sure he would have let you work the siren and the flashing lights."

I narrowed my eyes. "I'm maintaining the relationship, remember?"

He smirked. "Oh, I don't doubt that."

"For a guy who doesn't have to deal with that manuscript, you don't seem too grateful for the sacrifice I'm making."

"Uh-huh."

"Besides, it was research."

"Yeah, you two seem to do a lot of that."

"This is ridiculous." I turned toward the bodyguard. With a shrug Stephen took out his phone, probably to look for video of an iguana that played the harmonica or something.

"Mr. Yates," I said, offering my hand.

"Yes, ma'am." His grasp was strong but measured, efficient. His smile was so faint it made the Mona Lisa look like Julia Roberts.

"I'm Carolyn Neville."

"Timothy Yates, ma'am."

His eyes met mine but didn't stay there. He kept glancing over my shoulder, taking in the corridor, looking out for his employer's best interests, apparently.

"Don't tell me," I said. "Former military."

The corners of his mouth turned up slightly. "That's right."

"Where did you serve?"

"Military police in Iraq."

His answers were so short I had to wonder whether he'd taken half a vow of silence. Or half-vowed a whole one.

"How long have you been working for Willow?" I asked.

"About two years now."

"That's quite a vehicle she has. Does she ever let you drive it?"

He gave an unexpected chuckle. "Let's see. Maybe three, four times. An impressive piece of machinery. You into Jags?"

"Only from a distance, I'm afraid."

There was a pause, during which I remembered the way his hand had hovered over his chest at the park.

"If you don't mind my asking . . . do you carry a gun?"

He nodded. "I do."

"I've heard Willow doesn't care for guns."

"I guess a lot of folks don't. That's their right."

For a few moments he went quiet, then sat up even straighter. "They sure have a lot of *questions* about guns, though."

"Such as?"

"Mostly folks at work. They want to know what it's like to shoot somebody, which I'd just as soon not get into. Or they ask whether it's safe to let their kids get pellet guns or paintball guns or whatever. Couple of months ago a guy was writing a movie script or something and asked a whole bunch of questions to make sure he got the 'gun parts' right.

Drives me a little nuts, to tell you the truth. But people are what they are."

"Isn't *that* the truth? In fact, I had an author once who insisted—"

"Excuse me," he said suddenly, rising to his feet.

I twisted to see what he was looking at.

Luis and Willow had just emerged from a doorway down the hall. As they approached our little group, Stephen lifted his gaze from his phone.

"I've asked Ms. Hayly enough questions for now," Luis said quietly. "But I'm going to have a lot more—for Gerald."

"When?" I asked.

"Any day now."

I shook my head. "The police station may be a safe place, but we obviously can't stay here. What if Gerald finds us at the motel?"

Luis folded his arms across his chest. "We'll be watching him. That's what happens when you make the kind of threat Ms. Hayly says he made."

"How long will you watch him?"

"Until the powers that be decide whether or not to charge him. He'll be under constant surveillance. That should allow everybody to breathe a little easier, right?"

I checked my breathing. It didn't seem easier at all. In fact, I might need to breathe into a paper bag pretty soon, to avoid hyperventilating.

I hoped the police were on the right track.

If they weren't, Stephen and I might find ourselves neglecting to breathe at all.

CHAPTER 26

"Very good," Luis declared with the confidence of someone who'd just created the heavens and the earth. "I've got everybody's contact information. I'll keep you posted while we've got an eye on Gerald. Give you some idea of how long this might take."

Looking pained, Willow put a hand on my shoulder. "I'm sorry, Carolyn. This feels like my fault."

I shook my head. "It's not, really. Although I have to admit I'm a little tired of being stuck in motels and airplanes."

"Losing your job," she said.

"Getting sued," added Stephen.

I looked down at the glimmering floor. "Living on whatever happens to be in the vending machine. Listening to workmen banging on pipes, and—"

"Hold it," Willow said. "I have a better idea."

She spread her arms like a pope blessing the faithful in St. Peter's Square. "Carolyn . . . Stephen . . . I'd like you to come stay at my house."

I raised at least two eyebrows.

"It's perfect," she continued. "Stay with me and I'll feel a little less guilty about bringing all this down on you. Besides, if we all have to lay low for a while, we may as well do it together. Misery loves company."

She nodded at Yates. "Plus, we'll have our very own bodyguard."

"Willow, that's so generous of you," I said. "But I hate to impose."

"No imposition," Willow said with a wave of her papal hand.

Stephen looked doubtful.

"So, it's settled," Willow declared.

And, of course, it was.

She was, after all, Willow.

AFTER STOPPING by the motel for our bags, we drove toward Swan's Corners, toward Willow's house.

Stephen shook his head slowly. "My mom would blow a gasket if she knew I'd been invited to stay at Willow Hayly's."

"I've been in some nice places, but I can't imagine what hers must be like."

He grunted. "Maybe there are birds and bees and cigarette trees beside the crystal fountains . . . the lemonade springs where the bluebird sings in the Big Rock Candy Mountains."

I laughed. "Where did you hear that song? It's from, what, the 1930s?"

"I have eclectic tastes."

At length we passed the familiar Swan's Corners landmarks—the Paul Bunyan billboard, the Dairy-Freez, the used car lot, the street with Willow's name on it. But this time we kept going. As Willow had hastily noted on the back of her business card before leaving the police station, her house was 3.1 miles past the city limits.

We watched the NOW LEAVING SWAN'S CORNERS sign whiz by. After that, the businesses disappeared and then the houses were fewer and further between. Soon there were no buildings at all—save for an occasional barn or silo, sometimes accompanied by a rusting tractor.

I slowed when the odometer hit three miles. Sure enough, an unmarked, narrow road forked to the right. I took it.

The asphalt made a slow climb to the crest of a hill. Once on the other side, we saw it.

Willow's house.

It wasn't a house at all, really. It was more of a gated compound, an estate that seemed large enough to generate its own weather. The same gray granite that covered so much of Willow's headquarters was accented with red brick. The overall impression: a fortress designed by Martha Stewart.

"Gross," Stephen said.

I slowed the car further. "We seem to have entered another dimension."

I stopped in front of the black iron gate. A granite pillar with a keypad stood to my left. I punched in the code she'd jotted next to the map.

The gate clicked and slowly swung open. The Kia began to inch up the driveway, no doubt feeling out of place.

When I rang the doorbell, which sounded more like a gong than a chime, I half expected a butler to answer. But Willow did it herself.

"You made it!" she said and gave me another hug. "We beat you, though. Something about that car makes me drive a little too fast. Come in."

It was clear that Martha Stewart, or someone like her, had overseen the interior decoration, too. Countless shades of mocha, auburn, and russet, dashes of stainless steel and glass.

Three paintings of indeterminate subject but probably great import, one of which may or may not have been a Jackson Pollock. Floors clean enough to eat from, which would have been useful if we'd been barbarian germaphobes.

On one of the sofas, a cocoa sectional, the steadfast Mr. Yates was already sipping a beer. The sports jacket was gone, revealing a leather waistband holster. The way he was sitting kept me from seeing the gun itself.

"Can I get you a drink?" Willow asked.

Stephen looked at Yates. "I'll have whatever he's having."

"Carolyn?"

"Have any white wine?"

"Of course."

She disappeared into the kitchen, then reappeared with our drinks. "Don't worry, Carolyn." She handed me the wine glass. "I won't tell Philip or the lawyers I'm giving aid and comfort to the enemy. And speaking of the lawsuit, I'm still working on getting them to drop it."

"Thanks," I said.

"We're having salmon." She bent toward the bodyguard. "I'll need your help in the kitchen."

Without a word, he set down his beer and followed.

I wandered slowly around the room, absorbing the elegance. There were no pictures of Willow, no trophies. And no racket of kids in the next room, watching Cartoon Network on the motel TV. I took a deep breath and let it out a bit at a time.

The *snick-snick* of vegetable-chopping and the plink of plates drifted from the kitchen. I could see the sink from where I stood. Every half-minute or so, Willow or Yates would cross my line of sight. It was obvious they'd done this many times.

Suddenly they met in the middle. Willow stopped Yates by placing her hands on his biceps. Rising on her tiptoes, she kissed him quickly on the mouth. Then they moved on, resuming their culinary choreography.

My eyebrows went up. Guarding wasn't the only thing Mr. Yates had been doing with Willow's body.

The clanks and sizzles of cooking continued, joined by growing scents of garlic and ginger. From time to time Willow would poke her head through the doorway and assure us that it wouldn't be long before the meal began.

And finally it did, in the dining room, where a flame danced on the tip of a single taper in a silver candlestick at the center of a lacy, white tablecloth. There was grilled salmon, rice pilaf, and some kind of Frankensteinian orange cauliflower that tasted much better than it looked. The customary compliments were paid and in this case were earned.

"You know," Stephen said about halfway through the repast, "Carolyn's something of a gourmet chef herself."

"Really?" Willow asked. "Well, you must promise to cook us a meal while you're here."

I laughed. "Stephen's exaggerating. I've just collected some exotic cooking utensils, most of which sit in a drawer. I don't even know what half of them do."

"We'll see," Willow said.

When the meal came to an end and the table was cleared, there were contented sighs and multi-star reviews. "It's so nice to have a *real* dinner," I said.

Willow glanced at her companion. "I owe it all to Timothy. I don't know where he learned all that stuff about cedar planks and tarragon, but he did."

Yates shrugged. "Travel broadens the mind."

"So it does," Willow said. For a second, she gave him a look that seemed to speak volumes about their relationship, but I couldn't tell what the volumes were saying.

As if wanting to change the subject, she turned to me. "Have you seen *Women of Means*?"

"The series on Amazon?"

"That's the one."

"I've heard about it, but I haven't seen it yet."

"I just started binge-watching. You've got to join me, girl. Just you and me. That show would be guaranteed toxic to any self-respecting male. Tim certainly hasn't been able to tolerate it."

Yates squeezed out a hapless, halfway smile. "I tried."

She shooed him away with a wave. "You and Stephen go do whatever it is men do instead of being civilized. And try not to burn the place down."

Yates turned toward Stephen. "You heard the lady," he said, and led the way out.

I couldn't imagine what they'd do. Their odds of finding anything to talk about were practically nonexistent.

Willow got up and stretched. "Let's go to the theater room. You've got to see this show."

The theater room was downstairs, all soft lighting and plush burgundy carpets and curtains. About two dozen seats, the reclining kind, filled the space—except for the miniature concession stand, complete with bright red circus-style popcorn popper and soda fountain.

Willow dropped into a back-row seat, took a remote control from the cup holder, and pushed a few buttons. The screen, which was roughly the size of a double bed, sprang to life with a *Jeopardy!* question about the Ming Dynasty.

She thumbed the remote, not even looking at the buttons. I sighed, remembering the times I'd accidentally hit HDMI2 instead of HDMI1, upped the channel instead of the volume, or gotten thrown off the Internet entirely by my uncaring ISP.

"Girls' night out," she said. "The boys will probably be in

Timothy's study. At least that's what he calls it. No books on the shelves, just stuff he's gotten on his travels. One of those Arab swords from Iraq, a bunch of animal heads from Africa. Antique pistols. And of course his cigars." She shuddered. "Why can't he smoke a pipe? Fortunately, he confines the tobacco to his man cave."

She navigated her way to Amazon Video. "So," she said, "what's the deal with you and Stephen?"

My eyes widened. "What do you mean?"

"Let me know if you want me to shut up. But I can't help wondering whether there's something between you two."

Flustered, I reared back in my seat as if hoping to put more distance between us. "We . . . just work together. Why?"

"I know about these things. Slightly older woman, slightly younger man."

"Like you and Timothy?"

She leaned in my direction. "Can you keep a secret?"

"I think so."

"He's not just my bodyguard."

"I kind of figured that out."

"I suppose half the people at Willoworth have, too, but most of them are too polite to say anything." She paused. "Back to you and Stephen."

I cleared my throat. "We've worked together about five years. Sure, he's . . . not bad looking. Very smart. But my gosh, he's too young."

"How big is the difference?"

"I've got ten years on him."

She chuckled. "That's nothing. I've got thirteen years on Tim."

Desperate to change the subject, I looked at the screen. "Isn't it about time for the show to start?"

She patted me on the shoulder. "Okay, I get it. I'll button my lip. None of my business."

Pushing the button, she started downloading. The red line zipped from right to left, much faster than at home.

I sank into the recliner, still cringing. Sure, Stephen and I had a lot in common. Similar senses of humor, love of books and Chinese food, knowing the rules of editing and publishing and Words with Friends. But I was no cougar.

I also wasn't his type, spiritual speaking. I believed in things we couldn't see and he thought that made me mentally defective. It was sort of a dealbreaker.

I'd had my chance. The guy I'd been engaged to seemed plenty compatible, but in the end, he couldn't close the deal.

I just hoped it wasn't the last chance I'd ever have.

WOMEN OF MEANS was a show about female empowerment, at least according to Willow. I had no idea who the characters were, and every time Willow hit PAUSE to explain, I'd nod and wonder what she was talking about.

There was lots of glittery jewelry and designer dresses, the kind Hunter Thicke's wife probably bought at Neiman Marcus and Bergdorf Goodman with a platinum American Express card. Everybody had an attitude and a name that sounded like a shade of eye shadow.

When we got to a scene in which a cheekbony blonde scorched her boyfriend for not wanting to commit, Willow started clapping. "You tell him, sister." She turned to me. "Don't you just hate that?"

"Mmm-hmm." If only she knew.

But then I had another thought. Was she talking about Timothy?

She folded her arms. "Men think they can just—"

Suddenly the door banged open. Stephen stumbled in,

choking, coughing. The smell of smoke got stronger as he got closer.

At first I thought the house was on fire, but then recognized the smell. It stank too much. Cigar smoke.

He was holding up his phone, apparently unable to speak. Handing it to me, he proceeded to put his hands on his knees and hack hard enough to donate both lungs to science.

Luis was on the line. "Carolyn? Things okay there? Mr. Ames seems to be having some kind of trouble."

"I think he and Mr. Yates were doing something manly."

He paused. "Whatever that means. I tried dialing you, but it went straight to voice mail."

I flipped open my purse and checked the phone. "Must have turned it off during dinner. Sorry."

Timothy entered, looking sheepish. He gave Stephen a couple of whacks on the back.

"Anyway, I've got some news," Luis said.

"Just a second. I'll put it on speaker."

"We've had one interview with Gerald so far. He's under surveillance by an officer in a squad car. Gerald's home and hasn't gone anywhere."

By now Stephen's gasping had been downgraded to severe wheezing. His eyes were watering.

"When we interviewed Gerald, we found out he doesn't have a solid alibi for the day Tripp died. Or when you and Stephen were attacked. As for the noisy vehicle that peeled out of the parking garage, we've established that Gerald does own a Ford F-150 pickup."

He paused. "Bottom line, we haven't heard anything yet that would keep us from charging him. But we have a few more things to confirm."

"Sounds good," I said.

"Are you still on speaker?"

I pushed the button. "Not anymore."

"Sweet dreams," he said.

I felt myself blush. When I realized I'd pushed the volume button instead and made his words even louder, I blushed harder.

Willow burst out laughing. "*Sweet dreams?* Woo woo!" She waggled her eyebrows.

"I'll call you in the morning," Luis said, and hung up.

Willow scowled at Timothy. "That *smell*. Cigars are a filthy habit. Mr. Ames obviously wasn't prepared for it."

"I thought he knew not to inhale."

"They don't teach that in school anymore. Mr. Ames, we may have to bury your clothes to get rid of that smell." Bending toward me, she lowered her voice. "I had to do that with Tim's once."

She sighed. "Now, the two of you find something else to do. We want to finish watching our show."

Stephen finally tried his voice. "I'll just go to bed." He sounded like he'd been gargling with Drano.

Wishing him goodnight, I settled back in my chair. Willow did the same and hit PLAY. The parade of costumes and cleft chins resumed.

I hoped the police would hurry up and charge Gerald.

The sooner they did, the sooner I could get out of Xanadu.

...

CHAPTER 27

WHEN I OPENED MY EYES, EVERYTHING WAS IN THE WRONG place.

Or at least not in any arrangement I recognized. This wasn't the Swan's Corners Inn, the Saddleback Lodge, or the Southern Suites. It wasn't even my condo in Connecticut. It was way too nice.

The pillow felt smooth but firm against my cheek. *Ah*, I thought. *Willow's house.*

I looked around. The guest room was a showplace, like something on the National Register of Historic Places. There were a few small paintings, more restful than the ones downstairs. Waterfalls, mostly. It had no stainless steel or glass tables and everything seemed padded with no sharp edges.

I rubbed a few crumbs from my eyes. It had been my longest, deepest sleep since leaving home. Probably since I'd first heard about Willowgate. Maybe even since that last night *in utero*. This had to be a thousand-dollar mattress and worth every penny.

I got up and zipped open my suitcase, then hesitated.

Should I unpack? How long would I be here? Nobody seemed to know.

I stepped into the bathroom. The shower looked like something out of a science fiction movie, all gleaming plastic with mysterious fixtures and luxurious elbow room. The built-in body wash and shampoo dispensers were loaded and operational, unlike most I'd encountered, and the towels were thicker than peat bogs.

By the time I emerged from the bathroom, I'd decided I was in the mood to wear a long mint tee, deep cuff blue jeans, and sandals. Unfortunately, the only relatively clean outfit in my suitcase was my tweedy brown editor's blazer and a dark green skirt. Maybe Willow would let me use her washer and dryer later.

I made my way down the spiral staircase, not missing the elevator in the least. Or the Free Continental Breakfast.

Mr. Yates was already in the kitchen, making coffee. "Morning," he said. "Guess Stephen must have stayed up most of the night. After all that coughing, wasn't sure he was going to make it."

He walked to the pantry and pulled out a box. "Care for a Pop-Tart? I try not to eat them when Willow's up. She wants me to eat stuff like quinoa and yogurt."

"Cruel and unusual," I said.

"Got two flavors. Strawberry and Brown Sugar Cinnamon."

This was beginning to look like the Free Continental Breakfast. Or, worse, the Complimentary one. "Which do you recommend?"

"Strawberry. I know I've reached the bottom of the barrel when I hit Brown Sugar Cinnamon. Hardly a Pop-Tart at all. No frosting."

"Strawberry it is."

He turned to put two of them in the toaster. I could see the gun sticking out of the holster.

After pouring two cups of coffee, which were strong enough to pummel anything Starbucks had to offer, he placed my Pop-Tart on a saucer. We chewed and drank in silence.

"Sorry I'm out of the other flavors," he said after a while. "Don't know whether you follow Pop-Tarts, but there are more kinds than most people realize."

"Oh?"

"They've had just about every flavor you can imagine. Hot Fudge Sundae. Red Velvet. Gone Nutty, which is pretty much peanut butter and jelly, except there's another Gone Nutty with peanut butter and chocolate."

"Fascinating," I said.

"My favorites? Blue Raspberry and S'mores. And I don't think I'm alone in that."

He proceeded to fill me in on several other varieties, historical facts, and points of controversy. The previous evening's Man of Few Words apparently had been abducted by aliens during the night.

I looked up at the ceiling, hoping to convey that I was swiftly reaching the limits of my interest in this field. It didn't work.

"Pop-Tarts were tough to come by in Iraq," he said. "Maybe that's why I make sure I have a supply here. Like the man says, you don't know what you've got 'til it's gone."

"Iraq, yes," I said, ready to shift gears. "What was it like there?"

"Educational."

I waited for him to elaborate, but he didn't. I tried again. "Quite a phone call from the detective last night, wouldn't you say?"

He nodded.

"What do you think we should do while the police make up their minds about Gerald?" I asked.

He took a swallow of coffee. "Wouldn't *go* anywhere, if that's what you mean. Right now, this is the safest place on earth. I'll tell Willow the same thing if she gets it into her head to go the office. We've got more security here—higher gates, better surveillance system."

"And an armed guard."

"I go where she goes," he said simply.

"I'm sure she appreciates your . . . arrangement."

His smile was almost imperceptible. "Let's just say we have a mutually beneficial relationship."

Just then I heard a yawn at the kitchen doorway. It was Stephen.

"Do I smell Pop-Tarts?" he asked.

Yates got another coffee mug from the cupboard. "Two choices. Strawberry and Brown Sugar Cinnamon."

"Strawberry," Stephen said. "I could never say yes to Brown Sugar Cinnamon. It's not even a real Pop-Tart—no frosting."

The two of them began an agonizingly detailed discussion involving Frosted Wild Cherry and Printed Fun Sugar Cookie. I sensed my chance to escape. When I slipped out, they didn't seem to notice.

I climbed the spiral staircase. If I had to be stuck here, I could make better use of my time than watching a debate about artificial pastry.

I could, for instance, start thinking about my future.

What if Gerald really was the killer? I'd be free to go, free to return to a empty condominium in Connecticut, an overloaded credit card, and no salary to pay for either.

Maybe it was time to find out what I was going to do with the rest of my life.

Just in case I had one.

~

I DECIDED to take my thoughts outdoors.

The sky was clear, the breeze light, the sun industrious but not malicious. After checking to make sure the iron fence was still in place, I started wandering.

There was no front or back yard to Willow's mansion—only grounds, the sort of thing groundskeepers keep. A cobblestone driveway here, a garden there. I spotted a hippopotamus topiary, a koi pond, and a circle of lawn as plush and flat as a billiard table on which croquet might be played if this weren't Georgia.

I walked until I reached a trellis. Surrounded by white magnolias and their lemony fragrance, I sat on a steel bench with a butterfly design on the back.

Out came my phone. The time had come to preserve the remnants of my career.

I knew *Publishers Weekly* had job listings on the Internet. I'd never really been interested in them, except to assure myself that the grass was just as brown elsewhere. But now I found my way to those announcements.

There were 43 possibilities. My heart beat a little faster.

I narrowed down the list, weeding out the number crunchers, salespeople, designers, Marketing Analytics Managers, Art Directors, Publicists, and Audience Development Coordinators.

That left the editorial jobs.

All two of them.

I tapped a link to *Details*. One of the positions was editorial assistant at a large company down the street from Pendleton House, a golden opportunity for anyone with a talent for changing toner cartridges and a sizable inheritance to pay the rent. The other vacancy was in Chicago, a senior editor post requiring knowledge of Excel, HTML5, crowdsourcing, research impact metrics, and "non-Eurocentric literary concerns." *Perfect*, I thought. Except for, well, everything.

I looked at my watch. My job hunt, including the walk, had taken a total of nine minutes.

Standing up, I returned my phone to its resting place. I'd continue this another day, a day when the publishing industry more greatly valued editorial proficiency. Maybe April 17, 1921 would be a good choice.

I NEEDED DIRECTION. Not the kind I got from Marvin. The personal kind.

I checked my watch. What was Mikki Flaherty doing? Was it worth trying again to reach her?

Maybe I should call her work number. Her boss didn't like her to have personal conversations on the clock. But she could hang up if the timing wasn't right.

"Hey!" she answered. "Where have you been?"

"Where have *you* been? I've been trying to get hold of you for a week."

"My phone got stolen."

"I tried e-mail, too."

"I do everything on my phone these days. What's going on?"

"Very long story."

"Fortunately, the boss is gone. Tell me the whole thing. I promise to take it out of vacation time."

I launched into an explanation. The more I told her, the more she kept saying "You're *kidding*," and "*What?*" When I got to the part about being shot at, she practically screamed.

"Are you all *right?*" she cried.

"Sort of. I will be. My face got a little rearranged, but

maybe it's an improvement. But the reason I'm calling is to get your input on my resumé. You know me pretty well. Plus, you're in HR."

There was a long pause. "You're writing your *resume*? Now?"

"Can you think of a better time? I've been fired. I have one at home, but the last time I revised it was during the George W. Bush administration."

She sighed. "Yeah, okay. So . . . how would you describe your background?"

"Honestly?"

"Why not?"

I cleared my throat. "Well, I got my B.A. in English literature from a college that specialized in navel-gazing and turning out armchair revolutionaries."

"Sounds good."

"Then I signed up for a two-year Master of Fine Arts program. But the faculty was a bunch of pretentious twits. It was a huge waste of time, so I quit after six months."

"Not sure you want to put it that way, but keep going."

"For a year I was adjunct professor of literature at a small liberal arts college. Most of my students could barely read, much less write."

"Um . . . let's come back to that later."

"Okay. To sum it all up, I guess I'd say I've spent most of my life as an editor, working my way up from a small press to one of the biggest. The experience has taught me that publishers tend to be cowards, writers tend to be incompetent, and readers tend to have no taste."

There was a long silence.

"It's perfect, except for one thing."

"What's that?"

"It sounds too much like a suicide note."

"You said to be honest."

"I take it back."

I sighed. "Maybe I should do this another time."

"Yeah. You need a chance to reflect. And to get off your meds."

We talked a little longer about people at church and what they were doing. And how there was nothing the police could do about her stolen phone.

Finally she said, "Well, I'd better wrap this up. I don't have much vacation time left."

"Thanks for talking," I said.

"And thanks for not asking whether I've been thinking of you like I said I would. It hasn't been twice a day, but close. One is close to two, right?"

"Right," I said.

"Come home, Carolyn."

"As soon as I can. Assuming they let me."

After she hung up, I wished I could feel her forehead touching mine.

CHAPTER 28

WHEN I GOT BACK TO THE KITCHEN, STEPHEN AND TIMOTHY were done talking about Pop-Tarts and finishing their coffee. Willow was finally up. She was looking at something in the pantry.

"There are Pop-Tart wrappers in this garbage can," she said.

Stephen raised a hand, looking unrepentant. "One is mine. Maybe three."

Timothy shrugged. "Just trying to feed our guests."

She shook her head. "That's poison, people. Now you'll have to eat an extra-healthy lunch. Things like flaxseed and hummus."

"Are we running out of *real* food?" Yates asked.

Willow shut the pantry door. "Don't you worry. Today's the day we get our weekly delivery."

"Wow," said Stephen. "Your groceries come right to your door?"

"I know it sounds snooty," she said. "But all the Willow sightings at the supermarket wore me out. By the time I left the store, my gelato would be melted. I couldn't—"

"What's that?" Timothy said suddenly.

He looked at me. My phone was warbling.

I checked the screen. "Hello, Luis. Let me put you on speaker, okay? We're all here."

"Everybody holding up?" he asked.

I nodded, which was kind of stupid.

"We're fine," Stephen said over my shoulder.

"Great. Here's the latest, as of about an hour ago. We've been looking into what Ms. Hayly said about Gerald's mental state. Only an expert witness could determine that. But we did find a guy who used to live next door to the Sacketts. His dogs were poisoned when Gerald was in high school."

"I remember that," Willow said.

"Nobody could be totally sure who did it. But the neighbor figured it was Gerald. Said he was a 'weird kid.'"

"No lie," she mumbled.

"We also talked to the owner of the furniture refinishing place next to Gerald's shop. Said they had a dispute over parking spaces a couple years ago and somebody slashed the guy's tires. Thinks it was Gerald but can't prove it."

"Wouldn't surprise me," Willow said.

"Oh, and the lady who owns the trophy shop. She said one night a few years ago she heard glass breaking and Gerald yelling. Both shops were closed. It was around tax time."

I raised an eyebrow. "Doesn't everybody do that at tax time?"

"Yeah, two people here said the same thing. Anyway, we're probably close. It's all pretty circumstantial, but we may have enough to hold him."

"Thank God," Willow said.

"No guarantees. Charging Gerald will be up to my boss. But I think he'd like to wrap this up ASAP. Maybe as soon as this evening."

"That would make us all happy," I said.

"I'll call you then. Bye."

The phone went back in my pocket.

"Maybe this evening!" Willow repeated. She put her arm around me and squeezed.

Then she looked me in the face and laughed at what she saw. "Carolyn," she said. "Smile, will you?"

"When the time comes."

"And when will that be?"

"When Gerald's in prison," I said, "and I'm not."

CHAPTER 29

LUNCH REALLY DID RELY HEAVILY ON FLAXSEED AND HUMMUS. Stephen and Timothy stuck with leftover salmon. They didn't seem to enjoy our conversation about empowerment much, either.

Afterward we drifted to separate regions of the house to await the inevitable gassiness and Sergeant Valenzuela's next call. I found myself peeking into a room that looked like a real study, unlike Timothy's testosterone sanctuary. Books lined the recessed shelves; there was just enough rosewood paneling and the mellow scent of Murphy's Oil Soap to thrill the most discriminating bibliophile.

There was also a desk with a bona fide blotter and assorted mementos presumably too personal for Willow's office. Not wanting to intrude, I turned my attention to her literary collection.

No organizing principle seemed to be at work on the shelves, except that the heaviest books were on the bottom. I noted yards of psychology, recovery, and financial titles. There were plenty of Pendleton titles, too, since Willow was on the "influencers" list that Our Friends in Marketing held so dear.

Next to some outdated new-age hokum about past lives and primal screams sat autobiographies of Willow's famous friends, most of them autographed. To my surprise, there was even a section of paperback historical romances, their covers full of parted lips, windblown locks, and brazenly embossed lettering.

Finally there were the books Willow herself had written, or sort of written. They started with *Worth It*, the memoir that had gotten us into this mess. It was the first edition, which I hadn't seen in years.

When I slipped it from the shelf, it fell open to the photo insert. The pictures were all black-and-white, since four-color printing had been deemed too expensive for that edition. Nobody had known it was destined for bestseller status.

Here was the photo of Willow as a preschooler. She stood next to her Aunt Annalynn, a somber and exceptionally over-weight woman in a shapeless tent of a dress. On the other side was Gerald, already tall and simian and pale. He was smiling. So was Willow, revealing at least two gaps where teeth had been. She looked happy. Maybe it was before he'd threatened her.

I was about to start reading the acknowledgments page, looking for my name, when I heard a noise behind me. Startled, I whirled.

It was Willow.

I held up the book. "Reliving past glories. Hope you don't mind."

She chuckled. "Lady, you belong in a roomful of books. Just don't tell anybody I have any romance novels."

BZZZZZZ, came a sound from the doorway, somewhere near her elbow.

"Aha," she said, going to the window and pushing the curtain aside. "Timothy and Steven's redemption draweth nigh. Take a look."

A white commercial van about the size of an ice cream truck idled outside the front gate. The name of a market was on the side, under a dancing celery stalk logo.

"Grocery delivery," Willow said.

She returned to the doorway and pushed an intercom button on the wall. "Do you come bearing Pop-Tarts?" she called.

"Absolutely," came a man's muffled reply.

"Then enter!" she said and pushed another button.

Slowly the gate swung open, then closed behind the van.

"Shall we?" Willow asked.

When we reached the living room, the doorbell rang. She peered through the peephole. "That's a lot of Pop-Tarts," she said, and opened the door.

There stood what seemed to be a cardboard appliance carton, almost large enough to hold a dishwasher, that had grown arms and legs. The box had the dancing celery stalk on it. The delivery man, I finally realized, had his arms wrapped around the box and was carrying it.

The box stepped carefully over the threshold. Willow shut the door behind it.

"Afternoon, ma'am," said the box. "Where would you like these?"

Somewhere, in a rear corner of my mind, there was a flicker of recognition.

The voice, the soft drawl. The long arms, the height.

The flicker grew to a warning light, and I took a step backward.

But it was too late.

With a grunt the box was lowered to the floor. A hand

plunged into a pocket, and I found myself staring into the barrel of a black revolver.

It was impossible. But the hand holding the gun belonged to Gerald.

❧

"Ms. Neville . . . Cousin Willow . . ."

He nodded, smiling politely. "I'll need you folks to toss me your cell phones. Then kneel on the floor, please, hands behind your heads."

Hands shaking, I complied. Willow did the same. My toss was more of a slide, to keep the phone from breaking. I wondered whether there was any point in caring. Chances are I'd never dial it again.

He didn't pick up the phones. When Willow put her hands behind her head, I saw her arms were trembling.

Slow footsteps came from behind me, then Stephen's voice. "What the—"

"Mr. Ames," Gerald said. "Thank you for coming. Afraid we won't be having any sweet tea this time. Just throw me your phone, if you will, and do what these folks are doing."

Without a word he followed the instructions, then knelt next to me. He might have been able to hear my heart hammering.

"Oops," Gerald said. "Missing somebody. Where's that bodyguard of yours, Willow?"

"I don't know," she said quietly.

He shook his head. "Well, the man obviously isn't doing his job. You really ought to give him his walking papers."

She stared at the floor, silent.

"I should thank you, cousin," Gerald continued. "You've made this family reunion possible. Been an awfully long time, hasn't it? You're looking well, considering the circumstances and all."

He paused again but got no response. I could hear a clock ticking somewhere.

"Has it been so long you can't remember what I promised?" he asked. "You think I'm not a man of my word?"

He sounded genuinely hurt. His voice was calm, under control. If not for the gun, I could have imagined him folding his hands like a grandmother as he had that day at his shop.

"The police have been asking me all kinds of interesting questions, cousin. The kind they couldn't ask unless you'd talked to them. They've been watching my every move. Not very well, I guess, because here I am."

My shoulders were starting to ache from keeping my hands behind my head. Trying not to move my elbows, I twisted my neck slowly slightly left, then right.

That was when I caught a glimpse of something outside the front window. It was Timothy, standing almost out of view, gun in hand. The weapon was pointing up.

He lowered it, no doubt trying to get a clear shot at Gerald.

Gerald turned toward me. I forced my eyes away from the window, just in time to see Stephen and Willow look away, too.

Gerald's eyes narrowed. Whirling, he aimed the gun at the window and fired.

The sound wasn't a pop. It was a sharp crack, an ice pick to the ears.

The window shattered. Willow gasped.

Timothy fell to the ground, out of sight.

I closed my eyes, ears ringing. Finally I opened them again, slowly.

Gerald stepped backward to the window and looked down.

"Too bad," he said without expression.

He turned to face the three of us again. "Up 'til now, you know, I'd never actually killed anybody. Ever."

He lifted the gun and trained it on Willow.

"But I think I could develop a taste for it," he said.

WILLOW WAS QUAKING, her hands still behind her head, straining at an invisible leash. "If you've killed him—"

"Oh, he looks pretty dead," Gerald said. "'Course, like I said, I've never killed anybody before."

"Liar!" she shouted. "You killed the blogger."

He shook his head. "Nope. Had no reason to. Never met the man."

Stephen made a disgusted noise. "You sure tried to shoot Carolyn and me."

Gerald shook his head again. "No, sir. Had no reason to do that, either—before now, anyway."

Willow dared to lower her arms, her hands closing into fists. "You've always been a liar. It took me years to understand it, but you're a sociopath. A high-functioning sociopath."

He tilted his head to one side, looking a bit wistful. "Now, that almost sounds like a compliment. Those *low*-functioning sociopaths must have trouble tying their own shoes." He paused and the wistfulness faded. "Hands behind your head, cousin. Rules are rules."

I lifted my chin, trying to look confident. "It's only a matter of time before Luis figures out where you are. He'll send a SWAT team or something."

"Actually, you're right, ma'am," he said. "Unfortunately, it's a matter of too much time. When they get here, things will be . . . over."

He glanced at his watch. "So, there's no need to rush. Kind of spoils it when you do. Learned that from our animal friends, didn't I, cousin?"

Willow glared at him but said nothing.

He turned toward me. "I bet you'd like to know how I got past the boys in blue and made it here. Kind of the elephant in the room, isn't it?"

I opened my mouth, then paused. I had no idea how he'd gotten here. But if I didn't keep him talking, there was no chance the police would arrive in time.

"I . . . do have a theory," I said finally, wondering what it was.

"Let's hear it."

"Well . . . first, you collected some old clothes and pillows. Made a dummy of yourself. Put it in the window of your shop to make the police think you were still there. Then you . . . went out the back door and . . . hailed a taxi."

He rolled his eyes. I forged ahead.

"You had the cab driver take you to a spot near Willow's gate and leave you there. Hid in the brush next to the road. Somehow you knew the supermarket delivery van just happened to be coming today. When it did, you got through the gate by . . . crawling under the van while the driver talked to Willow on the intercom."

He snorted. "Oh, this is good. Then what?"

"You slipped under the van and held on to the . . . chassis, or whatever they call it. While the van went through the gate. And somewhere between there and the front door, you killed the driver and took his place."

He shook his head, laughing. "I'd advise you to keep your day job, Ms. Neville. You don't seem to have a future as a detective."

I sighed. I didn't have a future at all. I started to pray, but he pressed on with his explanation.

"In the first place, my shop doesn't *have* a front window to put a dummy in. In the second place, getting a one-way cab ride to a spot in the middle of nowhere would look pretty suspicious, wouldn't it? Especially near a big celebrity's mansion."

I nodded.

"And the delivery van. Sure, I knew Willow had her food delivered. Plenty of folks knew that. The supermarket even had a commercial where she raved about it. But I didn't know when her delivery was. And what were the chances this would be the right day?"

I sighed. I should have asked Stephen. He was much better at making things up.

"The worst part," he continued, "is the part about the gate. I'm not Indiana Jones. If I'd tried to ride under that van, I'd be an oily spot on the driveway now."

He checked his watch again. "You want to hear what really happened?"

I listened for the sound of police cars slowly crunching to a halt outside the gate, or a SWAT team scaling the fence. Nothing.

"Go on," I said. "Take as long as you like."

"So, the cops think I'm still at the shop. But I slipped past the one who was supposed to keep an eye on me by changing out of my coveralls into these old civvies I keep in the back. Next, I walked out the service entrance, then about a mile. Lousy neighborhood. Found an old beater Toyota and hot-wired it. Figured the owner wouldn't report it as stolen right away. Then drove it to a spot about half a mile from Willow's place and pulled over."

"Very clever," I said.

"Stood by the car with the hood up, waiting for somebody to come by. But it had to be somebody Willow would let through the gate. UPS truck, delivery van, Postal Service, utility company. Anything official-looking."

He paused, then lowered his voice. "Finally a supermarket delivery van shows up. I flag it down, tell the driver my car's dead and so's the battery in my cell phone. I ask if I can use his phone to call a tow truck. He says no but offers to dial 911. I thank him, then pull out the gun before he can dial. I tell him to get in the back, then have him put duct tape over his mouth. I tape his legs together. I drive the van up to the gate and buzz to be let in. Willow, bless her heart, buzzes me in."

He tapped the cell phones into a little pile with his foot. "And no, I didn't kill the driver. No need to. Although the poor man probably isn't in the best of shape, considering the duct tape and his appetite for oxygen."

He looked at his watch once more. "My, how time flies."

I listened again for any hint that help was on the way. Nothing.

Keep stalling, I thought.

"Gerald," I said, "surely a careful planner like yourself knows it's impossible to get away with this. You have no way to get out of here."

"You don't say."

"If you're going to hold us hostage and negotiate with the police for safe passage, they'll storm the house as soon as you shoot anybody. Which it seems you're bent on doing."

His smile was faint. "I know."

"But—"

"I don't plan to survive this, Ms. Neville. Why should I? Everyone will believe Willow's story, not mine. You know perfectly well I'm going to be charged and convicted no matter what." He paused. "Let's just say I'm not about to spend the rest of my life in prison when I can end things my way."

Willow shook her head. "It's always all about you, isn't it?"

Gerald shrugged. "I know, it's really all about *you*. But what can I say? After all, I'm crazy. You said it yourself."

He took still another look at his watch. "Well, even though we needn't rush, we don't literally have all day. Time for you folks to lie down, eyes closed."

I did so. I was almost glad to, since the muscles in my arms were on fire and my shins throbbed from kneeling.

But I wasn't entirely comfortable. As I lay down, I was certain that the smooth, perfectly polished oak floor against my cheek was the last thing I'd ever feel.

Right before the bullet.

As my eyes closed, I finally started praying. I figured it was time.

CHAPTER 30

ONCE MORE I LISTENED FOR A NOISE IN THE DISTANCE, FOR any hint that help was on the way. Still nothing. The cavalry wasn't coming.

There was no sound from Stephen. He probably wasn't praying, but you could never tell. I wanted to nudge him one last time to get ready, but it was too late.

Willow sniffed, but only once. I'd never talked to her about anything remotely spiritual and had no idea where she stood. Only God could answer that one.

My heartbeat thudded in both ears. I couldn't let it end this way, especially not for Stephen. I had to try something, anything.

"Gerald," I said, my eyes still closed. "You know this isn't right. Or even necessary. Let Stephen and Willow leave. If you have to shoot someone, I'm right here."

About 10 feet to my left, Stephen cleared his throat and addressed Gerald. "Look, man, I'm a bigger target. You shoot one of them, I'll be all over you."

"And they say chivalry is dead," Gerald mocked. "In that case, I'll just shoot you first."

Suddenly, from the little pile of surrendered smart-phones, there was a noise. Jungle sounds. A monkey's gibber-ing, the shriek of some exotic bird. Stephen's ringtone.

I managed to raise my head just enough to see Gerald twist toward the racket.

Now.

With a grunt I pushed myself up from the floor and lunged toward him. *Knock him off balance. Get the gun. Something.*

Unfortunately, my cramped leg muscles weren't up to it. I went down like a sack of potatoes, short by at least three feet.

Gerald looked down at me, his expression emptied of compassion. And fury. It held no emotion at all.

Yet somewhere he found the zeal to kick me in the side of the head.

It was a work boot, hard rubber, driven like a piston. If there were no steel cleats in the sole, there may as well have been.

The pain was beyond words, including *excruciating*.

I gasped. My eyes squeezed shut. Tears sprang up and seeped out.

"I didn't say 'Simon says'," Gerald drawled.

My head throbbed. Moments later some emergency backup system kicked in—shock, endorphins, whatever. I was slipping away, as if being absorbed by the floor itself. *Let your mind count backward from 99. There is no tension, only peace.*

"Now, folks, keep your hands and arms inside the car at all times," Gerald warned. "Time to get this over with. You first, Mr. Ames."

His words drifted in the air, but not for long. A single gunshot splintered the silence.

"Oh, God," Willow cried, seeming far away.

It wasn't a cry of pain. She hadn't been hit. Nor had I.

I swallowed.

Stephen.

I could barely breathe.

My eyes squeezed tighter.

I didn't want to open them again. Ever.

~

I HAD to open them eventually, of course. It took at least 10 seconds to focus.

When I could see, more or less, I almost forgot the agony in my face. There was a body on the floor.

It was Gerald's.

A perfect circle of blood spread slowly beneath him.

I raised my gaze, looking for the one who'd fired the shot.

Timothy.

He was outside the window, apparently having pulled himself up enough to fire. He swayed slightly, blinking, the gun still in his hand. The shoulder of his shirt was soaked with blood. The wound didn't look fatal.

He's not dead, I thought, though not very clearly. What had Gerald said about not having killed anyone yet? If he was right, he was still right. He hadn't killed anyone yet after all. But that was too complicated. I'd have to think about it later.

Something was dripping from my chin and down my neck.

"Carolyn," said Stephen's voice from somewhere. "You're bleeding."

I touched my chin. I looked at the red shine on my hand as if it belonged to someone else. I wanted to say something, but nothing came out. What would happen if it did? My cheek was starting to swell. If I tried to talk, how much would it hurt? Would there be a scar?

Not knowing what else to do, I crawled to where Gerald

lay. After pushing the gun away, I attempted to take his pulse with my fingers on his wrist.

I didn't detect one, but then I couldn't sense much of anything at the moment. The blood under his body was soaking my skirt. I couldn't tell how much he'd lost and didn't know what it would mean anyway.

I looked up. Willow had gone to the window, trying to help Yates. He appeared to have sunk into the bushes again, unconscious.

Stephen ran to the pile of smartphones and grabbed his. I heard him saying Willow's address and words like *shooting* and *ambulance* and *right away*.

I picked up the gun, not knowing what to do with it. I was careful to point it at the floor. Was it the one that had killed Zane Tripp? Or the one from the parking garage? Or both?

Or neither?

I knew only that it was the gun which, two minutes ago, was about to kill us all.

STEPHEN THANKED the 911 operator and hung up. As soon as he did, his phone made jungle noises again.

Sighing, he picked up. "Hello, detective."

Putting the phone on speaker, he leaned against the wall, next to the cardboard box with the dancing celery on it.

Luis sounded agitated. I could picture him at his desk leaning forward, more forward than ever. The words poured out of him. "I couldn't get Carolyn. Listen carefully. Problem at this end. The guys watching Gerald went into his shop to ask him a couple more questions. He was gone. Can't believe he got around surveillance. I don't want to scare you, but it's possible he headed your way."

He paused, but Stephen said nothing.

"So, shelter in place," he added. "Lock everything you can —gates, doors, windows. Don't let anybody in. Don't take any chances, just in case. For the moment we don't know where he's gone."

"*We* do," Stephen said wearily.

"Huh?"

He turned to look at me, wincing at what he saw. "Get here as soon as you can." Then he hung up.

Things started to get blurry. Closing my eyes, I began to thank God I was alive.

That, I believe, is when I finally passed out.

CHAPTER 31

THE NEXT 24 HOURS WERE A BLUR. EXCEPT FOR THE FIRST 18 or so, which were a total loss. I spent the latter lying semi-comatose in a hospital bed, heavily sedated with the same tranquilizer they must have used on King Kong.

When they finally let me out, my signature on the discharge papers looked as if I'd signed with my toes. The nurse made Stephen promise to drive me back to Willow's, where she'd invited us to stay until I recovered. Or died, whichever came first.

Now Willow and Stephen and I sat in Luis's cubicle, crammed like overly chummy sardines in front of his desk. Luis kept looking at me as if he thought he should kiss it and make it better but didn't really want to.

"At least your nose isn't broken," he said.

"Only nineteen stitches, a giant purple bruise, and a neck brace." The side of my face was still swollen, but I could form the words with impressive clarity.

"I wish you'd take more of the pain medication," Stephen said.

"I'm taking the smallest dose the doctor would approve."

"Why?"

"Too much at stake. I need to keep my mind clear."

"Don't we all?" Willow asked.

Luis leaned forward and folded his hands on the desk, as if to start the business portion of the meeting. "Ms. Hayly, how's Mr. Yates?"

"Still in the hospital. The doctor says he might get out in a day or two."

"Good."

"And I called the supermarket about our delivery man. He's fine, considering what he went through—the duct tape and everything. I promise to tip him extra next time."

Luis nodded, looking as if he were only half-listening. He frowned at his folded hands. "That leaves Gerald," he said. "He was still alive when the paramedics came. Just barely. But he died last night in intensive care."

There was a moment of silence. Not the flag-at-half-mast kind. Just silence.

"I'm sure we all have mixed feelings about that," he said.

"Not me," Stephen said. "I'm pretty much in favor."

Luis tipped back in his chair. "Now, here's what this means. If Gerald had survived, he would have been charged with the murder of Zane Tripp. And your attempted murders. But he's deceased and can't be prosecuted. So, the case is what we call 'cleared.' It's closed." He paused. "So technically, you're all free to go."

Willow heaved a massive sigh. "Free at last."

I frowned. "Even though Gerald said he didn't kill Tripp and wasn't the shooter in the parking garage?"

"That's right," said Luis.

"But why lie about that? He was about to murder the three of us and planned to be killed himself." My face and neck were starting to throb and not just because the painkiller was wearing off. "How can we be done here? The evidence against Gerald seems pretty flimsy."

Luis raised an eyebrow. "I'm listening," he said, sounding as if he'd rather not.

"Let's take the vehicle," I said. "Owning a pickup truck doesn't mean you tried to shoot someone in a parking garage."

"And?"

"And being suspected of killing a neighbor's pets or slashing tires doesn't make you a sociopath."

It was Willow's turn to frown.

The throbbing was getting worse. I chose my words carefully. "I'm . . . grateful Stephen and I aren't on the official suspect list anymore. But not if it means the real killer's still at large."

Luis tried to look at his watch without seeming to.

Willow put her fingertips together and gave me her best words-of-wisdom face. "Carolyn, would you rather be right . . . or happy?"

Stephen looked at me as if doubting I could answer in my current condition.

I shook my head. "That's not quite the brainteaser some people think it is. It's based on the premise that being wrong can make you happy. And no self-respecting editor could ever believe *that*."

Luis and Willow looked puzzled. But Stephen was impressed. "Whoa!"

Luis cleared his throat. "Well, all I can say is the police investigation is over. If the two of you want to chase wild geese, you'll have to do it yourselves."

I winced. The throbbing in my head seemed to spread.

I couldn't out-sleuth the entire Atlanta Police Department. But it didn't seem right to just let it go.

Or smart. Whoever had tried to kill us might want to tie up that loose end.

I snapped open my purse to make sure the vial of Tylenol 3 was still there.

Maybe more drugs *would* be a good idea after all.

~

In accordance with doctor's orders, it was Stephen's turn to drive. That was how, around lunchtime, we ended up at a park near the police station, reviewing a row of street vendors who sold everything from barbecue to more barbecue.

"I love these carts," he said.

"I don't think I can chew," I mumbled.

"The doctor didn't say you couldn't. It's not like your jaw is wired shut."

"He didn't tell me not to go cliff diving in the Grand Canyon, either. But you won't find me doing that anytime soon."

"Suit yourself," he said. He pointed at a food truck painted to resemble a little red schoolhouse. "They have smoothies." He headed for a cart decorated with the likeness of a mustachioed Porky the Pig, ignoring the blatant trademark violation.

At the little red schoolhouse, I bought a Mango Banana Refresher, which sounded safe. The straws were roughly the size of clarinets, which at least meant I wouldn't have to suck beyond my current capabilities. Sitting on a bench, I began to drink, using the smoothie to swallow my two tablets.

The neck brace didn't make things any easier. I could feel the sweat pooling beneath it.

"Oh, good," Stephen said, parking next to me with a

plastic plateful of cruelly aromatic and attractive solids. "You found something."

"Yes. And it only cost as much as my night in the hospital."

He started eating. "Are you still worried about money?"

"Aren't *you*?" There might be a couple of Bible verses about God caring for sparrows and unemployed lilies of the field, but I suspected I was an exception.

"I wouldn't be worried if we were going home," he said. "But we're not, as long as you insist on hunting the great white whale."

"I'm not Captain Ahab. And don't ask me to call you Ishmael."

Just then a little boy, holding his mother's hand and wearing an Atlanta Falcons cap, walked past. He pointed at my face and whispered something to his mom.

"Don't stare," she said, and walked faster.

Stephen kept chewing. "I love kids," he said. "So, how do you want to wrap this up?"

"Leave no stone unturned."

"What stone is left?"

"For one thing, we never answered our question about the Sundstroms," I said. "They were on our list. On the white board."

"Norma and Eric."

I nodded. "Did Eric blame Tripp for putting his mother out of business? He would have inherited it. The police weren't interested, but nobody really ruled them out."

"How do we do that?"

"Talk to Eric. At work, probably, since Norma said he spends most of his time there."

"When should we do that?"

I looked at my watch. "Right about now."

His eyes grew wide. "Can I finish my food?"

"I guess so."

When he'd eaten the last of his sloppy pulled pork sandwich and wiped his fingers with at least three napkins, he pulled out his phone and started tapping. "If he's on LinkedIn, I should be able to find him."

A minute later he had. "Accounting firm of Harker Bledsoe and Associates. About three miles from here."

"Then let's go. And Stephen . . ."

"Yeah?"

"If this doesn't work, I won't ask you to look under any more rocks."

∾

THE ACCOUNTING FIRM of Harker Bledsoe and Associates occupied a long, low brick building with eyeshade-green windows and no personality. No doubt many who passed it thought that fitting.

The receptionist was a lady surrounded by FedEx envelopes and little porcelain kittens. When she looked up at my face and neck brace, she gasped.

"They say I'll be fine, eventually," I said.

"I—I certainly hope so."

"Is Eric Sundstrom in?"

"Yes, yes." It was clear she hoped to turn us over to anyone at all, so she could begin wiping the sight of my injuries from her memory.

She led us down a hall to the open doorway of a small office. There was Sundstrom, still lantern-jawed and brooding, still in the same blue suit but without the jacket, absorbed in something on the sprawling monitor of his computer.

"Mr. Sundstrom," the receptionist said, "these people would like to see you."

"Thank you, Doris," he said without looking up. The woman backed away, then nearly sprinted down the hall.

Sundstrom raised his chin. For an instant he turned his head slightly and squinted, as if we were almost, but not quite, familiar.

"We met at the nursing home," I said. "I'm Carolyn Neville. This is Stephen Ames."

"Yes," he said, but still looked confused.

"My face looks a bit different now, I suppose," I said.

"It does."

"It's a long story," I said.

He looked at his watch. "I'm afraid I don't have time for a long story. If you can boil it down, go ahead. And you may as well sit."

"Thank you."

I spoke as quickly as I could, given the state of my jaw. Eric already knew about Tripp, of course. I added the part about the parking garage and Gerald.

My head was pounding again by the time I finally I got to the big question: Had he resented Tripp for destroying his mother's business?

"Let me see if I understand this," he said without expression. "You barged into a nursing home and upset a terminally ill woman. And now you want me to incriminate myself so you can have me arrested for murder and attempted murder."

"We know it's a bit of a stretch," Stephen said.

I leaned forward, sort of like Luis, but it made my neck hurt. "You might look at it this way, Mr. Sundstrom. This is your chance to keep your mother and yourself off the suspect list."

He looked down at his desk. "My mother is already off the list. She passed away a week ago today."

The silence that followed was not golden.

I groaned. "I'm so, so sorry. If I'd known—"

"Look," he said, sounding more tired than angry. "I was certainly no fan of that idiot blogger. Or the effect he had on Mom, especially those last few months. But the truth, which I never told her, is that I didn't *want* to run a day care center. I'm an accountant, not a babysitter. And, frankly, the profits were marginal at best."

He picked up the DayTimer on his desk. "What was the date Tripp died?"

When I told him, he flipped backward a whole chunk of pages. "I was conducting an audit in San Diego that whole week. And yes, I have plenty of people who can vouch for that."

He straightened again. "And the day you were shot at in the parking garage. When was that?"

When Stephen told him, he stuck his hands in his pockets. "I don't even have to look that one up. My daughter's birthday. Took the day off. We all went to Chuck E. Cheese and a movie. It was awful, but she loved it."

He folded his hands across his chest. "So, I have an alibi, Ms. Neville. Two of them. I believe the police find things like that important."

I sighed. "They do."

"Now, I don't want to be impolite. But my family and I have had a pretty disastrous year or so. If you don't leave me alone, I'm going to call the police. From what you've said, it doesn't sound like they'd take your side of things."

"Probably not. We're sorry we bothered you, Mr. Sundstrom."

We passed the receptionist on the way out. She pretended not to see us.

Outside, Stephen turned to me. "Stone turned," he said. "Loose end tied."

I nodded.

But there was no closure. Odds were that someone, somewhere was getting away with murder. And my future. We were still off the Pendleton payroll. We hadn't verified Willow's story.

Maybe I deserved to be fired. I'd failed at everything I'd come to Atlanta to do.

The crucifixion was over and there'd be no resurrection.

BACK AT WILLOW'S, I rang the doorbell. She seemed to take a long time to open the door, and when she did it was cautiously, glancing left and right. I couldn't blame her.

Stephen crossed the threshold first. "We struck out with Eric Sundstrom," he announced. It sounded like he was tattling.

"Who?"

"Another person of interest," I said. "But not interesting enough."

She looked at me. "How's the pain?"

"On a scale of one to ten, about six-point-eight,"

"Must be time for your next pill," Stephen said.

I went to the kitchen sink. After taking the orange vial from my purse, I tapped a white tablet into my palm and swallowed it with a glass of water.

Nothing happened, of course. I'd waited too long, and it would take even longer than usual for the throbbing to ease again.

I started to walk back to the living room. But I could hear Willow and Stephen murmuring things like *only hurting herself* and *wish she'd give it up.*

Reversing course, I headed for the library. Willow had been right. I did belong in a roomful of books, especially right now.

As if with a bookmark, I picked up where I'd left off. Taking Willow's memoir from the shelf, I found the acknowledgments page. There was my name, tacked onto a list of Pendleton employees being nebulously thanked "for helping to make this book a reality."

I turned to the first chapter, sat down, and began to read. Five or six pages in, I stopped. I frowned.

I put the book back on the shelf, then pulled out one of Willow's later efforts, *Make Your Life Your Life's Work*. I glanced through the acknowledgments, read about a third of the first chapter, and frowned again.

I did the same with book after book, the whole Willow collection. *Never Say Someday*, *Give What It Takes*, *Your Secret Word*, *50 Ways to 100 Percent*. It took more than an hour.

Finally I put the last book, *Landing Square in the Winner's Circle*, back on the shelf. I sank into the chair and shut my eyes.

The high tide of pain was ebbing. But another kind of discomfort was taking its place.

A theory had started to build itself in my head. One I probably couldn't prove.

If I was right, Gerald had been telling the truth. He hadn't shot Zane Tripp or been in the parking garage that day. Someone else had and could target us again.

I could think of only one way to find out.

There was a lot to do before tomorrow and a lot to lose if I didn't do it right.

CHAPTER 32

IT WAS TIME.

The time being the next day, 10:07 a.m., at the headquarters of Willoworth International. The wall clock told me so.

I stood in the Liberation Room, down the hall from Willow's office. It was a major upgrade from the Business Center at the Southern Suites. A rectangle of dark woodgrain tables was the main attraction, with a black plastic conferencing phone, sleek and futuristic, sitting in the middle like a UFO. The gray suede walls were mostly fitted with white boards, their trays loaded with erasable markers no doubt fresh from their boxes and juicy as raspberries.

Seven people, not counting Stephen and me, had gathered at my invitation. I'd e-mailed each participant, explaining that the goal was to bring resolution to recent events so everyone could move on. It must have sounded convincing; Willow, Stephen, Luis, and Philip Minor were there. Even Timothy was on hand, having been released from the hospital just in time. He looked pale, but no less square-jawed.

One of Willow's lawyers was there at her request. He was

squat, sandy-haired, jacketless, wearing a name badge that said ROBERT VIDIC. He shook my hand and smiled, despite the fact that he'd filed the lawsuit against me.

Finally there was Willow's extremely longtime administrative assistant, Melodee Luther, bustling about with Southern charm under a cotton-candy wad of white hair, bringing the attendees beverages and pencils. She'd done the same that day in Willow's office, fetching us countless cups of coffee and tea. The only thing she lacked was an apron, one with quilted strawberries on the front and an enormous bow in back.

Low murmurs and random titters of conversation were everywhere. Most everyone was talking to someone or listening. Willow to Melodee. Luis to Stephen. Minor to Vidic. Only Yates and I abstained.

I reached up, trying to adjust my neck brace. The skin was moist under the foam. I longed to yank the contraption off, but the zone from my collarbone to my scalp still ached.

The pain was a 3.6. It was the best I could do, having switched this morning to regular Tylenol. I needed clarity of thought, among other things.

At 10:14 I cleared my throat.

"*Excuse me,*" I said, using my italicized voice.

Willow and Melodee, to their credit, quieted and faced me first. The others took longer to cooperate.

"Before we start," I said, "I'd like to express my appreciation to Melodee Luther for her help."

She put a modest hand to her cheek.

"Melodee," I asked, "how long have you worked for Willow?"

"Twenty-one . . . no, twenty-two years."

There was a smattering of applause, mainly from Willow, Minor, and Vidic.

"You're to be commended for your loyalty," I said. "Hard to find these days."

"Hear, hear," said Minor.

I paused, then cleared my throat again. "I'd like to begin with a fable. It's based on a true story."

I pulled an index card from my pocket. My handwriting, as my fourth-grade teacher Miss Bagley had noted more than once, was still outstandingly legible.

Once upon a time, there was a very wealthy king with a humble servant. The servant always did as he was told, working his fingers until they bled for the sake of his master. He sacrificed day in, day out, year after year. Yet he never received the credit or reward he deserved, even after helping the king build a royal treasury for which there was no rival.

But time took its toll. One day the servant learned it was all about to end. The king was going to replace him. After all that labor, all that patience.

It was so unfair. The servant vowed to right this wrong by revealing secrets to the king's enemies, to bring his reign to an end. Revenge, the servant thought, would be sweet.

I FLIPPED THE CARD OVER.

Soon the servant reached his goal. He betrayed the king, who was quickly deposed and driven into exile.

I PUT the card back in my pocket. "And that is the tale of Willowgate."

I could have heard a pin drop. In fact, I think I did.

Most of the faces around the table looked confused. A few turned toward Melodee.

Her eyes grew large. "Why are y'all looking at me?"

I folded my arms. "Maybe because that sounded like the story of a loyal, selfless administrative assistant. One who's been fetching coffee and taking notes for twenty-two years— and doesn't have much to show for it."

She gasped. "But . . . that's not me at all. In the first place, Willow has always treated me kindly."

"Of course," I said.

"In the second place, I'm not one of those people who thinks she's above serving coffee and taking notes."

"I know."

"In the third place, Willow deserves every bit of success she's had. She's the hardest worker I've ever met."

"I don't doubt it."

She rose from her seat. "And in the fourth place . . . I've stayed with Willow because she's like . . . the daughter I never had." Her voice broke. "I'd never hurt her like that."

I looked down at the table, the neck brace creasing like a double chin.

Standing up, Willow proceeded to lean over and give Melodee a hug, then looked sternly at me. "Carolyn, I don't get it. To accuse this lady of—"

"Of nothing," I said, still looking down. "This isn't Melodee's story."

"Whose is it, then?"

I looked up. "You'll have to ask Mr. Minor," I replied.

∼

MINOR, who was still wearing a black turtleneck to make us all Think Different, raised an eyebrow. But then he lowered it and, with a chuckle, shook his head.

"Ah, the knowledgeable Ms. Neville. I see where you're going with this. You're implying that your little fable is about me."

"Am I?"

"It's obvious, isn't it? I've been working with Willow nearly as long as Melodee has. But like her, I've been one of Willow's staunchest supporters."

He paused, probably waiting for me to fire back. I kept my powder dry.

"I know I'm not your favorite person," he continued. "We've never gotten along since that first book. And now I've had the audacity to encourage Willoworth to hold you accountable for your actions."

I kept quiet, trying not to notice that the pain in my face was rising to 4.1.

"This *is* a revenge story," he said. "*Your* revenge. Perhaps, thanks to your injuries, you just aren't yourself. Or your medication is giving you hallucinations."

"Maybe," I said. "Maybe not." I went to the nearest white board but didn't pick up a marker. As far as I was concerned, brainstorming was over.

"Before you went to work for Willow," I said, "you aspired to be a motivational speaker and author yourself, didn't you?"

"Well, I wouldn't put it—"

"Your self-published book, *Stressed for Success*, is out of print. Used copies are still available on Amazon. No reviews."

He shrugged. "Hardly unusual. Most books don't stay in print. In fact, most never earn back their advance. You know that."

"No one bought the book because you had no platform,

no way to promote it. You lacked the charisma to make it big on the speaking circuit."

"Oh, now you're just trying to make me feel better."

"But you had to make a living. You decided to hitch your wagon to Willow's star."

"I was fortunate to have the opportunity," he said, nodding in the direction of his employer.

"But *your* wagon never quite made it off the ground. The acknowledgments pages in Willow's books make vague references to your 'contributions.' But you've never gotten cover credit as a co-writer."

He laughed. "You know perfectly well ghostwriters don't get their names on books. That's why they're called ghost-writers. I'm lucky to be mentioned at all."

"I noticed this morning that your office isn't much bigger than Melodee's. And judging from Google Street View's perspective on your neighborhood, Willow hasn't exactly been sharing the wealth with you."

Willow frowned at me but said nothing.

He folded his arms. "Writers and editors in Manhattan might make huge salaries, Ms. Neville, but they don't in Swan's Corners. If I'd been disgruntled about money, I could have left years ago."

"But things changed. Now you saw the handwriting on the wall. After years of being Willow's guide and confidant, you were yesterday's news. Like the servant in the fable, you'd outlived your usefulness."

"Ridiculous. Willow has never said anything remotely like that to me."

I walked to another white board, picked an eraser off the floor, and returned it to its tray. "She didn't have to. The signs were everywhere. A new creative team was moving in with the Worth TV channel and it was ignoring you. Our first day in Willow's office we heard you say it. They never copied you on anything."

He waved dismissively. "An oversight. Don't tell me things like that don't happen in New York."

"You responded by trying to seem more relevant, closer to the cutting edge. You wore leather jackets and tried to look like a certain innovative computer magnate. Not too effective, I'm afraid."

I walked behind his chair and stood there. "Maybe that explains why Willow told me during a walk at the park that she might have kept you around too long."

Willow sat up straight.

"She'd never say such a thing," Minor said, his confident baritone sounding slightly less so. He turned toward her. "You didn't, did you?"

She hesitated.

"I . . . don't recall," she said finally.

For the first time I saw anger flash in Minor's eyes.

An instant later it was gone.

But not forgotten.

He put his hands behind his head, then stretched out his arms. "Even if that were true, it wouldn't mean I wanted to 'end Willow's reign' or 'destroy her empire.' I'm not the type to hold a grudge."

"Oh, obviously not. But someone is." I turned toward Luis. "I've asked Sergeant Valenzuela to bring a few photocopied pages from the envelopes found in the blogger's house."

"Right here," Luis said, handing them over.

"Envelopes?" Minor asked.

"Oh, hadn't you heard? The police found anonymous messages from an informant. I think you'll find them interesting."

I gave him the papers. He accepted them as though they'd been generously dusted with anthrax.

"Please do us the favor of reading an excerpt aloud. Your mellifluous voice would enhance the experience, I'm sure."

He swallowed, then began to read.

Dear Mr. Tripp:

I've . . . seen your blog, and . . its . . . quite . . . informative.

HE EMPHASIZED THE *ITS*, as if wanting everyone to know it was missing an apostrophe. His pauses were clumsy. It was so awkward, in fact, that he almost seemed to have forgotten how to read at all.

It could reach a much bigger audience. . . I think with a little. . . . or rather . . . a much bigger audience, I think . . . with a . . . little help.

HE PICKED up the glass of ice water in front of him and took a drink, then continued.

And I would like . . . to give you that help—with a story this . . . that many people would be interested to hear. And deserve to hear, as the one they've been told is . . . a lie from beginning to end. . . .

"THAT'S ENOUGH," I said. "You seem to be having difficulty."

"Probably because I've never seen it before."

"Or because you want us to *think* you haven't. Just as you wanted to disguise your identity with a few punctuation and spelling errors. A professional writer like yourself would never make such mistakes, after all."

He took another drink.

"But you didn't disguise everything," I said. "Old writing habits die hard. Too many em dashes and parentheses. Too many *howevers* and *ands* starting sentences. I saw them in these pages when Sergeant Valenzuela showed them to us. When I saw them in so many of Willow's books this weekend, I finally realized where I'd seen them before."

He folded his hands on top of the pages. "I doubt I'm the only person on earth who's used too many em dashes or parentheses for your taste," he said.

"But you're the only one who wanted to make Willow pay for the way you felt she'd treated you all those years. Now that your career was about to end, you decided to take her with you."

"How dramatic."

"You'd known from the beginning that parts of Willow's story couldn't be verified or didn't ring true. You'd known the 'repressed memories specialist' was at least questionable. You'd done enough fact-checking to know some things Willow had said in her interviews with you didn't add up. You fed your conclusions anonymously to Zane Tripp. He blew the whistle."

Minor shook his head. "If I were the source—which of course I wasn't—it's hardly against the law to expose a book you're convinced is fraudulent. Which of course it wasn't." He turned to the lawyer. "Isn't that so?"

"It is," Vidic said. "Though I should point out that murder and attempted murder would be entirely different matters."

Minor sighed and looked at the wall clock. "This is all very interesting. Still, I have a lot of work to do. I'd guess others do as well. Can we cut to the chase? As in less imagination and more evidence? Things like fingerprints. Bullets."

Luis leaned forward. "No fingerprints. No fibers. Nothing useful from ballistics." He turned my way. "I like evidence too, Ms. Neville. Maybe you can help me out by explaining a few things. For instance, why wasn't Mr. Minor scared off by Tripp's dummy surveillance camera? It's not like he was an expert."

I studied my fingernails, trying to look smarter, then looked around the room for assistance. I was about to give up when I saw Timothy Yates. He was starting to doze off, no doubt due to his painkiller. I was jealous.

"I believe Mr. Yates is something of an expert on that," I said. "I'll defer to him."

Willow tapped Timothy on the arm. "Wake up," she whispered.

"Yes, ma'am," he said. He squinted at me. "What was the question?"

"Can most people tell the difference between a real surveillance camera and a fake?"

"Yes, ma'am, if they spend any time on the Internet." He paused. "Not as easy as it used to be to spot a decoy, though. The cheapest dummies are still plastic. They might have one cable instead of two. But these days the good fakes look real. Of course, they're expensive."

"Mr. Tripp was on a tight budget," I said. "Let's assume he had one that was easy to spot. Could Mr. Minor have done a little Googling on his phone and figured it out?"

"I guess he could have."

Luis looked skeptical. "Just because he could have doesn't mean he did. You said that about Gerald, Ms. Neville. Remember?"

Unfortunately, I did. Too bad he did, too. I missed the Luis with the shy smile, the bringer of ice cream.

"And another thing," he said. "Why was Tripp's door unlocked when you and Mr. Ames got there? It's not like Tripp opened the door because he knew Mr. Minor. They'd never met in person, right?"

I examined my cuticles again, even though it hadn't helped with the first question. "Maybe . . . when Tripp answered the door, Mr. Minor pulled out the gun and backed Tripp inside. After firing the shot, he left—and didn't lock the door from the outside."

Luis looked unconvinced.

Suddenly Stephen waved at him. "Excuse me. But Tripp didn't know *Gerald*, either. How did *he* get in?"

Luis paused. "I hadn't thought of that."

"Maybe Carolyn's . . . I mean Ms. Neville's . . . idea about Mr. Minor not locking the door makes sense."

Exhaling, I made a mental note to thank Stephen later. I couldn't give him a raise anymore, but maybe I could afford a subscription to *Entertainment Weekly*. Unless we were in jail.

Luis turned and looked at Minor with something like suspicion.

At least that's what I hoped it was.

I was running out of arguments.

And the pain was up to 6.9.

MINOR TOOK off his Steve Jobs glasses, blew on the lenses, and put them back on.

"And I suppose, Ms. Neville, that you've also invented a *reason* for me to kill Mr. Tripp. You know, a motive. It's kind of a tradition."

"No invention needed. You'd reached your goal—entangling Willow in a scandal guaranteed to bring her down. But Tripp couldn't let it die. As Mr. Ames once pointed out, he was on a roll, getting more attention than ever. He had to stretch his fifteen minutes of fame."

Stephen was smiling, apparently pleased to be quoted.

"Tripp started believing he really was an 'indie journalist,'" I said. "He started investigating on his own, not just regurgitating what you sent. You knew he might figure out who you were and blog it to the world. You'd never work again—not just for Willow, but for anybody. He wouldn't stop unless you made him."

Minor pressed a hand to his forehead as if enduring a migraine. "Truly absurd. I'm embarrassed for you." He paused and lowered his hand. "No doubt you've come up with an equally far-fetched reason for me to shoot at you and Mr. Ames."

"Simple. When Stephen and I started looking into Tripp's murder to clear ourselves, you were afraid we'd uncover the fact that you killed him. You had to stop *us*, too."

Minor returned to his condescending smile, though maintaining it seemed to take more effort. "Quite a plot, all right. Since you've gotten yourself fired, you might try your hand at novels."

"Too hard," I said. "But when it comes to storytelling, you show great promise yourself. Take that tale you told me. You said you and Willow hate guns."

"We do."

I turned to Timothy, who now seemed fully alert. "Mr. Yates, I believe you mentioned to me at the police station that a fellow employee had asked you a lot of questions about guns. Said he'd finished a script for a movie and wanted to make sure his facts were straight. Who was that?"

"That would be Mr. Minor, sir."

"When did he ask you those questions?"

"Oh, I guess three, four weeks ago."

"Not long before Zane Tripp was shot?"

"That's about right."

I pivoted toward Minor. "Now, if Sergeant Valenzuela were to ask you politely for a copy of your finished action movie script, could you give it to him?"

The condescending smile had vanished. The only sound was a cough across the table. Melodee, I think.

"You weren't fact-checking a script, Mr. Minor," I said. "You were deciding how to kill Zane Tripp."

He glared at the ceiling, probably considering how to do the same to me.

Luis leaned forward again. "Mr. Minor, refresh my memory. What kind of vehicle do you drive?"

"A Toyota Scion and a Yamaha motorcycle."

"Last time I looked, most motorcycles were pretty loud," Luis said. "Where were you at the time of the murder, and when Mr. Neville and Mr. Ames were under fire in that parking garage?"

Minor's indignant inspection of the ceiling tiles was unwavering. "I've already told the police I was working. And no, I can't prove it. Sometimes I work from home, or I have to do research on location."

Luis nodded. "So, you have no alibi." He paused. "Like Gerald."

Minor tore himself away from the ceiling and leaned toward Willow. "You know me," he said. "We've worked together for almost twenty years. Tell them. You know I could never do these things."

Willow stared at her coffee cup. Finally she raised her head. "Do I, Philip?"

I waited.

He was cornered. He had to be.

Luis looked at him. "I don't suppose you have the gun with you," he said.

"Of course not. I mean, I hate guns. Why would I carry it? Even if I had one . . ."

He glanced around the room, his bravado only a memory.

It was now or never. I got up, my chair scraping the floor.

I threaded my way around the table and knelt next to Minor's chair. My knees still hurt, but I tried to concentrate on his face.

"You didn't mean for it to happen," I said quietly. "You didn't want to shoot anybody. You just wanted the truth to be told."

He stared at the floor.

"But that blogger wanted more. Attention. Rewards. Things you'd never gotten."

There was a long pause. I held my breath.

Finally I got to my feet. "You didn't set out to kill anyone in the beginning. You wanted people to know what happened. Wouldn't it be a shame if they never found out? You can let everybody in this room know the truth. You can let the whole world know."

He lifted his head, but only enough to stare at the tabletop.

I waited for the confession.

It didn't come.

PANICKING, Minor sprang to his feet. He strode toward the door.

"Ow," said a voice. It was Timothy, yanking his revolver from its holster with his good hand. He pointed it at Minor.

"I wouldn't do that, sir, if I were you."

Minor halted, his hands in midair.

"I wouldn't, either," Luis added. "We're not done yet."

Minor lowered himself into the nearest chair and looked at the floor again. His expression was unreadable.

Luis looked at Timothy. "I appreciate your effort," he said. "But you can put your weapon away. The City of Atlanta was kind enough to give me one, too."

Wincing the pain, Yates holstered his gun.

Willow shook her head. "After all these years, Philip. After all we've been through." She fixed him with a withering look. "I can't believe it. Can't believe you tried to destroy everything we worked for. Much less what you did to that poor young man and tried to do to Carolyn and Stephen."

Minor raised his chin. His eyes narrowed. "Is that a fact? A bit hypocritical for such a self-centered, selfish—"

Vidic, the lawyer, held up his hand. "I'm not your personal counsel, Mr. Minor," he said drily. "But if I were, I'd advise that you resist the temptation to express yourself further."

The muscle in Minor's jaw flexed. He had to be grinding his teeth.

"Sounds like good advice to me," Luis said. He drew out his service revolver. "I'll have to ask you to place your hands against the wall, Mr. Minor."

He complied. Luis patted him down.

"Please sit there on the floor if you would."

When he did, Luis handcuffed him to a leg of the conference room table.

"You're under arrest for the murder of Zane Tripp and the attempted murder of Carolyn Neville and Stephen Ames. You have the right to remain silent. Anything you say can and will be used against you in a court of law. You have the right to consult with an attorney and to have that attorney present during questioning. If you can't afford an attorney, one will be provided at no cost to represent you."

He put his gun away.

For a few moments nobody seemed to know what to do or say.

Finding a chair, I tried to collapse into it without making too much noise. I needed a pill. Maybe two.

Finally Melodee got up and did her best to smile.

"Would anyone like a little more coffee?" she asked.

CHAPTER 33

AFTER LUIS CALLED A BACKUP OFFICER, THEY TOOK MINOR away.

Stephen leaned toward me. "He won't look good in an orange jumpsuit, either," he whispered.

I fished the pills from my purse. There was a bottled water dispenser in the corner. After swallowing two tablets, I belatedly remembered to thank God for Tylenol. And the fact that we wouldn't be spending next Christmas in a federal penitentiary.

Then I remembered. Even if we were cleared, we were still jobless. I'd won the battle and lost the war.

I sat down, staring at the white boards. They seemed blanker than ever.

IT TOOK another day before Willow would talk about what happened.

Stephen and I were still staying at her house. We tried not to bring it up.

When she was ready, though, she was all business. Reconvening six of us—herself, Timothy, Stephen, me, Melodee, and the lawyer—in the Liberation Room, she sat at the table and watched us wonder what she had in mind.

Finally she turned to Melodee. "Please get Pendleton House on the phone. Hunter Thicke."

The magnificent Ms. Luther went to the black plastic UFO in the middle of the room and started punching buttons. A loud dial tone filled the place like an air raid siren. Punching the volume button rapidly, she turned it down.

Eventually there was a click. "This is Hunter," said the voice. There went my gorge again, rising like all get-out.

"Hunter, this is Willow Hayly."

There was a pause. I could hear the gears turning in his head, weighing his options, wondering what was going on. As usual, they didn't turn quickly.

"Willow!" he said at last. "What a surprise! Always delighted to hear from you."

She smirked. "I'm sure. Hunter, there have been some developments down here you need to know about."

"I'm all ears."

She launched into an explanation of what had happened since Zane Tripp's death. It was condensed, but she hit all the key points. She neglected to mention my face, but I decided not to hold it against her.

"Ms. Neville and Mr. Ames are here with us," she added.

Another pause. The gears quit turning. His Friends in Legal couldn't save him now.

"You mean . . . right there in the room?" he asked.

"In the flesh."

"Well . . . Carolyn . . . Stephen . . . hello."

"Hi," we said, more or less in unison and with well-curbed enthusiasm.

"Hunter," Willow called, "It won't be long before this gets

out. It'll be on every Facebook comments page and talk show in the country."

"I hope not," he said.

"No, it's good. Philip was right about one thing. When people learn I was a victim, not a villain, our brand will be stronger than ever. The tour could sell out. Chronicle Merkel might want to get that *Worth It* film in the can ASAP. Maybe even move up the go-live date of Worth TV to take advantage of the publicity. In other words, this could be a new and very profitable era for our partnership with Pendleton House."

Another pause. The wheels were grinding again. He had to find a way to flatter her without committing to anything.

"Willow, you've always been a big-picture thinker. That's what Pendleton loves about you."

"Which brings me to the reason for my call," she said. "I've heard a rumor that, due to a misunderstanding, Carolyn and Stephen are no longer employed by Pendleton House. If that's the case, I won't be able to maintain that partnership anymore. I may even hire the two of them myself, since Mr. Minor won't be back."

She let this sink in, though the density of the receiving party would have made that an awfully long process. "What would you prefer?"

I couldn't hear him hyperventilating, but that was probably due to the lowered volume on the speaker phone.

"A misunderstanding, yes. No doubt about it. Our . . . friends in Legal and HR . . . misspoke themselves. I never got a reply to my e-mail from Carolyn or Stephen, and—"

"Perhaps they had more pressing matters to attend to. Such as survival."

"Exactly. A miscommunication, that's what it was."

"Crossed wires," Willow said.

"Happens all the time," Stephen added.

I just rolled my eyes.

"So, we'll put this unpleasantness behind us going forward," Hunter said.

"With the understanding that Carolyn and Stephen are reinstated," Willow replied.

"Of course."

"With all their expenses reimbursed."

Another pause. He must have been writhing in his executive chair. "You took the words right out of my mouth," he said, choking.

"A joy doing business with you," Willow said. "Here's to our continuing partnership. Have a lovely day."

She nodded at Melodee, who hung up.

I could see Hunter lying on the floor of his office, spent. But it was only a matter of time before he'd find another way to be rid of me. I'd have to enjoy this while I could.

Willow turned to the lawyer. "While I'm at it, I want you to drop the lawsuit against Ms. Neville immediately."

He smiled. "I thought you'd never ask."

For reasons unknown, my pain level suddenly dropped to about three. Maybe even two.

Willow leaned back in her chair. "Melodee, Mr. Vidic . . . you can go now. Thank you."

When they were gone, she stood up, went over to Timothy, and planted a kiss on his cheek.

"My goodness," I said. "That's practically a public display of affection."

She grinned. "I hope you two can come back in a few months. Probably beginning of October. When Tim and I get married."

"About time," I said, and nearly crushed her with a hug. I hoped she wouldn't take my comment as judgmental, but it was true.

I shook Timothy's hand, the good one.

He gave a little smile. "Yeah, I guess it *is* about time. Recent events have convinced me life's too short not to commit yourself."

"And we're not wasting time," Willow said. "We've already planned the menu for the wedding reception."

"Don't tell me," I said. "Pop-Tarts."

Yates nodded. "Yes, ma'am," he answered.

NEXT MORNING, we stowed our bags in the Kia, waved at the Southern Suites, and headed for Hartsfield-Jackson International Airport.

There was one more stop to make, though. Luis's office. To say goodbye.

I was groaning, looking out the window. "I can't do this. I feel so guilty about stringing him along, letting him think we could get his book published. Then leaving him with nothing but a blue shoebox full of . . . well, you know."

"Yeah, I know. But you did what you had to do."

I said little else before we reached the police station. We nodded at the desk sergeant, who still looked drowsy but recognized us and waved us through.

Soon we were walking past the crayon drawing into Luis's cubicle. We sat down and waited for him to lean forward, which of course he did.

"Well, it's been real," he said.

"Luis," I blurted, "I just want to say that—"

He raised a palm. "I know. The two of you have put a lot of effort into my book and were looking forward to doing more."

Neither of us said anything, but we tried to look inconsolable.

He looked down at his desk. "I don't know how to say

this, so I'll just say I'm sorry. I finally heard from that TV producer I sent the first draft to a year ago. The friend of a relative of a friend, remember?"

"Yeah," Stephen said.

"So last week I get this contract in the mail. These guys want me to let them turn *Hard Bargain* into one of those streaming series, you know. A 'Hulu original.' They said it could be the next *Sharknado*."

Stephen's jaw dropped. Mine followed.

"You're kidding," I said. "I mean . . . congratulations. That's great."

"They said it was great satire."

I closed my eyes, wondering what Jonathan Swift would think.

"I don't even have to make any changes," he added.

Stephen looked around as if searching for a brick wall to bang his head against. One needed a wall like that for this sort of thing. It was still another confirmation of the collapse of Western civilization.

As if we needed any.

～

Delta Flight 1950 to LaGuardia was crowded. We were in Row 16, seats A and B.

I was reading Anne Tyler's *Breathing Lessons* on my Kindle. Stephen had finished the in-flight magazine. Now he swiped away at his smartphone.

"So, you figured out how to use Google Street View," he said. "That was how you knew Minor wasn't rich."

"It's not as if I can't do *anything* on the Internet myself," I said.

"I know. Impressive."

"Thanks."

"I hear Willow's fan club is pretty happy. Guess their faith has been rewarded." He put the phone in his lap. "Not sure how much to believe of Willow's story. But *she* seems to believe it."

I settled back in my seat. "I'm sure she does. Probably always will. She has too much invested in it to do otherwise."

"You don't mean money."

"Emotionally. Emotions are a powerful thing."

We sat in silence for a moment. Or at least as much silence as one could find in a Boeing 737 at 35,000 feet.

He cleared his throat. "You know . . . at Willow's house, when Gerald was about to shoot, you tried to get him to take you instead of us, and he hurt you . . ."

He lifted his hand from the armrest as if he might reach toward me but stuck it under his arm. "Just wanted to say thanks," he said.

"You . . . did the same thing," I said. "You told Gerald you were a bigger target."

He looked away. "Just a dumb joke. Couldn't think of anything else. Maybe I wanted to leave 'em laughing."

There was so much I wished he knew. About leaving this world and getting into the next.

I'd keep trying. Without being too obnoxious.

I jumped a little when a flight attendant pushing a beverage cart tapped me on the shoulder.

"Is there anything you'd like?" she asked.

Yeah, I thought, *there is*.

There were a lot of things I wanted.

Today, though, I'd settle for the plane landing in one piece.

A LOOK AT: MURDER MOST
IRRITATING (A CAROLYN NEVILLE
MYSTERY BOOK 2)

When a big Seattle pharmaceutical company's "miracle" drug kills several people, a dedicated researcher blows the whistle.

Pressed to come up with an instant bestseller about the case, book editor Carolyn Neville and her sidekick Stephen Ames are stunned when the scientist is poisoned.

Trying to produce a book, they face a grieving widow, an opportunistic police chief, an impossible deadline—and jail.

For fans of Horace Rumpole, Monk and Stephanie Plum, the Carolyn Neville Mysteries are full of laugh-out-loud suspense.

Order Now!

ABOUT THE AUTHOR

John Duckworth is a novelist, editor, playwright, scriptwriter, cartoonist, and father of twins. After earning his bachelor's degree at Linfield College, he spent 35 years in the publishing industry as a curmudgeonly editor, product developer, and author, working with people like Ken Blanchard, Dr. Kevin Leman, Richard Foster, and Calvin Miller, producers like VeggieTales, organizations like Focus on the Family and companies like Random House, Thomas Nelson, NavPress, Group Publishing, Zondervan and Rainfall Toys.

After producing nearly 250 issues of weekly publications *Power for Living* and *FreeWay*, he created seven multi-volume series of youth ministry resources. He's edited or rewritten hundreds of books, articles, and lesson plans.